White Chocolate Moon
and other stories

by

Michael Levins

FIRST EDITION,

Copyright © 2009 by Michael Levins

Published in the United States by Michael Levins (thanks to Lulu.com), Raleigh, North Carolina.

This book is a work of fiction. Names, characters, places organizations, and incidents are the product of the author's imagination or are used fictitiously. Any resemblance to any actual events or locales or persons living or dead, is entirely coincidental.

Library of Congress Control Number: 2009903409
ISBN – 978-0-578-02174-4

Printed in the United States of America
10 9 8 7 6 5 4 3 2 1

Cover design by Kelli Jansen, Michael Levins, and Matt Levins
Cover photograph by Kelli Jansen.
Photo of moon by Eric Smith used with the permission of Gayle Harte of Gayle's Chocolates (*www.gayleschocolates.com*).

To order additional copies of this book or other books by Michael Levins, go to **http://stores.lulu.com/m_levins1027**

Dedicated to my parents.

For Milton Levins, who taught me courage, integrity, honesty, and a love for baseball.

For Mildred Levins, who taught me to appreciate all things artistic and beautiful and to have a voice.

"Sometimes you're supposed to just let the experience happen. You have to allow it to be and just feel it."

Martin

"The game is not played without hints. You just have to learn to pay attention."

Master Azar

Table of Contents

White Chocolate Moon.. 1

The Shaving Brush 27

Cerulean Blue 43

No Time Like the Present.. 75

The Trial 93

Do Over 111

End of Cycle 129

How Darnell and Crazy Joe Saved Earth from Annihilation 149

The Healing 171

Tech Support.. 187

Star Maker, Inc. 213

Payback.. 231

Dear Santa.. 243

White Chocolate Moon

"No, I'm sorry; Mr. Dinsmore does not grant any interviews. Thank you for calling."

"Hello? No, I'm sorry; Mr. Dinsmore does not make any public appearances. Thank you for calling."

"Hello? No, I'm sorry. . . What? Well, that's interesting. Yes, I'll ask him." Esther Rodriguez tentatively knocked on Clayton Dinsmore's door.

"Yes?"

"Mr. Dinsmore, I'm sorry to bother you but. . . ."

"Miss Rodriguez, I hired you to keep the world away from me. That includes you too. What could possibly be so important that you would interrupt me while I'm writing?"

"That was the White House calling. They're putting together a program celebrating the twenty best American novels of all time. Your book, *White Chocolate Moon,* is listed as number fifteen. You've been invited to attend the ceremonies."

"I don't do public appearances, Miss Rodriguez. I thought I was clear about that."

"But Mr. Dinsmore, the White House!"

"I don't care what color the house is, I don't do public appearances. I don't do interviews. I don't do autographs. I only write. Now please leave me alone."

"Yes sir, sorry to bother you."

Clayton Dinsmore returned to his work. His computer was switched on. He was staring at a blank page. He waited patiently for inspiration to

1

come to him. He had been waiting for twenty years and there was no sign of it coming any time soon. He let out a heavy sigh. A bird at the window momentarily distracted him.

Dinsmore leaned back in his chair. Three walls of his study were lined with books, only one of which was written by him. There were several signed photographs lining the wall in front of him. Every influential writer of the twentieth century appeared with him, shaking his hand. There were pictures of two presidents and several actors who had appeared in the film adaptation of *White Chocolate Moon*. There were several framed awards including a Pulitzer Prize. Sitting centrally on his desk was a Best Screenplay Oscar.

He couldn't take the silence any longer. He notified Miss Rodriguez that he was going out for a walk. Dinsmore left through the back door of his mansion, as he did nearly every day, and began the long trek around his 200 acre estate. He carried a cane. He didn't really need it but it served as a walking stick as though he were going on a hike. He wound through the fruit orchards and the vineyards, waving to the people working there. He followed the trail along the woods and to the bridge that crossed the small stream. In a grove of pine trees, he sat down on a bench as he did almost every day.

The success of *White Chocolate Moon* and some good investments had paid for the estate and set Dinsmore up so he never had to work again. But he wanted to. He desperately wanted to, and couldn't. Every day he literally walked through the fruits of his labor, the outward manifestation of his enormous success. And every day he would give it all up for just one more success. Hell, he'd even settle for a failure.

He'd written *White Chocolate Moon* in six months. He wrote it out

2

in long hand in a notebook in the bedroom of a tiny apartment and at a local library. The story flowed faster than he could write it down. He saw so clearly the characters, the plot, the nuances, the accents, the sounds of the city, the dialogue, the conflicts, the solutions. It all flowed as a single vision, clearer than anything he could see with his real eyes. In fact, the only challenge as he was writing the novel, was remembering to eat every now and then.

Almost immediately upon finishing the book, he got a call from an old college friend who had just taken a job in a publishing house and was trolling around for new material. The book was an instant success. Dinsmore was a guest on every television show. He traveled the country doing book signings and interviews. *White Chocolate Moon* was at the top of the national best seller list for four months. A movie deal netted him a six figure contract. When the movie won five Oscars, the book sat on the best seller list for another five months. Clayton Dinsmore was hailed as the new Ernest Hemingway. He was set for life. Until he tried writing a second novel.

He waited patiently for inspiration. He waited for the pictures to return, for the ideas, for the characters to visit him. For twenty years he waited. The first five years, he sat at his typewriter, having faith and making excuses, hoping each day that maybe it would come the next day. The next five years he pretended to himself that inspiration might still show itself. He was like a bride jilted at the altar, refusing to believe the truth of it. For several years after that he was like a man having already lost several hundred dollars in the slot machine but desperately refusing to leave lest he be absent when the jackpot finally would hit. Now he just sat, lonely, defeated, staring at the walls as if in an abandoned broken down bus station still hoping to catch the 515 out of town.

He sighed deeply, sitting there among the pine trees feeling sorry for himself, trying to talk himself into accepting that one book was more than enough to ask for and that at least he had this gorgeous estate to retire in. Daily he tried to talk himself into believing that he was incredibly lucky, but now even the ability to do that was beyond his imagination. Every day he walked just a little more stooped over, just a little slower, expending much of his energy releasing heavy sighs and wracking his brain trying to figure out the answer. He'd had the vault opened and it was full of treasures but he'd lost the combination and couldn't open it again.

For a while he even tried retracing his steps. He purchased the building where his former apartment had been. He went there every day, pad and pen in hand, waiting, waiting, waiting. He tried to force it. He thought maybe he could just jump start the process, writing about anything. Maybe if he could just start somewhere, anywhere, the floodgates might once again open but the more he tried, the more elusive the pictures became.

At one time he had thought he must be the luckiest man in the world to be a writer. Actors could rehearse by themselves but they needed a whole company of players and a theater to perform their craft. Even graphic artists needed expensive materials and equipment. All a writer needed was a pen and paper, or so he once thought. Now he knew they were worthless without inspiration. It had come so easily, so automatically so long ago, that he had taken it for granted. He hadn't paid attention to how he did it, what produced it, what kind of trance state or frame of mind had allowed the flow of images.

Enough of this, he thought. He arose from the bench to complete the path around his vast property, toward the back hedges, around toward

4

the front again through the second woods. Soon he would be back to the house. He was not in a hurry. There was nothing waiting for him there. The second woods emerged onto a path along the south fence. As he rounded a turn, his foot caught on something or maybe there was a bit of moisture that made the path slippery. He didn't know. He never saw it. Down he went with a thud.

Dinsmore stayed on the ground until he was satisfied he hadn't broken anything.

"Hey Mister, are you okay?"

A young woman about twenty years old ran toward the fence. She climbed up and over it and leaned down to help him up.

"I'm okay," said Dinsmore. "Don't bother about me."

"It's no bother," she said. "Let me help you up."

"I'm okay. Oooh! Well, maybe I could use some help. Who are you? Do you live around here?"

"Uh, I was just taking a walk. I just happened to be passing by. Lucky for you, huh?"

"Oh yeah, this is my lucky day. I think I hurt my knee."

"Let me help you back to your house."

"I don't want to trouble you."

"It's no trouble."

She helped him up and had him put his arm around her shoulder for support. They slowly made their way back to the house. Miss Rodriguez was out in front looking for him, alarmed that he hadn't come back sooner. "Mr. Dinsmore. Are you okay? Shall I call the doctor?"

"No! No doctors." They helped him into the house and onto the sofa in the main living room.

"Thank you, Miss . . ."

"Whitney. Collette Angelina Whitney."

"That's quite a name. Very mellifluous."

"Thank you."

"So, you live around here, do you?"

"Uh, no."

"No?"

"No."

"Well, what were you doing here?"

"Uh, well, I was kind of hoping to meet you." Dinsmore let out a deep exhausted sigh.

"I'm so sorry to hear that. You seemed like such a charming young lady. Well, you've met me. Please be off with you."

"Mr. Dinsmore, can I just have a few moments of your time?"

"You've already had them. I don't do interviews. I don't do appearances. I have a list of charities I donate to. There's nothing I have for you."

"My mother was Mary Whitney."

The name took all the wind out of Dinsmore's lungs. He looked at once shocked, frightened, puzzled, and sad.

"Did you say 'was'?" he asked barely in a whisper.

"My mother died several months ago."

"I am very sorry to hear that. Please sit down."

"Thank you, Mr. Dinsmore."

"Give me a few moments to digest this. I haven't thought of your mother in years and yet I think of her every day. Now that I look at you, I can see the resemblance. Please, tell me about her."

"There's not a lot to tell. We lived in California. She ran a bookstore."

"Hah! That doesn't surprise me. She loved books. She always felt more at home in a book than in the real world. Funny how the memories start flooding in once you prime the pump. And your father? He must be a very wonderful man, a very lucky man."

"I don't really know much about him. I never met him, ... until now."

"Me? Are you telling me that I'm your father? That's impossible!"

"My mother told me a few weeks before she died."

"She never told me. Why didn't she ever tell me?"

"She didn't want to interfere with your career. Please Mr. Dinsmore, I don't want anything from you. I didn't come here to make any trouble. I'm not asking for anything."

"If you didn't want anything, you wouldn't be here."

"I'm not asking for any money or anything."

"Money is all I have. You tricked me. How long have you been lurking around my property? I don't have anything for you. I can't tell you who you are."

"I'm sorry to have bothered you. This was probably a bad idea. I'll leave now. I'll be at the Bell Motel until Saturday at noon in case you change your mind. After that, I'll never bother you again. I'm sorry to have disrupted you." Collette rose suddenly from her chair and abruptly turned her back to Dinsmore and exited the house.

Dinsmore sat in silence staring at the door, still hearing the echo of it slamming shut behind her. Another heavy sigh. Miss Rodriguez flitted into the room asking him if there was anything he needed. He waved her away. Slowly, far too slowly, he pushed himself off the sofa. He felt like a man of ancient years even though by most standards in his early sixties he would still be considered young. He felt the pain in his knees and shoulders as he climbed the huge curved staircase. In his bedroom, he entered the closet and pulled down from a high shelf, a carved wooden box. He fished around in his desk drawer for the key to it and with yet another heavy sigh, he opened it.

With a shaky hand, he held up a photo of a much younger Clayton Dinsmore posing in a bathing suit with the ocean behind him. Holding his hand and smiling at him was the young fresh happy face of Mary Whitney, Collette's mother. Looking at the picture, he could hear the roar of the ocean and the musical sound of her laughter. He could see the scene unfurl in his mind. After the picture was taken, he lifted her up in his arms and dumped her in the surf. She got up splashing him. They embraced and kissed, a salty but sweet kiss, carefree and full of promise. Looking at the picture now, her image was as foreign to him as his own. When was the last time he had laughed? When was the last time he had kissed a pretty girl? He continued rummaging through the wooden box. There were some ticket stubs from a movie and a playbill from a theater. And there was the candy wrapper from a bar of white chocolate from the Moon Chocolate Company. He won it for her at a carnival and they ate it together holding hands and proclaiming their love for one another.

He dug deeper looking for the letters. He didn't want to read them but couldn't turn away from them. Three letters encompassing an entire lifetime. He pulled the first one out of its envelope and read it:

Dearest Clay,

I can only say this summer was pure magic for me. I never dreamed life could be so exciting and wonderful. I am so much in love with you now and forever.

Yours always,

Mary

And the second letter:

Dear Clay,

Needless to say I am disappointed that you will not be able to visit me at Christmas. I certainly understand the demands and pressures you are under and with the deadline approaching and all. I will be thinking of you. Can't wait to see the book.

Yours,

Mary

Clayton pulled out the third letter and read it too. He'd meant to throw it away many times but kept it, maybe out of a sense of penance.

Clayton,

I heard about you and Elizabeth. I can't say at this point that I was surprised but that doesn't mean I wasn't still deeply disappointed, not just for myself but because I, perhaps too naively, assumed or hoped better of you. I have no regrets. It was a joy and an honor to have shared a small but intimate space of time with you and to have known you. I wish you only good luck

and success and will eagerly follow your career, but from afar.
Please do not call me again.
  Mary

"And for what?" he said out loud. "I don't even remember who Elizabeth was. Mary, why have you come back to me now? Why are these doors being forced open? You never should have told her. And she never should have come here to tell me. Is this my punishment now after twenty years, still paying for my stupid mistakes of the past?"

Over the next few days, Collette busied herself taking walks and visiting little shops. Each day she would spend the afternoon under the shade of a tree in a park sketching pictures of the children at play. Each day when she returned to her room, she checked to see if she'd received any phone messages but the red light remained unlit. When Saturday morning arrived, she took a shower, went downstairs for an early breakfast, and packed her things. She sat on the bed and waited until precisely twelve o'clock before getting up to leave. She was in good spirits. She wasn't disappointed. She'd had no real expectations of the trip, only hoping that she would at least make contact with him. She'd done that. If he needed to be so closed off that he couldn't see her, well that would have to be okay. She could respect it even if she didn't understand it. If it had been her, she would have been eager to meet anyone who had taken so many pains to contact her, even a stranger, let alone a daughter. But that was her. Whoever he was and whatever life had done to him, well that was his problem. She was glad her mother hadn't stayed with him. But then again, if she had, maybe he'd have been a different person. But none of that mattered now. It was time to go. As she reached for the door to leave, there was a knock on it that startled her. She figured if he would have changed his mind, he would have called or had one of his servants call. She didn't expect to see him actually standing there outside her door.

"Hi," she said simply, not knowing quite what else to say.

"Hello," he replied, just as uncomfortably. Her surprise at seeing him there at least equaled his own surprise at seeing himself there. They stood, looking at each other, not quite knowing what to do next.

"Would you like to come in and sit down?" she asked.

"No. Uh, thank you. I have a car waiting outside. I was thinking, I mean, would you like to come out to the house and have lunch with me?"

"Sure," she said.

"Bring your bags. You can stay at the house. I mean, I'd like you to stay for a few days. That is, if you want to."

"Yes, I would like that." Collette grabbed her bags and followed him. He said nothing throughout the car ride.

When they arrived at the house, Dinsmore directed Miss Rodriguez to take Collette to one of the many guest rooms on the third floor. Collette was invited to settle in and then to meet him in the dining room in a half hour.

They sat on opposite sides of a huge table that could easily seat fifty guests between them. There was a single setting at each end of the table with several vases full of flowers between them. A small lunch was served. They ate in silence. The only sound throughout the meal was the clinking of silverware and the ticking of a grandfather clock standing against one wall.

After the meal, Dinsmore invited her into his study. Her eyes widened at the sight of all the books lining the walls from floor to ceiling. He had her sit in an overstuffed chair in front of his desk.

"Did you enjoy your lunch?" he asked.

"It was great," she replied.

"Your room is adequate?"

"This is very uncomfortable for you, isn't it?"

"Yes it is."

"What made you change your mind?"

"When I didn't hear from you again I convinced myself that you were telling the truth when you said you didn't want anything from me. And . . ."

"Yes?"

"Frankly, I had to see your face again. It is extraordinarily like your mother's. Tell me, what do you know about your mother and me?"

"Not a lot. Only what I can deduce by the fact of my existence."

"Yes, your mother and I were lovers. But that doesn't begin to describe it. You know that my book was about us?"

"I didn't know it at the time I read it. I kind of guessed at something like that after she told me."

"What, er, what did you think of it, my book I mean?"

"I wrote a paper about it in college actually."

"Yes?"

"Well I kind of liked it and I didn't."

"Yes?"

"On the one hand it was an extraordinarily beautiful and tragic love story. The ending made me ache with yearning for a different outcome like when I read *Romeo and Juliet*. You just wanted it to go a different way. It broke my heart. I cried every time I read it."

"What didn't you like?"

12

"I just didn't understand it. I didn't understand why it didn't end differently. The two characters so obviously loved each other. They didn't have the obstacles that Romeo and Juliet had. They didn't have feuding families separating them, or illness like in *Love Story* or war like in *Doctor Zhivago* driving them apart. Their obstacles were all internal. I just didn't see why they couldn't overcome them, why their love wasn't stronger. I always blamed the guy. It seemed to me he always had a wall between himself and his feelings, like he was always just standing behind something and never really touching it, like he was playing a role or wearing a mask or something, like he wasn't fully within himself. Do you know what I mean?"

He was glaring at her. She hadn't been paying attention but had just gone on talking. Suddenly she realized. Suddenly she remembered she wasn't just discussing a book with a teacher or with a friend, she was discussing it with the author and worse yet, with the character himself.

"I'm sorry. That was very presumptuous of me. I hope I haven't offended you. I'm very sorry. Sometimes I just speak up like that. I don't know what I'm talking about. I only got a 'B' on the paper. Forgive me." He held the glare for a bit but then softened. Another deep sigh.

"You see, that's the problem with schools these days. You should have gotten an 'A' on that paper. Obviously you saw things even the author failed to see but how could I see them? If I had, it would have been a different story. You want to know why the characters in my book failed to stay together? Since we both know who we're talking about, I'll answer your real question.

"When I met your mother, she was working at the library. I went there nearly every day, at first for the books, later for a quiet place to work, but later still, just to see her, just to see her face. I will spare you the

13

intimate details. Suffice to say we began spending every free moment together. And of course she also invaded my writing. I had only to glance over to her desk and be filled with inspiration. We were together throughout the publishing of the book, through all the hoopla and public display. And then at some point it all just ended, just like in the book. She didn't like the ending either."

"But what happened? You see what I mean? You're not telling the whole story."

"You're very much like her; relentless. Okay. I'll try again for your sake, perhaps for my own sake. When I met your mother I was a struggling young writer. I was filled with ambition. No, that wasn't it, I was filled with passion. I lived for my work. Your mother was also filled with passion but of another kind. She became like a drug to me almost as powerful as writing. I was addicted to her laughter, her carefree smile, her grace of movement, her lyrical voice, how she made me feel.

"And she knew books. My God, she knew books. She could quote passages from just about any author I could name. I introduced her to Bellow and they talked for hours. I couldn't keep up with them. We spent an evening with Steinbeck and he was equally fascinated with her. I was almost a bit jealous and insecure.

"But I discovered the trap too late. You see, she knew books but she didn't know writers. She didn't understand what it took, the sacrifice we have to make in real life in order to create our fictional worlds. She went through the motions. I'll give her that. She made a valiant attempt to be supportive but when I needed to be alone, when I needed to stay up all night, when I needed to get drunk, and ultimately when I needed . . . other comforts, she couldn't keep up. She wasn't up to the challenge. I saw her

14

as weak and I resented her for it. I felt she'd betrayed me, that she hadn't lived up to the promise, that she hadn't kept her part of the bargain.

"You ask why the characters in my book failed to stay together? Because, ultimately, they both just stopped trying. Because at some last straw moment someone stepped over the line and the other reacted and they went to their separate corners to lick their wounds and blame each other and passively watch it fizzle away without lifting a finger to stop it. They were exhausted, emotionally, sexually, and every other which way. So there it is in a nutshell. Now do you understand?"

"No. I'm sorry, I still don't. I still don't understand why you both let that happen."

"What do you want from me? It's old ancient news. It's a dead story. Leave it alone. Leave me alone. Why did you come here? Why do you have to shake these ancient cobwebs and raise the dead? Just leave me here to wither and die. I'm just a dried up old prune. I don't have anything for you. Please, just leave me alone. I'm sorry Collette. I tried. For Mary's sake and for yours I tried. But I can't do it. I don't have any answers for you. Please, just leave me alone." He put his hands on his head and lowered it. She quietly backed out of the room.

Esther Rodriquez found her in her room packing her things.

"Why did you come here?" asked Esther.

"Don't worry, I'm leaving. The whole thing was a stupid mistake."

"That wasn't an accusation. It was a question. Sit down, dear. Tell me why you came here."

"I don't know. I wanted to meet him. I wanted to find out about him. I wanted to find out about myself I guess. I don't know. I didn't know what else to do. My mother died. I broke up with my boyfriend.

Things were crumbling all around me. I didn't have anything else to hold onto."

"So you were looking for a little stability. You thought your father would welcome you with open arms and you'd have a home again."

"I guess. I don't know. It sounds pretty silly when you put it like that."

"And now you're going to give up and leave?"

"I'm making him miserable. I can see the pain I'm causing him every time he looks at me."

"He's happier than I've seen him in years."

"That's a pretty sad statement. Are you serious?"

"No, actually I'm joking. What can I say? He's a crusty old goat and always has been for as long as I've known him."

"How long have you been working for him?"

"About twelve years."

"How do you put up with it? And why? What are you exactly? The housekeeper? His secretary?"

"I'm his faithful dog. I look after him, I'm loyal to him, I take his abuse, and besides that, he thinks I'm a bitch."

"Not my idea of a good time."

"I'm not here to have a good time. I'm here to do my job. Underneath all that crust is a good heart. He's a little boy who had his toys stolen and he can't understand it and he can't accept it so he goes into the playroom every day and hopes they'll turn up. And when they don't, he has temper tantrums. But he has never given up hope. You have to give him credit for that. Now what about you? Are you going to give up? Can't you give him a little more time?"

16

"Why should I?"

"Why shouldn't you? I swear, people have it so backwards. Young people who have all the time in the world are always in such a hurry. Everything has to be accomplished yesterday. Old people nearing the end of their lives with little time left have learned to take things slowly and be patient. I think you should stay. I have a strong feeling about it. I think you're supposed to be here."

"I don't know."

"Give it a few more days. Take a walk around the grounds. There's an old bicycle in the garage. I see you have some sketch pads. I would suggest the pine grove near the stream. You could draw some great pictures there." Collette eyed her as though seeing her for the first time. She hadn't really regarded her as anything more than a servant. But there was a deep inner strength and wisdom there that she hadn't noticed. More importantly, Collette now saw her as a friend. She softened and smiled and began to unpack again.

Dinsmore rode the crest of conflicting emotions sitting alone in his study after she left. The room was full of her absence. Was it Collette's he so acutely felt or was it Mary's all over again. Gone now were the heavy sighs, replaced instead with a slow fullness of breath, bittersweet, tasting of a life not lived. "The unexamined life," Socrates had said, "is not worth living." Perhaps he had it backwards, thought Dinsmore. Perhaps the unlived life isn't worth examining. He felt the pressure of his down turned eyebrows, always on the verge of sadness. He thought of Collette's, always on the verge of laughter.

Without thinking or even remembering doing so, he turned to the computer. His fingers began moving by themselves, remembering how to communicate, just like in the old days. They came alive on the keyboard. Without thinking, without planning, he finally after all those years, was able to bypass the brain and find his link back to the source of inspiration.

It was her eyebrow that linked her with her mother, the way it curled up to one side with tentative laughter and the slightest touch of sadness and irony. The single silky curved and delicate hairs, each innocent as individuals, but together, conspiring together, they took his breath away. Her eyebrow, holding evil thoughts and pranks and jolting at his heart with the slightest quiver. She didn't have to say a word. It was all in her eyebrow. Just as hers turned up, his own turned down. He was not laughter and innocence. He was floundering in a morass. And although he prayed that the laughter of her eyebrow and the twinkle in her eye could somehow pull him magically from the bog of death, it was the more likely outcome that if their hands should clasp and hold each other and became as one, that he would, in fact, win that tug of war and pull her down with him. But how could he let go and lose her forever? On the other hand, how could he hold on and lose himself? That was the way it was with laughing eyebrows that ultimately laughed at him.

He was startled to see that he had written. He cried with relief like the junkie finally scoring dope and injecting himself, feeling the relief of the fix, all the pain disappearing or at least temporarily masked until the next wave of desperation hit.

When it finally came to him, after all those years, he laughed at how effortless it was. He'd forgotten. It didn't come from the mind. It came from the fingers. You don't think and then write about it. You use what you've written to tell you what your thoughts are. Why had it suddenly come back? What made it so easy again after all those years? It was her, of course. Like her mother before her. What key did she possess? What was it she held over him? But then he read the words and then he knew. It was as if a message was sent from Mary herself, finally forgiving him and letting him know his penance was over. Finally he understood everything.

He found her sitting in front of a row of maple trees. She didn't hear him approaching, engrossed as she was in drawing the family of trees just beyond the creek. The bicycle lay on the ground beside her along with her backpack. He watched her fingers, furiously manipulating the pastel chalks. She had it too. She too, was addicted. He could tell, just by watching her fingers even before taking in the picture itself. He could tell from the fact that she was unaware of his presence, standing behind her, looking down at the life unfolding on the paper. He could tell by the trees coming to life on the paper, holding more life in fact, than the real ones standing in front of her. He'd never noticed those trees before. He never fully saw them until he saw them through her eyes and fingers. He didn't realize they were a family, clinging together, guarding each other, living their lives in peaceful tranquility. He wasn't just looking at the trees. He could see them looking at him.

He carefully sat down beside her, gently entering her frame. She was not startled but eased him gently into her field.

"What do you think?" she asked him.

"I couldn't write it any better than that. It's all there. It's not just the trees I'm seeing for the first time and understanding through your picture, it's all of life. How do you do it?"

"Really? You think it's any good?"

"You really don't know, do you? It's just as well. Best not to think about it."

"No, please tell me what you think."

"I have a friend who is a master at the game of checkers. I've never seen him beaten. I've never seen anyone come close. He knows the game. He can see ten moves in advance. And yet, he takes little pleasure or pride in that because he can't play chess to save his life. It's the same with me. I know I'm a decent writer. But I also know that a great poet could take any hundred pages of mine and condense them into ten lines conveying even more meaning than I was able to. Your picture takes that poem and condenses it into a single image.

"I've passed this way almost every day for years. When I've bothered to notice those trees at all, I've seen . . . . just trees, not much more. Maybe I'll note the changing of colors in the fall or the fresh buds in the springtime. But in your drawing I see what I missed. I see a story I would need a hundred pages to convey. I don't know how else to express it. It's beyond words. It's a feeling, an essence, that even a poet couldn't capture."

"Really? I don't know. I just liked how they kind of stood together like that behind the creek. It's just a drawing. I didn't think it was that good."

"That's probably why it is. Collette, I have something to tell you. I was up in my office and I was suddenly able to write again. After all those years and without even expecting it or even trying, it just suddenly came back to me."

"That's great."

"But what came with it was understanding. Funny how you think you know something but the knowing of it was only a way of blocking what was really true. All those years I blamed your mother for abandoning me and taking inspiration away with her. She didn't abandon me. I drove her away. I can see it now. I was afraid. I was afraid of being happy. I was afraid of losing my edge."

"You thought you had to be Van Gogh."

"Yes, I guess that's a good way to put it. But ultimately the joke was on me. In losing your mother, I suffered all the more, and inspiration went with her. I lost the ability to write. Now that you're here, I seem to have regained it. I still don't fully understand. I still don't know where it all comes from. How do you do it? How do you allow that flow and still live a life?"

"You're asking me? You're asking me for advice?"

"Yes, I am."

"Well I don't know. I don't know that I've ever thought about it. I just draw pictures."

"But how do you deal with the tortures of being an artist?"

"What tortures? It gives me joy to draw pictures. I don't think about it. I just do it. I think . . . no, never mind."

"Please tell me."

"Listen, I don't know anything. I'm just a kid. Believe me, I don't have anything figured out."

"Collette, please tell me."

"Well, it's like the character in your book. He wasn't fully alive. He wasn't fully in his body experiencing life through his five senses. He filtered everything through his mind first. That's why he was always a step behind. You know what I mean? I don't think you're tortured because you're an artist. Forgive me for saying this but I think you're just a tortured man who happens to be an artist. I have friends like you who think they have to suffer to produce anything worthwhile. But you don't have to be Van Gogh. You can be Chagall. His art is full of joy and warmth and whimsy. I think you have to strike a balance. For me, drawing is like emptying the cup but first you have to fill it. You think you have to make a choice between living a life and expressing it. But you have to do both. First you have to live, and then after you've had experience, then you can express it in art. I think when you sent my mother away, you stopped living and then you just had nothing to say anymore."

Dinsmore at first frowned, his brow furrowed but then relaxed. "Yes. I see it. Again, you've drawn a perfect picture. I see it now. What a waste. What a waste of a life I've been. What a fool I am."

"But your life isn't over. I see now why I had to come here. I thought it was for me but it was for you too. Esther was right."

"Esther! What's Esther got to do with it?"

"She persuaded me to stay and keep trying with you. She's a very special person. She can see the pictures even before they're on paper."

They walked back together to the big house. Dinsmore saw that Esther was flustered. "What's the matter?" he asked her.

"I'm sorry. Forgive me. I was cleaning in your study. I didn't mean to look at it. I couldn't help noticing."

"You read it?"

"I'm sorry. It was on the screen. At first I just glanced at it, but I couldn't pull away. Mr. Dinsmore, you're writing again!"

"Yes, it seems that I am."

She then turned to Collette. "Oh thank you. I knew it would happen. I knew you could inspire him."

"It wasn't her, Esther. Don't make the same mistake I did. It wasn't her and it wasn't Mary. It was me all along. When Mary left me I stopped living. If you dam up a river you don't just block the flow of the water, you block the flow of everything moving in it."

Dinsmore spent the rest of the day writing. He worked for hours but in the timeless time of creation. He barely noticed the words as they appeared almost by themselves on the screen in front of him. He took joy in the process as though seeing an old friend again after many years. He delighted in the twists and turns the story took, leading him in directions he couldn't have anticipated. It didn't come from him, it came through him. And when it stopped, he rested, not with the panic he had felt for so many years, but rather like tucking in a child for the night and wishing sweet dreams, knowing that in the morning the joys and miracles would continue again.

He left the office as though awakening from a good night's sleep. He found Esther and Collette sitting together in the den. Esther was knitting something and Collette was sketching her doing so. They were surprised to see him as if not expecting him to surface for many more days.

Collette's sketch allowed him to see Esther as never before. He hadn't realized how devoted she was to him. He hadn't realized the sacrifices she'd made. He could see the young girl she once was, full of dreams and wonder. He could see the wise old woman she was destined to become.

"Marvelous," was all he could say.

"I'm glad you came up for air," Collette said. "I wanted to talk to you. I was thinking about leaving in the morning. I need to get back home."

"What are you going to do?"

"I don't know. There's a young man back there waiting for me. At least I hope he's still waiting. He wanted us to get married but I wasn't sure I was ready. I'm still not sure but I have to give us a try and find out. I suppose I'll have to find a place to live and get a job too. I can't keep living on Mom's inheritance."

"Let me help you."

"I don't want anything from you. I told you, I just wanted to meet you."

"But you've given me so much. I don't mean just because I'm writing again. I mean because I'm living again. You've given me my life back. And more than that, you've given me a daughter. I'm very grateful to you for that. I still don't feel very much like a father but I'd like to try to make a go of it. I want to help you if you'd let me."

"I can't take any money from you."

"Why? Are you trying to be Van Gogh?" She laughed and turned red. "You're too old for me to give you an allowance. If you can't accept a gift, then consider this: I want you to design the cover of my next book and I want you to promise me that you'll accept from me whatever I pay you for it."

"Okay. You've got yourself a deal."

"So, you're leaving in the morning?"

"Yeah, I figure with you writing again, I'll just be in the way. You're going to want to keep working."

"Well, actually that's not the case. I'm setting it aside for a while."

"Really? Why?"

"Because Esther and I are going to the White House to meet the

President. Would you like that Esther?"

"Madre de Diós! Are you serious?"

"Yes I am. I need to fill my cup before I continue writing. Please call them back and let them know we're coming. And take this credit card and buy yourself whatever you want to wear to it."

"Nice going, Dad," said Collette. "I think there's hope for you yet."

Dinsmore choked up a bit. "I like the sound of that. Never thought I would but I do, especially coming from you. I'm very proud of you, daughter."

"I'm proud of you too, Dad." He reached out his hand to her. She grabbed it and pulled him close and hugged him.

The Shaving Brush

"I still don't understand why I have to move," said eighty year old Nellie to her daughter, Abby.

"The papers are already signed," said Carter, Abby's husband. "We've been over this a hundred times."

"It was just a little fall," said Nellie. "We can move the bed down here and I won't have to use the stairs."

"Mom, it wasn't a little fall. You broke your hip. What if something like that happens again and there's nobody here to take care of you?"

"I'm a big girl. I can take care of myself."

"Mom," said Carter, "it's just a house for goodness sakes. It's just wood and glass and bricks, that's all. It's an investment."

"It's not a house. It's a home. You've never lived anywhere for fifty years. You don't understand. You've never had a house as the one constant in your life, watching over you as people were born and died. It's not a thing, Carter."

"What Mom is trying to say," said Abby.

"What Mom is trying to say," interrupted Nellie, "is that sometimes I don't know how you managed to have the good sense to marry my daughter in the first place, unless you thought she was just a good investment." Abby stifled a laugh.

"Mom," said Abby, "they'll take good care of you there. You'll be safe and you'll have your meals provided for you. Besides, you don't want to see this old house getting any more rundown than it is already. The garden is getting overrun with weeds and the siding is falling off. It needs a new coat of paint and probably will need a new roof next year. Come on. It's just too much for you. Someone else will move in here and they'll love your old house and take care of it for you."

"Well if you put it that way, I suppose you're right."

"Finally!" said Carter. "Can we schedule the garage sale now?"

"The what?" asked Nellie.

"Carter, did you have to bring that up now? She's just getting used to the idea of moving."

"What garage sale?"

"Mom, you have to be realistic," said Carter. "There's no room for all this stuff."

"Stuff! This isn't stuff. This is my life."

"Stop it, both of you!" yelled Abby. "I'm tired of being the referee between you two. It's tearing me apart. Carter, go wait in the car."

"I don't appreciate being talked to like that."

"Just go." Carter slinked out the door.

"Mom, as insensitive as Carter can be sometimes, he's still my husband and he's right. I can't help it if he isn't able to sugarcoat everything for you. I feel like I've spent my whole married life being a translator between you two. The thing is, there's no room where you're going for all of this. It's hard for me to part with it too. I thought it might be a good idea to sell off as much of it as we can. If you'd rather donate it to charity, we can do that instead."

"I suppose you're right. There's no room for it. There's no room for me, either."

"Mom, please. Don't say that. I'll tell you what. You can put whatever price you want on anything. And if you don't like the buyer you don't have to sell to them. That way you'll know that the right people are getting the right things and they'll take care of them for you. And anything you really want to hold onto, we'll take home and find some room for in the attic."

"Carter won't agree to that."

"Well, he'll have to. Carter has to face up to things and accept changes too, just like we all have to. Have we got a deal?"

"Okay."

"I'll buy you some stickers and you can put prices on everything. It'll be fun. And listen Mom, Carter is a good man. He's been a good husband and a good father. He's just not like us. He's more like Dad was."

"Don't you say a thing like that! Well, come to think of it, you're probably right. Your father drove me crazy plenty of times. Funny how time passes and all the memories smooth out and leave only the good ones. I know your father and I had some pretty big fights over the years but I certainly don't remember what any of them were about. You know what I remember the most?"

"What?"

"I remember him shaving. I used to love watching him shave. He always looked so serious and so manly lathering up the shaving brush and dabbing it on his face, standing in front of the mirror so straight and proud. Isn't that silly to remember something like that?"

"No Mom, it isn't silly. I think it's sweet. Listen, I have to go. Carter will be fuming in the car waiting for me. I'll come back in a couple of days with those stickers and we can price everything. Remember to take your medicine and call me if you have any problems."

The day of the garage sale arrived. Abby and Carter dragged

everything out of the house and set it all on tables on the driveway. Nellie sat patiently in a wheelchair with her two great-grandchildren. Four year old Jesse was a whirlwind of activity, running up and down the driveway, exploring all the little items on the tables, playing with toys, riding a tricycle, and throwing a ball against the wall. Six month old Kaylee sat in a stroller next to Nellie's wheelchair. Nellie was a bundle of nerves trying to keep tabs on Jesse to make sure he didn't do too much damage. Before the sale even opened, Jesse had managed to spill a cup of milk, bump into one of the tables sending silverware sprawling across the driveway, and whenever nobody was looking, he would poke his little sister and make her cry. Nellie loved her great-grandchildren, but she mostly watched them with wonder from a distance, as one watches a fast moving storm. Kaylee was too young to know Nellie existed and Jesse was too busy.

There was another crash as a pile of phonograph records toppled off a table. One of them escaped its sleeve and was rolling straight for the street. Carter ran after it and Nellie had a good laugh watching him, thinking he probably hadn't run for any reason in many years.

As people started arriving, Nellie sat patiently like a guard at a bank, making sure nobody stole any of her precious things. "Well Kaylee," she said to her great-granddaughter, "we're just in the way now sitting in our wheelchairs. There's no room in the world for either one of us I guess. You're not old enough to matter and I'm too old." Kaylee munched on her pacifier contentedly. "You see, that's how the world is. There's only room for walkers. If you can't walk you don't fit. Then they just put you in chairs that have wheels on them. We have a lot in common, you and I."

A man was looking intently at an old toaster. He picked it up and brought it to Abby who whispered something in his ear and pointed to

30

Nellie. The man looked over to Nellie and brought the toaster to her. "This is a fine toaster, Ma'am. I sure would love to have it. If I had a fine toaster like this I'd take real good care of it."

"Don't be so condescending. I may be old but I'm not stupid. Take the toaster. You can tell my daughter that I officially approve."

"The thing is, Ma'am, we had a toaster like this when I was a little boy. I miss all those things we all took for granted. They got old and we threw them away without even thinking about it. Things may work better nowadays but we sure don't get attached to them as much. You know what I mean?"

"Yes I certainly do."

"So the thing is, I'd really like to have this toaster because it reminds me of all the toast we made for peanut butter sandwiches when my brother and I watched television late at night. I just wanted you to know that."

"You're a nice man. Thank you for telling me that. You can have it for free."

"Oh no, I wouldn't think of it. Somebody went through a lot of trouble putting all those little stickers on everything. I want to pay the price that's on the sticker. Otherwise it's no deal."

"Well, thank you. Thank you very much." The man went off to pay Abby. As he was leaving he waved to Nellie and wished her good luck. Nellie gave a satisfied smile. Maybe this wouldn't be as bad as she'd feared.

Jesse snuck around to his sleeping sister and untied her sun bonnet. It fell off her head. She continued to sleep so Jesse poked her in the ribs. She woke with a start and began crying. Abby rushed over to her, picking her up and comforting her.

"Mom, didn't you see that her sun bonnet had fallen off? Why didn't you say anything? Poor little Kaylee." By this time Jesse had slipped off and was hiding behind one of the tables, smiling with satisfaction.

"I don't know why you had to bring them," said Nellie. "Where's Jenny?"

"She had to go to a class."

"And she left you with the little ones? Doesn't that girl have any consideration at all?"

"Let's not get into that discussion again, okay Mom? Jenny's doing the best she can."

"She could do better. For one thing, she could marry that good for nothing who fathered those children. I honestly don't understand these kids today. In my day we would have hidden away in shame having a child out of wedlock. Jenny's had two of them and instead of casting her out, you've taken her in and made things easy for her. I just don't understand it."

"Mom, there's nothing easy about Jenny's life. But it's her life. She has to make her own choices. Now she's going to school at night and on the weekends and she's working during the day. She's trying to better herself so she won't have to depend on her boyfriend. I'm very proud of her."

"Boyfriend, you call him. Hah!"

"What's this, Dad?" A boy about twelve years old held up Chester's shaving brush.

"Wow, I haven't seen one of those in years," answered his father. "That's an old shaving brush." He could see the puzzled look on his son's face. "You used to have to use those before there was canned shaving cream. You'd put special soap into a shaving mug and then stir it up with the brush to build up lather and then you'd brushed it on your face. That's how they made shaving cream back in the old days. My grandfather used to have one of those."

"Can I buy it?"

"What would you want it for?"

"It'll make a cool mustache on a snowman next winter."

"Well, I guess so. What's the price on it?"

"Fifty."

"Oh, I think we could afford that." The man gave Nellie a half-dollar. Instead of taking it, she kept her hand out as if expecting more money.

"That's fifty dollars," she said.

"What? Are you kidding me?"

"I most certainly am not." The man took the half dollar back.

"Better put it back, son. Maybe we can find one of those for you in a thrift shop. Fifty dollars is a bit too much."

Carter, hearing the conversation, ran up to Nellie incredulous. "Are you crazy?" he asked her. "Nobody in his right mind is going to buy that. You're never going to sell that for fifty dollars." Nellie just smiled contentedly. Carter went around to the various tables checking price tags. He sputtered and fumed. Then he grabbed Abby and pulled her into the garage supposedly so nobody could hear him but he didn't exactly talk in hushed tones.

"What's going on here?" he asked her. "Did you see those price tags?"

"Yes, I saw them. I helped her make them."

"Are you crazy too? This is ridiculous! Nobody's going to buy any of this stuff. I was wondering why things weren't moving faster. This is a joke. I gave up a golf game for this charade!"

"Carter, lower your voice. She'll hear you."

"I don't care if she hears me. What's the point of going through with this anyway? I swear Abby, you've put me through some pretty crazy stuff over the years but this, by God, is the worst. I'm getting out of here."

"Where are you going?"

"I don't know. I'll get a cup of coffee or something. If I stay here I'll say something I'll regret." Just about that time, Jesse poked Kaylee, waking her up yet again and making her wail. Abby rolled her eyes and went to attend to her granddaughter.

By lunchtime only a few things had been sold, mostly things Nellie didn't care about and had priced reasonably. Abby went into the house and got out the sandwiches they had made the night before. Nellie wasn't hungry and Jesse didn't like boloney. Kaylee was fussy but ate the baby food that Jenny had packed for her. In the middle of feeding her, Abby heard a crash. Jesse had been bouncing the ball off the wall and catching it. He fell backwards and knocked into a table sending cups and saucers crashing to the driveway. Abby looked to the heavens and took a deep breath. Then she calmly picked up the pieces and took them inside to throw away.

Shortly after lunch, a man carefully inspected Chester's old rocker recliner. He sat in it and extended the leg support. He rocked it and swiveled it and leaned back to recline in it. Then he got up and approached Nellie.

"I'd like to buy your old recliner but, I don't know. Two hundred dollars is a bit more than I can afford. The leather is a bit worn on it. Do you think you could come down on the price any?"

"Absolutely not," she said.

The recliner was Chester's special chair. She saw visions of him at parties with a room full of people, telling long drawn out stories, waving his arms dramatically, holding everyone spellbound. She saw him watching television, yelling at the screen when his favorite team was losing. She saw him holding newborn Abby and lifting her into the air. She could hear baby Abby squealing with delight. She saw him sitting in the chair after he'd gotten sick. She saw him skinny and frail. She saw him coughing and wincing in pain. She saw herself trying to feed him soup and him too weak to eat any of it. She saw his face with whiskers overgrown when he no longer had the strength even to get up and shave.

"You see," said the man, startling her out of her memories, "I wanted to get it for my father. He's getting kind of old and it would be perfect for him. I can't really afford to get a new one for him. He lives at the Parker Retirement Home and what with the costs of keeping him there and all. Well, it was just a thought. I can understand your not wanting to part with it. It looks like it has a lot of memories for you."

"Wait! What did you say?"

"I was just saying that . . . ."

"Did you say the Parker Retirement Home?"

"Yes. That's where my father is living now. He was getting too old to keep up the house and all."

"Does he like it there?"

"Oh yes he does. He didn't think he would. It took a lot to talk him into agreeing to go there. He's a very proud man, you know. Worked twenty-five years in a factory. It took him a while to get used to the change but I'd say he kind of likes it there now. They've got a great support staff and good food. He's made a lot of friends there."

"What's your father's name?"

"John Hamilton."

"I'll have to look him up when I get there. Would you do me a favor?"

"Sure if I can."

"Would you take that old chair for free?"

"I couldn't do that. Let me pay you something. It's worth at least fifty dollars I'd say."

"No, you take it. It would make me very happy if you would."

"Gosh, I don't know what to say."

"Just say 'Thank you'. That should suffice."

"Thank you. Thank you very much. My father's really going to enjoy that chair. His back's been hurting him a lot recently even though he won't admit it."

"Really? Well you see that heating pad on the table there? It fits perfectly into the back of the chair. You take that too."

"Wow. I don't know how to thank you."

"You already have."

The man went back to his van and pulled out a dolly and soon the chair and the heating pad were gone.

"That was a nice thing you did, Nels."

Nellie looked up and saw her beloved Chester standing over her. He looked like he did when they were first married. He wore a crisp white shirt. His brown leather suspenders held up his straight black trousers. He stood strong, young, and proud. He pulled up a chair and sat next to her.

"Well, good Lord, what are you doing here?"

"I'm always nearby, Nellie. You know that. You talk to me every evening. I always hear you."

"I miss you Chet. I miss you every day of my life."

"I know that. But we'll be together again soon enough."

"Is it nice where you are?"

"It's nearly perfect. There's only one thing missing."

"What's that?"

"Why, you of course."

"Well don't rush me, dear." Chester laughed. She'd forgotten the healing power his laughter always had on her. "Honestly, Chet, I often wonder why I'm still here. I'm certainly no use to anyone."

"You are, more than you can ever realize."

"Oh Chester, I can't stand the thought of letting go of all these things. It's like losing you all over again."

"But they're just things, Nellie."

"But those things hold such dear memories."

"No they don't. The memories aren't in those things. They're in you and you can keep them. Before we bought this old house, it held someone else's memories. The house itself is just brick and wood and glass after all."

"Oh God! You mean Carter was actually right about something? That's pretty hard to accept."

"Now you stop getting on about Carter. He's Abby's husband and he's a good man. He works hard and he's faithful and loyal. You can't ask for more than that."

"I could."

"Well, that's another story. Your standards were obviously higher."

"Yeah, go on about yourself. Oh Chet, you were always able to help me see things clearly. I think that's what I miss the most. Everything's so confusing these days. The world's turned topsy-turvy. I don't understand anything anymore."

"It's not your world anymore. It belongs to Jesse and Kaylee here. It'll make sense enough to them. And they'll grow up brave and strong just like we did. And you'll be with me and we can watch it all unfold together. I have to go now. Goodbye my dearest. I'll see you again soon." He stood up, holding Nellie's hand and then he disappeared in a mist.

"Mom? Mom? Are you all right?" Nellie hadn't noticed Abby standing in front of her.

"Yes dear. I'm fine. I'm fine now."

"You looked like you were going to faint."

"I'm fine, dear. Really."

"Well, this man wants to buy Dad's desk. I know you wanted two hundred dollars for it. He's willing to pay one hundred. I told him I'd ask you."

"What? Oh, sure. One hundred dollars? That would be fine."

"Are you sure? I know that desk has a lot of memories for you."

"Oh don't be ridiculous, dear. There aren't any memories in the desk. They're all in me. And I get to keep them. Sell the desk. Sell everything. I don't need those things anymore."

"Are you sure?"

"Yes I'm sure."

Jesse, bored to tears, came stalking by, trying to bother Kaylee again. "Why do you do that?" asked Nellie.

"It's fun," answered Jesse.

"Yes but it bothers her."

"I don't care. I don't like her."

"Oh? And why not?"

"I don't know. She's stupid. She can't do anything. And she smells really stinky when she poops in her pants."

"She's just a baby. You did that too when you were a baby."

"Did not! Well, maybe I did but I still don't like her. I wanted a baby brother. Girls are stupid. They're no fun."

"But if you had a baby brother, he would be exactly the same until he got older anyway."

"Well maybe but it's still fun making her cry."

"Is it? Well I've got an idea that might be even more fun."

"Really?"

"Yes, really. You see that thing on the table over there?"

"That brush with the wooden handle?"

"Yeah. You know what that is?"

"It's a shaving brush. I heard you talking about it before."

"No, it isn't a shaving brush. That's just pretend. It's really a magic brush."

"It is?"

"Sure. But its magic can only be revealed to brave young boys. Are you a brave young boy?"

"I sure am."

"Well then I can tell you its magic power. It's really a tickle brush."

"It is?"

"Sure. You go get it and rub it against Kaylee's nose and see what happens." Jesse scampered over to the table and retrieved the shaving brush. He rubbed it against Kaylee's nose and she let out a tiny laugh.

"Do it again," said Nellie.

Jesse did it again and again and soon had Kaylee squealing with laughter. Every time she laughed, Jesse laughed too. "You see how much fun that is? And you don't have to run and hide and get in trouble like when you make her cry."

"It is fun. I didn't know she knew how to laugh. She's funny."

Late in the afternoon, Carter returned. He looked around at the tables and was immediately upset all over again. "Abby, why did you put everything away? We still have a couple more hours left."

"I didn't put anything away. We sold it all."

"What? You're kidding me."

"No I'm not. We sold everything. We have almost five hundred dollars here and Mom's taking us all out to dinner."

"But how? Everything was overpriced."

"Oh, I brought the prices down on everything," Nellie said.

"You did? But I thought you didn't want to part with any of it. All those memories."

"Oh don't be ridiculous, Carter. They're just things. Now let's all go out to dinner and make some new memories."

"Can I push Kaylee's stroller?" asked Jesse.

"Well I don't know," said Carter. "Maybe I'd better."

"She's my sister. I want to push her. You push Granny Nellie."

"What happened here?" asked Carter.

"I don't know," said Abby.

40

"Chet," said Kaylee.

"Did she just say Chet?" asked Carter.

"No. She couldn't have. I think she just coughed."

Cerulean Blue

The man in the black suit showed up again, the third time that week, and he was making Lesley very nervous. And even though there were other tables available, he waited for the booth under the painting.

"Gus, do you know that guy?" Lesley asked the owner of the diner.

"Your guess is as good as mine," answered Gus. "I think he likes your painting."

"Maybe, but he creeps me out. Do you think I could take the booth and see if I can get any information?"

"It's okay with me if it's okay with Jan but it looks like you're too late. Jan's already over there."

As Lesley tended to her customers she kept glancing at the man in the black suit who again ordered only a cup of coffee and a sweet roll and again spent most of his time staring at the painting.

Lesley had painted it for Gus as a gift. It was a portrait of Gus's wife who had since passed away. Gus hung it on the wall directly across from the cash register where he could always see it. When Lesley heard that Greta had taken ill, she began the portrait from a photograph. Lesley didn't like painting from photos. She preferred live subjects. But this was to be a surprise gift. Nobody could have predicted how quickly Greta's health would fail. She didn't live to see the painting completed. The look in Gus's eyes when she gave it to him was worth the labor and expense it had taken to create it. It was one of those times when an inner knowing took over in Lesley. She'd learned to trust that inner voice. It hadn't failed her yet.

Gus was completely devoted to his Greta. It was why he chose to name the restaurant Gigi's. Everyone always kidded both Gus and Greta,

43

asking who Gigi was. But the name was really G for Gus and G for Greta, Gigi's. They had started the business together and because they'd never had children, they threw all their energy into it and each other.

Going to Gigi's restaurant was a weekly event for Lesley and her parents for as long as she could remember. When she was little, she would wander into the kitchen and talk to the cooks and dishwashers. Sometimes they would place her in a huge metal soup cauldron and pretend they were making Lesley soup. When Lesley was in grade school and learning to count, Gus would hoist her onto his lap and teach her how to run the cash register and make change. Gus came to be known as Grandpa Gus. On one occasion, Lesley's father completely forgot to pay the check. It just felt so much like visiting family at Gigi's he didn't even think about it. An hour later it hit him and he was so worried about it, he jumped into his car and drove back to the diner. Gus refused to accept his money. Instead he pinned the check to the wall. "If it felt so much like family in here that you forgot to pay, that's payment enough," he said. "Go on home." Later Gus framed the check and kept it permanently on the wall.

When Lesley was in high school and old enough to work, Gus gave her the job he'd promised her when she was seven. When he heard that Lesley aspired to be an artist, he bought her her first easel and paint set. Now her painting of his beloved Greta hung on the wall of his restaurant. He wasn't able to look at it without feeling a fullness deep inside himself. It reminded him of his love both for Greta and for Lesley.

Lesley cornered Jan near the condiment station and asked about the man in the black suit. "I don't know anything about him," said Jan. "He sure seems to like your painting though. I've tried talking to him, you know, asking him about his day and stuff. That usually gets people talking.

But other than ordering his coffee and sweet roll, I haven't heard much out of him. At least he's a decent tipper, though."

After the morning rush, Lesley raced on her bicycle to the Junior College where she was taking an art class. Most of her friends from high school had long since finished college but Lesley could only afford to take a single class each term. Several years earlier, her father had had an accident at the factory where he worked and he had been on disability ever since. It took him nearly half the day just to be able to stand up straight. Lesley's mother worked at the local Wal-Mart and occasionally filled in at dinner time at Gigi's restaurant.

When Lesley arrived home that night she kissed her father's forehead and asked him how he was feeling. At first he was annoyed at her blocking his view of the television but quickly shifted and pulled her close to him.

"How did school go today, Ressie?" he asked her. When Lesley first learned to talk, "Ressie" was as close as she could come to pronouncing her own name and the nickname stuck.

"It was good. We had a model come in. Those are my favorite classes."

"Can I see your work?"

"Sure." Lesley pulled out her sketchpad from her backpack. Richard immediately blushed and turned away.

"You have people in your class walking around naked?" he asked.

Lesley laughed. "She's a model, Dad. It's an art class. You can't be that much of a prude or I wouldn't be here." Richard blushed again and turned his attention back to the safety of the television set. It always unnerved him when his daughter reminded him that she was an adult. He still thought of her as the little toddler dancing in the living room, pretending she was Cinderella at the ball.

"Dinner's almost ready," called out Lesley's mother, Ellie, from the kitchen. Richard turned off the television and began extricating himself from the large recliner, wincing from the pain in his back. Lesley put down her things and went to help him but he brushed her aside.

"I can manage," he said. "It's only a little back pain. I'm not a cripple, you know. I'll probably be back at work in a couple of weeks." He'd been saying that for three years. And every time Lesley heard it, it choked her up, knowing what a strong proud man her father was and how much his emotional pain eclipsed the physical.

"Car's been acting up again," said Ellie. "I think it's the transmission."

"I'll take it over to Jake's in the morning."

"He's fixed it three times already. Doesn't seem to stay fixed. I think we ought to be thinking about getting a new car."

"Thinking about it is all we can afford to do."

"There's a used Chevy down at Simpson's lot. We could take out a loan. There's no use giving our hard earned money to Jake every other month."

"I suppose you're right. I hate to get deeper in debt though. Things just don't seem to be getting any better."

"It'll turn, Richard."

He slammed his fist on the table. "It pisses me off, Ellie! It pisses me off! I don't care so much about not having a car that works. I don't care if we can't get a new air conditioner or that the garage is falling apart. But damn it! I hate the fact that Lesley's got to work instead of going to school full time. A man who can't provide for his own child is only half a man."

"Daddy don't. Please don't do that to yourself. It breaks my heart to see you like this. Things are hard enough for us. I don't want you feeling bad on my account. I don't mind. Really."

"You don't mind? You don't mind that all your friends finished school a year ago and you're still struggling along class by class? You don't mind that they go traveling and dress up and go to parties that you have to pass up?"

"That's right. I don't mind. Franny's parents are divorced, and Teri's parents should have been, and don't forget Alfred's father who was killed in the same accident you got hurt in. I won't have you talking that way. At least we still have each other and we're still together. Compared to them, I consider myself very lucky so please don't be hard on yourself. Mom's right. Thing's will turn around and even if they don't, we still have a lot to be thankful for."

After a long sullen silence, Richard spoke up again. "You're right, Ressie. I'm sorry. I just get so tired sometimes. I keep waiting for things to change and I forget to appreciate what we already have. It's hard to remember sometimes. I just want things to be easier, just a little easier, that's all I'm asking for."

"Well maybe it would be easier if you just stopped struggling so much," said Ellie. "You don't have to work right now. Stop fighting it. You're healing. Maybe if you'd just accept that, you'd heal faster or at least have a little more enjoyment out of your life. There's no shame in not being able to work. God just gave you some time off because you refused to take it yourself. Allow us take care of you for a change."

The next morning, the man in the black suit was back again. As he

47

was paying his bill, he got into a rather lengthy discussion with Gus. Lesley stole glances at the cash register in between taking orders and delivering them. Gus shook his head. The man pointed to the painting several times. Gus just kept shaking his head and at one point he was waving his arms like he did when he was upset. The other man put up his hands to calm Gus down and then he left.

"What was all that about?" she asked him later.

"What was what about?"

"That man. What were you arguing about?"

"Don't concern yourself about it. It was nothing."

"Grandpa Gus, you look me in the eye and tell me the truth."

"He wants to buy the painting."

"Of Greta? My painting?"

"Yes. I told him she wasn't for sale and the son of a bitch started arguing with me."

"Well, did you explain why you couldn't sell it?"

"I certainly did. I told him my Greta wasn't for sale and if he didn't stop asking I would punch him in the nose. That's what I told him. I don't care if he is half my age. My Greta isn't for sale."

"Well maybe he didn't understand."

"No, he didn't. He just kept offering me more money. It was an insult to my Greta. She's not for sale, not even for two thousand dollars."

"Two thousand dollars? Are you serious?"

"She's not for sale."

"Yeah, I know but maybe I could paint something else for him."

"Oh my goodness, you're right. Lesley, I didn't think. He got me so worked up. Go quickly before he drives off."

She ran out of the restaurant and looked up and down the street but he was gone. Gus apologized a dozen times the rest of the morning. Lesley waved it off but inwardly she was a mess of emotions. The thought of anyone willing to pay that much for one of her paintings delighted her and frightened her. It gave her goose bumps thinking about it. On the other hand, she had no idea who the man was and after his heated discussion with Gus, she was sure she'd never see him again anyway.

For the rest of the day, she couldn't stop thinking about the man in the black suit, wondering who he was and why he was so interested in the painting of Greta, and most of all, the fact that he was willing to pay so much money for it. She made up all kinds of fantasies about it. The painting reminded him of a lost love and he'd give anything to have her near him again. Or it reminded him of his mother and it made him feel warm again thinking of her making him soup and tucking him in bed at night.

When she got home that night, she didn't say anything about it. She could just imagine how disappointed her parents would be to have been so close to even a small windfall only to have it slip out of their hands again. There was nothing she could do about it so it was better not to even mention it.

Her father was in a considerably better mood that night. After dinner, Lesley rubbed his back with lotion, which always cheered him. They watched some television together but Lesley's thoughts drifted several times back to the man in the black suit.

The next morning Lesley looked at the door every time she heard someone enter the restaurant but the man in the black suit did not show up. The following morning, however, he did and he was accompanied by another man; that one wearing a blue suit. They waited by the door passing up several tables and booths so they could be seated under the painting of Greta. This time Lesley got there before Jan did.

"Good morning, gentlemen. What can I get for you?" It seemed they had forgotten they were in a restaurant. They hastily glanced at the menu as though ordering food was an afterthought. She wrote down the order and then said, "You seem to be very interested in that painting. May I ask why?"

The man in the black suit regarded her for a second and decided to answer. "We want to buy it."

"It's not for sale," she said. "It's a special painting. I can't imagine Gus ever parting with it."

"He wouldn't tell us who the artist is. Would you know?"

Suddenly the boldness drained from her as their eyes focused on hers. Suddenly she was like a bird being offered a handful of food but afraid and tentative. "No. No I don't. I, I better get your order in." She left the table. They continued to study the painting.

It bothered her the rest of the day. Should she have told them or shouldn't she? Why had she lied to them? What was she afraid of? After class she caught up with her friend Salem, another girl in the class.

"Are you crazy?" said Salem. "Why did you tell them that?"

"I don't know. They made me uncomfortable. And Greta's painting isn't for sale anyway so what's the difference? It isn't mine to sell."

"Lesley, you're an artist. You have other work. Those guys want to buy. For God's sake, we wait our whole lives for an opportunity like that. Most of us never get a chance to sell our work. Why would you turn them away?"

"I don't know. It just doesn't seem right to sell art."

"Then what are you doing this for? I thought you wanted to be an artist, Lesley. You want to work your whole life in that diner and only have this as a hobby? If you want to be an artist, then sooner or later you're going to have to get out of your shell and declare yourself."

"It scares me. Okay? There, I've said it. I'm not ready to be out there. It's weird enough having that painting hanging at Gus's diner. I'm not ready."

"You're not ready to be successful? Well, ready or not, the customers are coming so you better make a choice. If you want to get anywhere you better put your fears aside and get out there and run the race."

"Yeah, but what if I'm not that good? What if I'm just fooling myself?"

"Well, as far as I can see, you've got some real customers with real money. If your work isn't good enough, that's their problem. Come on, Lesley, think of what you could do for your family. You're always talking about how tough things are for you. Here's a chance for you to do something about it. If it were me, I'd get out there and talk to those guys and take their money. It's time for you to stop being an artist and start being a salesman."

As much as it scared her to think about it, she knew Salem was right. Unfortunately, the guys in the suits stopped coming to the restaurant. Gus noticed her moping over the next couple of days. She didn't have her usual cheery smile.

"What's the matter, little angel?" he asked. "Is everything all right at home? You have clouds over your head."

"You remember those guys who wanted to buy your painting?"

"Our painting. Yes."

"Well, I feel like I missed a chance. I could have sold them something else. And now they're gone. I feel like I blew it."

"I see. Well, there's a lesson in there for you, isn't there? You have to take advantage of opportunities when they're in front of you."

"I didn't know it was an opportunity. Well, I guess I did. I just got scared. And now they're gone."

"Yes, they're gone. So you've learned something?"

"I don't know Grandpa Gus. Life seems awfully confusing sometimes."

"Well, if it's any consolation, it doesn't get any easier when you're older." Lesley laughed and relaxed a bit. Gus rummaged through the drawer under the cash register. He found the small card he was looking for. "So maybe this will help," he said. "They left a business card. I would have given it to you sooner but I thought you weren't interested in doing anything for them. You must have changed your mind. You must have found some courage. Good. Now you go for it, Lesley. For as long as I've known you, I looked forward to having you work here. And for as long as you've been working here, I've looked forward to replacing you. You're an artist, not a waitress. Now go and be an artist."

Lesley hugged him and gave him a kiss. "You're the best, Gus."

She went into Gus's office. Her hands shook as she made the call.

"Abernathy Advertising Company. How can I help you?"

"I'd like to speak to Stanley Howard please."

"Just a minute, I'll see if he's available. Who should I say is calling?"

"Uh, well, he doesn't know me. My name is Lesley Hart. I'm the

52

artist who painted the portrait he wanted to buy at Gigi's Restaurant."

"Just a moment please." A minute later, a booming voice came on the line.

"Hello? You're the artist?"

"Yes, I'm the artist."

"Great. He's decided to sell?"

"Uh, well, no. I'm afraid not, but I was thinking that if you were interested, I mean, I could, well, I have other work and I could even paint something new for you. I mean, if you were interested."

"Can you bring some samples to my office tomorrow morning? You have my address?"

"Yes. Could we make it in the afternoon? I work in the mornings. Oh, wait, I have class tomorrow. Could we make it the next day?"

"Well, I'd have to check my schedule."

"Wait a minute. Never mind. Let's make it tomorrow morning."

"Great. Be at my office at ten."

Lesley arrived the next morning at the offices of Abernathy Advertising Company. She was led into a conference room. Stanley Howard and a few associates laid out her work on the large table. Lesley felt like she did at the doctor's office, exposed and vulnerable, examined and pored over. Only this was worse. She sat nervously on the side and watched their expressions. Finally Stanley left the table and approached her.

"These are good. They're very good. But they aren't what we're looking for."

"Oh. I see. But you wanted the painting in the diner."

"Yes, that would have been perfect."

"Perfect for what exactly?"

"You've heard of Mama Larson's oatmeal?"

"Sure, who hasn't?"

"The Larson Company is looking for a new agency to handle them and we are vying for the business. I'm convinced that the key is to present a definitive image of Mama Larson herself, a nice homey oatmeal breakfast made by a kindly grandmother kind of image. We just can't seem to find the right face. Your painting would have been perfect. That painting showed all the goodness and gentleness we want to portray. Now the question is, could you do it again? Could you paint another one like it?"

"I don't think so. That portrait is Gus's late wife. It wouldn't be right. He'd never agree to it and I don't think I could either."

"It doesn't have to be her. What I'm asking is whether you could get those qualities again with a different face?"

"Oh. Well, that's different. Yes, I could try."

"Of course we would pay you for your efforts whether we used the portrait or not. Would a thousand dollars be enough for you?"

"A thousand dollars?"

"We could make it more if that isn't enough."

"Are you serious?"

"Okay, I can see you drive a hard bargain but your talent appears to be worth the investment. Why don't we just make it an even two thousand dollars? Of course there would be more if we get the account. In that case we could probably go as high as an additional ten thousand and of course if they go national, well, that would get you additional residuals and royalties amounting to maybe around fifty thousand, maybe more."

Lesley couldn't answer. She was too dumbfounded. Stanley called his assistant who arrived moments later with a check. Lesley took it and stuffed it into her pocket, gathered her paintings and stumbled out of the office.

Later on her way home after class, she stopped at a bank and deposited the check taking out a hefty sum for herself. She bought a bouquet of flowers for her mother and a vibrating heated cushion for her father to help ease his back pain. She wanted to take her parents to a fancy restaurant for dinner but after some discussion they decided that only Gigi's would do for the celebration. Gus was very glad to see Richard out of the house and feeling better. As dessert was served, Lesley gave her mother an envelope containing two hundred dollars.

"What's this for?"

"I'm paying you to be my model. I want you to pose for my painting of Mama Larson. Your face will be famous, seen all over the world."

"Me a model? That's ridiculous. No I couldn't. Believe me, nobody wants to see my face when they're trying to enjoy their breakfast."

"There's no other face I'd rather see," answered Lesley. "Besides, if you won't do it, then I won't either. I'll call the whole thing off. They want a sweet, kind, and gentle face. I don't know anyone who better fits that description than you, Mom."

Ellie pulled off her glasses and dabbed her eyes with a napkin. She reluctantly agreed to do it.

Over the next two weeks, Lesley worked daily on the painting. Although Ellie was getting excited at the thought of becoming famous, modeling was much more difficult than she thought it would be. She was required to hold a pose for what seemed like hours and invariably her nose would itch or she would yawn, or her head would drift. She would get hungry or have to use the bathroom. Lesley tried to remain patient with her but every interruption broke her concentration. When the sessions completed each day, Lesley would cover the canvas and not allow anyone to see it.

Finally it was finished. Richard poured glasses of wine for the unveiling. He and Ellie settled themselves on the sofa and Lesley lifted the cloth off the painting. Ellie gasped and then cried. Like Greta's portrait at the restaurant, this painting showed everything, inside and out. The visage on the canvas was strong and proud but gentle too, filled with warmth and humor and courage. Ellie was deeply touched, seeing herself through her daughter's eyes. She felt complete as a woman and a mother. Richard shook his head with disbelief and felt immensely proud of both his wife and his daughter. He kept noticing tiny details and pointing them out, marveling at the depth of Lesley's vision and her ability to portray it.

After allowing enough time for the painting to dry, Lesley wrapped it up and took it to the Abernathy Advertising Company. Everyone there concurred that it was exactly what they were looking for and an even better choice than the painting at the diner. The next step was to show it to the client and they planned to do so at a festive black tie reception in the Crystal Ballroom at the Blasingame Hotel.

Richard fussed and fumed at the idea of having to wear a tuxedo. He didn't even own a suit. "It's a waste of money. No, I won't do it. You go without me."

"Dad, don't be ridiculous. We're going to get something like ten to twenty thousand dollars if they want the painting. I think we can afford a hundred for a tuxedo for you. And besides, if you don't go I'm not going either."

"What if run into any of my friends down there?"

"They probably won't recognize you," said Ellie.

Ellie decided to wear a relatively new dress that she wore to a cousin's wedding the previous year. Lesley was undecided. Gus had an old gown of Greta's he had kept but it was quite atrocious. Lesley tactfully explained to him that it was just too good of a dress for her. She went to several shops but couldn't find anything she liked. Then Salem showed up with a slinky red gown with tiny straps. She had done a modeling job and they paid her by giving her the dress she'd modeled.

"Oh, I can't. It's too much."

"Try it on," said Salem. "You might as well use it. God knows I'll never get a chance to wear it. Besides, it isn't really my style."

Lesley reluctantly agreed and clomped up the stairs to put the dress on. A gorgeous sophisticated woman came back down the stairs with tears in her eyes. It fit perfectly. She loved it. She hugged Salem, who promised to come by on the night of the party to help her with her hair and makeup.

When the big night arrived and they entered the ballroom, it was as if they had emerged into a different world. Richard was very uncomfortable, especially if anyone came up to him asking who he was. He felt like apologizing for not being anyone important. Although nearly everyone was drinking champagne from tall spiked crystal glasses, Richard convinced the bartender to get him a beer which he drank out of the bottle at a table he found in an out of the way corner of the room. Ellie stayed with him even though she would have preferred to look at all the beautiful gowns and talk to people. That left Lesley to wander alone trying different hors d'oeuvres. She found one she thought would be sweet but it was very salty and made her gag and cough.

"It's caviar," said a voice behind her. She turned around to see a very handsome young man about her age looking very sharp in a tuxedo that did not look to be a rental. "You kind of have to get used to it. It's actually fish eggs."

"I know what caviar is. I've just never tried it before."

"Sorry. I didn't mean to offend. I'm Derek. What's a lovely lady like you doing in these shark infested waters? You must be somebody's daughter."

"Actually I'm . . ."

"I wonder if that's her coming in now. No, couldn't be."

"You're looking for someone?"

"I'm supposed to be on the lookout for the artist. She must not have arrived yet."

"Oh, well actually . ."

"I figure she must be some matronly old crone, probably with wild gray hair and a mustache, wearing some dowdy faded dress smelling of mothballs. You know how artists are. I mean real artists, not like all these phony advertising types. So whose daughter are you? I haven't seen you around before."

"I'm the daughter of the woman in the painting."

"Oh! Do you know the artist then? Have you met her?"

"Well, not exactly. Who are you? Are you one of the phony advertising types?"

"Please, don't insult me. Oh, I work for the company but only under duress. My father owns it. But no, I'm not an advertising guy. No way am I going to be stuck here the rest of my life. I want to be a real artist."

"So, what's stopping you?"

"Money of course. My dear old Dad won't give me a penny. He says I have to start at the bottom like he did. 'It builds character, son'. I've got news for you. It doesn't build character. It just builds resentment. I hardly ever saw him growing up and all the time he excused it saying he was doing it all for me. And now he won't share any of it with me. But then again, I'm probably just fooling myself."

"What do you mean?"

"Well, I've dabbled you know. I've tried my hand at painting. Some of my stuff is kind of okay. But then I see something like that portrait of your mother and it's like, jeez, I could never be that good. That's a whole different level. I mean my stuff looks okay but then you see a painting like that and you can just feel it. You know what I mean?"

"I hadn't really noticed."

"That's because you don't have a trained artist's eye. What kind of work do you do?"

"I'm a waitress in a small diner."

"Yeah, you see? I don't mean to put you down, but you have to have an artist's eye to really appreciate it. It pisses me off too, because all these goons in here see when they look at a painting like that is money. I feel sorry for the poor old bat who painted it. I hope they pay her enough. They're going to chew her up and then when they're done with her, they'll spit her out. And I'm ashamed to say I'm part of it. I'm supposed to find her and pour on the bullshit and convince her that selling her soul is the noblest thing she can do for our great society. Don't tell anyone but that idiot Howard forgot to get her to sign a contract. Boy is he in trouble. Got us into a bit of a pickle. Want to get a breath of fresh air? I want to show

59

you something."

"Well, I suppose I can slip out for a little while."

"It's okay. They won't officially present the painting for another half hour or so. They have to wait until everyone's sufficiently plastered. They're more pliable then. It's an old advertising trick. Anything to bypass judgment and get people to come around."

Derek took her by the hand and led her out of the ballroom toward the bank of elevators. She was amazed at how easy it was to go with him. They went to the top floor. Derek forced open an unmarked brown door behind which was a staircase. At the top of the stairs was a thick metal door that was unlocked. It opened to the roof of the hotel twenty stories above the street.

"You see that?" he said. "That's real art." The city spread out below them. The sky was just darkening. It had that deep rich fullness of cerulean blue. Small tufts of clouds hung motionless. The tiniest crescent of a moon punctuated the sky and just a few tentative stars began waking up to the night. There was a cool clean breeze that felt like cold water splashing against their faces, waking them up.

They stood there watching the world without saying anything. Lesley was startled to notice he was still holding her hand. It felt warm and protective. She felt safe in it. She looked up at him. He had a great face. She thought she would one day want to paint it before it changed. His face struggled against the world, yearning to be free. It held reserves of humor and goodness that would one day come out to full expression. She wanted to help them come out. She wanted to free the little boy inside who just wanted to feel the wind blowing on his face as he swung on the swing in the playground just a little too high, just enough to scare himself and impress

60

the girls.

He noticed her looking at him and realized he was still holding her hand. He quickly let go even though he wanted to hold on. He wanted to tell her how exquisite she looked, how her beauty rivaled the rich blue sky, how her face changed every second and gave full expression to each nuance. She had bright dazzling eyes lit from within. He had to look away.

"We'd better get back," he said.

When they returned, a man was standing next to the painting with a microphone in his hand making a speech. He briefly mentioned the painting but the speech was more a seduction of the potential client, extolling the praises of Mama Larson's products and especially her oatmeal. He went into a long Norman Rockwell scenario of a long ago time in simpler days when Mama Larson's oatmeal was served to eager pristine young children who never misbehaved and there was no evil in the world. Finally he tied in the painting as the symbol and embodiment of Mama Larson and how this new ad campaign would not only restore the product to its former greatness, but would transform the world back into the Garden of Eden it once was.

"And now I'd like to introduce the young artist who painted this masterpiece, Lesley Hart. Lesley, would you come up here please?"

To Derek's utter amazement, Lesley left his side and walked through the crowd to the man with the microphone as the people applauded her. When Lesley turned around she looked straight at Derek with a triumphant smile on her face. He'd been had and he knew it. And it was his own doing. He realized he'd never even asked her her name. He was embarrassed, trying to remember all the things he shouldn't have said to her. As he watched her standing there at the front of the ballroom basking in everyone's admiration, he was proud of her and all the more attracted to her.

When they were together again he said, "I'm so embarrassed. You must think I'm very stupid."

"I think you're sweet."

"Is that a good thing?"

"Yes, that's a very good thing."

"Okay. But would you please forget all the dumb things I said?"

"That wouldn't be much fun. I think I'll probably remember them until I'm a matronly old bat with a mustache and mothballs."

"Oh God!"

"And of course I'll do whatever I can to make sure you remember too."

They were interrupted by Stanley Howard, the man in the black suit, now in a black tuxedo. "Congratulations, Lesley. You and your painting are a big hit. I think we've got this account in the bag. Can you come by on Thursday? We'll sign all the papers then?"

"Yes, I'll be there."

After he left, Derek said to her, "Be sure you read them first. Get yourself a good lawyer. I don't want them to hurt you. You're too good for them."

"I'm sure I'll be fine but thank you. Will I, uh, see you again?"

"Just let somebody try and keep me away. Yes, I would love to see you again. Maybe you can teach me how to paint."

On the strength of Lesley's painting, the Abernathy Advertising Company landed the Mama Larson account amounting to a multi-million dollar deal. Lesley showed up on the appointed day to sign the contract. She didn't bring a lawyer as Derek had suggested. She trusted herself to know what to do. Before signing, she had a few questions.

"When you're finished with the painting, I get it back, right?"

"Yes, of course."

"And how much are you paying me?"

"You're getting twenty thousand dollars up front." Lesley made a quick intake of breath as her heart started beating faster.

"Okay, sounds pretty good." She was just about to sign but stopped and asked, "Oh, one more thing. When do you think I'll get it back?"

"Probably in about a month. Our artists will have to work on it to make the necessary changes. It should be returnable soon after that."

"Uh, what necessary changes? You didn't say anything about any changes."

"I didn't? I assumed it was understood. It's normal procedure. Just about all original art goes through some changes before final usage."

"But what kind of changes?"

"Please understand, Lesley, our client loves your painting. But they pictured Mama Larson a bit older and a little heavier. They're just going to do some touchup along those lines. They'll put a few pounds on her, color the hair gray, add a few wrinkles, and put an apron on her."

"Wait a minute. You can't do that. That's my mother."

"It's standard procedure."

"Not with my painting it isn't."

"I'm afraid it's too late. The deal has been struck. We're set to go into print production in a month."

"But you can't. I won't let you."

"Lesley, sweetheart, this is business. This is the way things are done. I'll tell you what. Let's sweeten the deal a little. This was going to be a surprise but I'll tell you about it now. We're going to be doing some television commercials. I can probably guarantee we can hire your mother to do the commercials. On a national ad, the residuals and public appearances could set you all up for life. That's something professional actors dream of getting. What do you say?"

"I say give me my painting back. My mother isn't for sale and neither am I."

"Young lady, it's just a painting. You can paint others. You're holding up a million dollar deal here. Okay, I'll tell you what. Take your painting back. Think about it. Okay? I'll call you in a couple of days."

He called as promised. And every day after that. At first he was gentle, trying to convince her how good it would be to have the freedom all that money would give them. Her father could get the best medical care. He wouldn't have to worry about going back to work. She could afford the best art schools. Her family could get a bigger house. When that didn't work, he pushed harder, playing on her guilt and accusing her of being self-centered and childish, holding up a big deal and inconveniencing many people, possibly putting their jobs at risk.

Lesley was adamant. She would not let them deface her painting. But the more he worked on her, the more doubt crept in. He was right, after all. There were wonderful things she could get with all that money. It was only one painting after all. What would be the harm? Her parents told her it would have to be her decision to make, but Lesley could see the pain of financial pressure weighing down on them and all the more so now, with a way out.

Salem thought she was crazy to waste a second thinking about it. "It's money, Babe. Take it and don't look back. There's plenty of time for principles later." Gus sided with her. He only had to look at his beloved

Greta and imagine anyone trying to change a brushstroke on that painting.

She had to ask Derek. Surely he of all people could see both sides of it. They met for dinner. "I just don't know what to do. Is it selfish of me not to want to help my family? I want to. I'd give anything to help them, or so I thought. I just don't know what to do. You have to help me, Derek."

"Can you trust me not to be on their side?"

"If I can't trust you then I can't trust anyone. I think maybe in a strange way, you're the only one I can trust."

"Lesley, I'll tell you the truth. That account means a lot to the company. They've been struggling. If they don't get that account, there will be a lot of layoffs. They've been counting on it. And it's not just that one account. In the advertising game, each account that's won sells the agency to the next one they chase after. It'll build their reputation with other companies if they have the Mama Larson account.

"Now let's look at your side of it. Your father's been ill. The right medical treatment could help him. Your house is small and old. Your mother's been working her whole life. Instead, you could be looking at a healthy father who could go back to work if he wanted to but probably wouldn't have to. Your mother could get herself a garden in a new house and not have to worry so much. You could go to the best art school anywhere and attend full time. If it were me, I wouldn't think twice about it. I'd go for it."

"You really think I should?"

"I said if it were me. But you aren't me. You're you. I have no idea what it's like to have talent like yours. I don't know where it comes from and I don't know how fragile it might be. I wouldn't tamper with it. You don't just make isolated choices, Lesley, you move through them and they change you. I don't know what it would do to you. I don't know who you would be on the other side of it. I don't know if it's just a matter of selling a painting or if it's selling your soul, but I do know this; once the deal is done, there's no turning back again."

"But that goes both ways. I could be wrong if I sell it and let them change it. But I could just as easily be plagued with guilt the rest of my life if I don't; if I pass up this opportunity not just for myself but for my family as well."

"That's true. So you have to do what feels right. And only you can know what that is. But if you ask me, I think it's better to make your choice based on what you want, not what you're afraid of. I think it's about time I made some important choices for myself too."

That night Derek waited for his father to come home to have it out with him. "How can you do this to that girl? How can you and your goons put this kind of pressure on her? I swear, you're like a cancer, eating up all that's good. Here's a girl with more talent than I can ever imagine having and all you people can think about is cashing in on it and destroying her work. You should be ashamed."

"I see. Are you finished blaming me and the advertising industry for all the evils in the world?"

"Yeah, I'm finished. I'm finished working for you and I'm finished talking to you. I don't know why I even bother. I've never been able to tell you anything."

"If you're finished, can I ask for the courtesy of your listening to me for a minute or two?"

"Yeah, go ahead and defend yourself. Tell me how business is business and all that crap."

"Actually I was hoping to use my own words rather than the ones you constantly put in my mouth."

"Fine. I'm listening."

"I doubt that but I'll continue regardless. First I want to say that I am extremely sorry that I am such a disappointment to you. Every father hopes his son will be proud of him. You seem to be ashamed of me. It's ironic that you so despise the way I earn money but at the same time you want to get your hands on as much of it as possible. You son, are a hypocrite.

"No, don't interrupt me. I'm not finished yet. Now what exactly are my crimes? I sell advertising. I use the talents of artists to do the selling. You make it sound like I tie them up and force them to work against their will. Every year I get dozens and dozens of resumes from young men and women who desperately want to work at my company. They are not slaves. Yes I take advantage of their talents, just as you take advantage of the talents of musicians when you buy tickets and go to their concerts. That isn't slave labor, it's commerce. You don't mind it when you're the recipient of other people's labors, but you seem to have this deep resentment when it comes to producing anything yourself.

"Now lets take the case of this young artist you seem to be so captivated by. Did I steal her painting? Did I force her to paint it? Did our people make any changes on it without her consent? It is true we seem to have placed her in a position of having to make a very difficult choice. Too bad. Life's like that sometimes. Are we pressuring her to make the choice we want her to make? Of course we are. But we're not threatening her. We haven't kidnapped her parents, holding them ransom until she does what we want. I may be a lot of things but I am not the evil monster you make me out to be. You have no right to question my ethics. It isn't fair and it isn't warranted. I think if you look deep inside you'll see that. And I hope you'll come to learn that you're only hurting yourself with all that resentment.

"I do have to agree with one thing you said, however. I've been doing a lot of thinking about it myself recently as I see you slipping away from me, hating me even. You said you've never been able to tell me anything. I'm ashamed to admit that's true. I've never been around. I worked and slaved and built up a business I am immensely proud of. I fooled myself into believing that I was doing it for you and your mother so you could have the best things in life. But now I see those weren't the things you wanted from me. You wanted me and I wasn't there for you. I missed your ballgames and your school plays and even some of your birthday parties and that is why I think you have such resentment against advertising. It's really me you resent. Well as I say, I've been doing a lot of thinking about things lately. As I contemplate retirement, I find I have no family to come home to. Your mother divorced me and you're about to do the same. As I get older, I realize that in many areas that really mattered, I've blown it. I have failed as a father and a husband. And I'm sorry. And if you can't forgive me, then at least know this: mine was by far the greater loss.

"Please try to understand. You were this tiny helpless baby and you terrified me. You were so full of need and I had to provide for you. So I dug in and worked and worked and worked and all of a sudden one day I looked up and you were all grown up and I'd missed everything. I didn't know how fast it would all go. I'd give anything to have one day of it back again.

"Well son, if we had a better relationship you wouldn't have had to come to me maligning me and my whole profession. You could have come to me and told me that we had a problem and that you wanted my help and I would have helped you. So I intend to solve this thing because in your own way, you have asked for help."

"Dad."

"Yes."

"I'm sorry. You're right. I've resented you for as long as I can remember. It's like an elephant I carry around with me everywhere. It's weighing me down. And it's selfish and self-centered. I've only been looking at how you failed me but I guess I failed you too. I haven't given you enough credit and respect and gratitude for the sacrifices you've made. I'm really sorry. Maybe we can make a new beginning."

"I'd like that son. I'd like that. Now at the risk of falling into my old patterns again, I have some business to attend to. I have some phone calls to make. I intend to set this right. And maybe after that is done, assuming I can pull it off and still make this deal, maybe we can take a long vacation together."

Lesley was up late watching an old movie. She was startled to hear a knock on the door. She was even more startled to see Wendell Abernathy himself on the other side of it.

"I'm sorry to bother you so late. Please don't be alarmed. Can I come in? I'd like very much to talk to you."

"Sure. Come in. Is everything okay? Is Derek okay?"

"Derek's fine. Everything's fine."

"I'm sorry I've been such a bother to all of you. I'll sell the painting. You can have it. Make any changes you want. I've been acting immaturely. I need to grow up and live in the real world. It isn't too late, is

69

it?"

"Please Lesley, hear me out. First of all I want to tell you that I just fired Stanley Howard."

"Why? Because of me?"

"No, because of him. I didn't realize he was putting so much pressure on you. That was stupid of him and it was bad business. I got where I am in business by working hard, not by working people. In business, you have to know how to wheel and deal, that's certainly true. But the advertising business is supposed to be filled with creative people and you can be creative in business too. It wasn't you who should have been pressured; it was Harry Sloan, the head of the Larson Company. I made a few phone calls tonight. I told Sloan if we couldn't go ahead with our plans with the painting as is, then the deal was off."

"Oh my goodness, wasn't that a terrible risk? What if he would have said no?"

"It wasn't a risk and he couldn't say no."

"Why not?"

"Because of you. Because of your painting. It is so full of childlike innocence. You don't gain anything by killing the golden goose. Talent like yours must be valued and nurtured, not co-opted. So if you will accept my apologies and if you will sign these papers we will have a deal."

"These are different papers."

"Yes they are. We're going to pay you less money up front because we are guaranteeing that you retain ownership and control of the painting. However, you'll notice we are also guaranteeing that your mother will be the face of the product and we will pay her for public appearances, television commercials, and other residuals. She will become as familiar a

70

face as Betty Crocker's. You'll also notice on page four that we have made your father eligible for any and all medical care that he might require and he will have a job with our company if he wants one. He won't need one but I'm guessing he might want one. And of course there's a desk available for you any time you might want it."

"Why are you doing all this?"

"Because you're worth it. And because you've helped me get my son back."

"I didn't do anything to do that."

"Lesley, after years in business and in sales I know a thing or two about people. You are a very talented young artist. A talent like yours comes along very rarely. It's pure and comes from deep within you. It's easy for you. But your real talent is being the bright star that you are. Your talent is your ability to touch people and bring out the best in them. I am honored to have had you touch our lives. You heal people just by being around them. You've touched my son and me and now we have a new beginning. And with any luck, maybe someday you'll join our family. A father can only hope."

Six months later the Hart family gathered together in their new house. Richard called Ellie in from the garden. Grandpa Gus finished up in the kitchen, putting popcorn in bowls and passing them out. Salem was in the kitchen helping him. Wendell Abernathy showed up at the front door. "Am I too late?" he asked. Derek gave him a hug. It made Wendell a bit uncomfortable but he was forcing himself to get used to it.

"No, Dad, you're not too late."

Richard looked at his watch and hurried them all to the sofa. He turned on the television set. It was a game show. Some woman was

71

jumping up and down and screaming, having just won a jackpot of a few thousand dollars. The show faded to a commercial.

"You remember how life used to be?" There were images of children playing on the sidewalk, roller skating, riding bicycles. "Life begins at breakfast time. Start your children off the right way with Mama Larson's oatmeal, a healthy breakfast for healthy lives. They're your children. You want what's best for them. Give them a head start in life." Then suddenly, there was Ellie on the screen. The real Ellie, watching the television, gave a small shriek. Everyone else shushed her so they could hear the Ellie on the screen. "Take it from me, Mama Larson. Every bowl of my oatmeal is made from the finest freshest oats. I wouldn't have it any other way."

They all applauded Ellie as Richard turned off the television set. "Oh my goodness, I looked terrible," said Ellie. "The television makes me look fat."

"You were great," said Lesley. "I bet they'll be calling you for acting roles soon. I bet you'll wind up on that soap opera you're always watching."

"You think so? I'll grab that Dr. Fulton and wring his neck for what he did to Violet's uncle."

"It's a great commercial," said Lesley to Wendell. "You did a great job."

"It's easy when you have a star performer like your mother and a great director like my son. Derek, I think you've finally found your niche. You're a natural."

"I guess there are all kinds of art. I just had to find mine," he said. "But Lesley's still giving me painting lessons."

"How are they coming along?"

"Well, I painted a watermelon but it looked more like someone's brains spilling out."

Lesley looked around her at her parents, joking and laughing and relaxed. It gave her a good feeling. Derek reached for her hand. She leaned over and gave him a kiss. Love and gratitude filled their eyes. She felt so proud of herself that she could make it all happen without having to compromise herself. She had it all. Her inner voice was still loud and true and hadn't failed her yet.

No Time Like the Present

Few people still lived in the town of Sunnydale, which for the past forty years was anything but sunny. That's why the sight of a stranger in town was highly unusual. But there he was just the same, holding his coat tightly around himself and clutching a small briefcase as the wind and rain stung him and the strange green lightning marked his path. Thomas Windon was a man on a mission.

He found the broken down house on Elm Street and banged on the door several times. The flashing lights in the basement window, matching the staccato green lightning above him, revealed that the man he came to see was indeed at home. Eventually Thomas tried rapping on the window itself and then, over the howling winds, he heard a voice and the sharp yipping of a small dog. When the door finally opened, Thomas looked down to see a man who looked far older than his years, sitting in a motor powered wheelchair. The dog was at his side and was barking manically. The man in the wheelchair motioned for Thomas to enter. It was then when the door was shut behind him that Thomas noticed that the man held a small gun that was aimed at him.

"Dr. McDonnell?" asked Thomas. "Dr. Wilson McDonnell?"

"What do you want?"

"I understand you're looking to hire an assistant." Thomas pulled from his back pocket a soggy rolled up newspaper from Harvard College.

"Are you crazy?" It took Thomas a few seconds to realize this wasn't a rhetorical question.

"I suppose I probably am. They say anyone who sets foot in Sunnydale must be."

"Can you cook?"

"Yes sir I'm an excellent cook."

"And you don't mind menial work? Cleaning up after me? Taking orders?"

"Whatever you need, sir."

"What about physics? What do you know about physics?"

"I have a Master's degree. I did my thesis on Grindor's theory of time travel and I've read all your articles and books as well."

"Take off your coat then and fix me supper. That'll be your room over there. I want a bowl of soup and some crackers in ten minutes. There's a red button on the wall near the sink. When the soup is ready, push the button. Don't bother me until then."

Dr. McDonnell turned his wheelchair to an elevator and disappeared back down to the basement. Thomas took off his dripping coat and hung it on the door to his room. Inside were a bed and a small desk with a lamp. He placed his briefcase on the desk. Rummaging around inside it, he found his cell phone, pulled it out, and made a call. Because reception was poor in the Sunnydale storm, he was barely able to make out the voice on the other end.

"I've made contact, Carla. I'm in. I'll call you in two weeks on his birthday in the afternoon. We'll know by then if I succeed or not. I miss you darling."

Thomas then headed for the kitchen and looked around for what he needed to make some soup for his new boss. He found several cans in a cabinet. Selecting one, he prepared it, watching the clock closely. At the proper moment Thomas pushed the red button. When he did so, he heard a horn blasting down below and Dr. McDonnell soon appeared at the elevator.

He rolled to the kitchen table and began eating his soup while occasionally passing a few crackers to his dog. When he finished, he motioned for Thomas to clean up the mess and told him to meet him in the living room after he had done so.

"Is everything in the kitchen exactly as it was before you arrived here?" he asked Thomas.

"Yes sir. I washed all the dishes and put everything away."

"That's good. I think you'll work out. I can't afford to have any clutter or distractions from my work. Now let me see your resume and identification papers."

Thomas retrieved his briefcase from the other room and produced the necessary papers hoping that Dr. McDonnell wouldn't notice they were fakes.

"Wait a minute! What's this? This can't be right." Thomas's heart leaped as he looked to where McDonnell was pointing. "According to this, you're only twenty years old. How could you already have a Master's degree?"

How could he have missed that? He had to think fast. "Oh yes. Well, you see, I don't like to brag but I was in kind of an accelerated program."

"Oh a boy genius. Something like that?"

"I don't like to brag, sir."

"Why do you want to work for me?"

"As I said, I've studied your work. I admire your theories."

"They aren't theories. They're facts. Sign this. It's a pledge of total and complete confidentiality. Nobody is to know you're even here. Do you understand?"

"Yes, sir."

"Good. In the morning we can talk further. I'll want two poached eggs and a slice of whole wheat toast and three strips of bacon. I want two tablespoons of milk and a half tablespoon of sugar in my coffee and I want a glass of orange juice. I want that at precisely seven thirty."

"Yes, sir." With that, Wilson McDonnell returned to the basement.

Alone in his room, Thomas breathed a sigh of relief. He didn't sleep well that night. The mattress on the small bed was lumpy. He hoped he would get used to it along with the incessant rumblings of thunder and the tapping of rain on the roof.

In the next few days Thomas saw little of Dr. McDonnell other than at meals. He had hoped or assumed that he would have a chance to see the laboratory downstairs but so far McDonnell had neither invited him down nor talked at all about his work. Thomas marveled at the sheer arrogance of the man. He had advertised for someone to take on the menial job of a housekeeper but someone who had at least a Master's degree in physics. How many people did he think would be qualified, let alone interested? He had interviewed him as if he expected dozens of people to show up and to have his pick of them.

It wasn't until his fourth day that Dr. McDonnell invited Thomas to sit with him in the living room and finally broached the subject of his work. The room was sparsely furnished with old unmatched tattered pieces that were rarely used. Thomas sat on a sofa, almost impaling himself on an exposed spring. Dr. McDonnell wasted no time with small talk.

"Tell me what you know about Grindor's theory," he said.

"Well, as far as I could understand it, the theory grew from the simple observation that the faster one traveled from point A to point B, the less time elapsed in the trip. His theory was that if one could travel at the speed of light, that no time would elapse at all and if one could go faster than the speed of light, time would actually go backwards."

"Do you think that's possible?"

"In theory, I think there's merit to it. But practically speaking it is considered impossible to reach such speeds."

"Correct. Quite correct. But supposing that it was considered differently?"

"How so?"

"Supposing that rather than thinking in terms of propelling a body from point A to point B, that instead we merely speed up the atoms making up that body."

"I would think that the body would disintegrate instantly. It would burn up. That would be like placing someone in a super microwave oven."

"Come with me."

It was the moment Thomas had been waiting for. They headed for the elevator. The basement extended beyond the foundation of the house. There were generators and computers everywhere. In the center of the room was a metal tunnel, resembling a walkthrough x-ray scanner used at airport security checkpoints. There were wires and tubes and pipes coming out of the sides, some of which were connected to a large console that had levers, switches, and a computer screen on it.

"Do you have any idea what you're looking at?" asked McDonnell.

"No," Thomas lied.

"I suppose in its simplest terms I would call it a time machine."

"How does it work?"

"I took Grindor's theory one step further. It is true that an object cannot travel faster than the speed of light, at least as far as we presently know, and it is true that a man's body would instantly burn up if his molecular structure were sped up. What this machine does is to increase the molecular structure of the space within this portal and it then becomes an entry into the past. You see? Even Einstein could not conceive of such a thing. All the great physicists focused only on the E of E=MC². All they thought about was the generation of energy. But I focused on C², the speed of light squared. If E=MC², then simple math will tell you that C²=E/M. I built a fusion reactor to generate the energy and focused it in that portal to increase the speed of light exponentially. With proper adjustments, I can calculate exactly how far into the past one will travel. I've been working on this for nearly fifteen years and it's almost ready. Now, let me hear the boy genius's thoughts on this."

"Well, assuming that it works, I can see a huge drawback immediately."

"And what would that be?"

"You can only make a one way trip. It's not reversible and even if it were, the machine doesn't exist in the past, nor the technology to build another one. And how would you reverse the field so time would go forward anyway?"

"That is all correct but irrelevant."

"Why is it irrelevant?"

"Because I only need to go one way."

"But why? Where would you go and for what purpose? Are you trying to change history? Do you plan on stopping an assassination or preventing a war or something?"

"No, nothing like that. I have no political cares at all. Let the world destroy itself. I don't care about anything like that."

"Then why?"

"To prevent this," he said pointing to his wheelchair. "To prevent this."

"What happened to you? Why are you in that chair?"

"It started a few days before my sixteenth birthday. I remember it so clearly. It was the day the storms began. I was running home from school. We lived in a house just down the street from here. As I was running, I noticed a small dog running alongside me, very much like this one. I even named this dog after the one I had back then, didn't I Muggs? Anyway, everyone was frightened by the onset of the storms."

"Does anyone have any idea what started the storms?"

"There are theories about a confluence of volcanoes and earthquakes or something. I don't know. It doesn't concern me. Don't interrupt me with stupid questions."

"Sorry, please continue. You were about to tell me about your sixteenth birthday."

"Yes. Well, as I was saying, on the day of my birthday there was a commotion outside. I heard a lot of sirens which was very unusual for our neighborhood. I opened the front door to look outside and Muggs ran out. When I chased after him I didn't watch where I was going and I got hit by an ambulance. I've been in this chair ever since and the pain has never subsided. If I can go back in time and warn myself, maybe I can prevent this."

"But that won't help you as you are now."

"I think it will. I think if I prevent the accident then I would be able to walk again. I will have changed the past. And even if that doesn't happen, I can at least save the me that is yet to be."

"And what will become of the present you?"

"I don't know. I suppose I would be stuck in the past and die there. I don't care about that."

"Dr. McDonnell. You're planning on testing your machine with Muggs, aren't you?"

"Yes, what about it? How do you know that?"

"Please listen to me carefully. Suppose that's the very dog that followed you home. Let's say you send him back in time. He appears in your past. You come running by on your way home from school and he picks up your scent and he recognizes you from now. And that's why he follows you home."

"So what? What if that's true?"

"It is true. In sending your dog to the past and interacting with it, you set a paradox in motion that ripped the fabric of time and that's what caused the storms to begin."

"Nonsense. That's impossible."

"Is it?"

"Of course."

"Why?"

"Why? I don't know. Why would sending the dog back into the past matter? Why would that set up a paradox?"

"The presence of this dog in your past proves the machine worked."

"What's the problem with that?"

"If the dog made it back there, why didn't you? Why weren't you able to warn yourself as you had planned?"

"I don't know. Something must have happened between the time I sent the dog and the time I went myself."

"No, you succeeded. You were back there too. I want you to look at something." Thomas pulled from his pocket an old yellowed clipping from a newspaper. It was the story of McDonnell's accident.

"What about it?" he asked after reading it.

"Dr. McDonnell, you can't be that stubborn. Please believe what's in front of you. The police found a crippled man loitering a block away from your house. When they approached him, he pulled a gun on them. The man was shot. The article clearly states that they never found out the identity of the crippled man. It was you Dr. McDonnell. You sent the dog that the younger you chased into the street. After the police shot you, you were in the speeding ambulance that ran you over. You caused the very accident you are trying to prevent."

"No! It can't be! I don't believe you. Wait. I know. I'll do it differently. I won't send the dog. Then the former me won't chase it into the street."

Thomas was greatly relieved. "I'm so glad you understand."

"Come on downstairs. You have to help me."

"With what?"

"I still have to go. I have to see. I have to make sure there isn't an accident anyway."

"But. No, Dr. McDonnell, you can't. I just explained it to you. That would still set up a paradox."

"No, it wouldn't. I won't have changed anything. I'll leave it the way it would have been. But I have to go see. I have to see for myself the results of my life's work. Don't you understand? I have to experience this for myself. If you won't help me, I'll do it without your help."

"Dr. McDonnell, I can't let you."

"You can't stop me." Dr. McDonnell pulled out the gun from under the blanket on his lap and pointed it at Thomas. He backed into the elevator. Thomas tried the door to the basement stairs but it was locked. He ran outside and busted through a basement window to try to stop him but by the time he got there McDonnell was gone.

It was the morning of Wilson McDonnell's sixteenth birthday. It was a beautiful sun shiny Saturday. Wilson's mother had gotten up early to make him a special breakfast; his favorite poached eggs and bacon.

"Where's Dad?" asked Wilson's little brother, Tommy.

"He had to go into town for something. He'll be back in a little while." Wilson finished his breakfast and helped his mother clean up afterwards. When his father returned he was carrying a strange looking case with a handle that seemed difficult to keep balanced.

"Happy Birthday, son."

"A dog? You got me a dog?"

"You said you wanted one. I know you wanted a big hunting dog but we just couldn't afford that. Mrs. Calley's dog had puppies. She gave me the pick of the litter. I hope you like him."

Wilson and Tommy got on the floor with the puppy. It climbed on them, licking their faces, barking, and jumping all over them. "He's great, Dad. Thanks, Mom. I'm going to name him Muggs."

"That's a stupid name," said Tommy.

"He's Wilson's dog," said their father. "He gets to name him."

"I still think it's a stupid name."

"Well we better clean this place up if you're going to have your friends over later," said Mrs. McDonnell. "We'll have to put paper down in your room and keep Muggs in there until he's trained."

The older Wilson McDonnell appeared a block away from the McDonnell house. Immediately the sky darkened. Clouds rolled in and the ominous green lightning began crackling in the skies.

The McDonnell family looked out the window of their house. "What in the hell is going on out there?" said Mr. McDonnell. "It was supposed to be clear all day today. Hmm! That's strange. There's an old guy out there in a wheelchair. He could be in trouble. I better call Jerry Hinton down at the police station. He might want to check it out."

Officer Hinton arrived and approached McDonnell cautiously. "Are you okay, old man? Can I help you?"

"I'm fine. Go away."

"It looks like some nasty weather is kicking up here. Can I help you get somewhere? Who are you?"

"Leave me alone." McDonnell turned his wheelchair around to face the police officer. As he did so, the gun slipped from his lap and fell to the ground. McDonnell got to it before the officer did. Now Officer Hinton became alarmed. He slowly backed away and headed to his car to radio for help. Soon, several more squad cars arrived with sirens blaring. McDonnell saw the door to his house open. He saw the puppy run out with the younger McDonnell chasing after it. One of the police cars careened around the corner and hit the boy who flew in the air and rolled over in a crumpled heap. His mother screamed. McDonnell cried out in vain. "NO!!!" Then he turned the gun on himself and pulled the trigger.

Thomas Windon called Carla to give her the bad news. He had

failed to stop McDonnell from using his time machine. The storms increased in their intensity.

"What do we do now?" Carla asked. "The storm seems to be getting worse. We have to stop this somehow."

Thomas picked up the yellowed newspaper from the coffee table to put back in his briefcase. Something caught his eye. The story had changed. It wasn't an ambulance anymore that had caused the accident, it was a police car. Thomas was stunned. Something must have changed back then that changed everything that had followed. It gave him hope and it gave him an idea. "We have to use the time machine and go back and try again."

"How far back do we have to go?"

"We have to go back fifteen years."

"Fifteen years? But why?"

"Think about it Carla. Anything less than that and we show up in McDonnell's basement. How would we explain that? We have to go back to before the time he moved into the house. Fifteen years ago this house was empty. We have to go back that far so we won't be detected."

"But fifteen years? Oh, Tom, that's like a prison sentence. What about having children? I'll be too old when we get back, if we ever get back at all."

"Carla, you know as well as I do that unless we succeed, there's no hope of having children for us or anyone else on Earth. And there won't be anything to go back to."

There was nothing else to say. Carla knew in her heart that he was right. She knew that the possibility of never having children was a price worth paying to save the entire planet. Thomas saw the fear and sadness in her eyes. "Don't worry," he said. "Next time I won't fail. I'll see to it."

Fifteen years later

Thomas wrapped himself against the wind and the rain. He knocked on the basement window. Soon McDonnell appeared at the door, his dog yipping at this side. McDonnell held a gun that he pointed at Thomas.

"I understand you are looking for an assistant," said Thomas. "I read your ad in the Harvard newspaper. Here are my credentials. I know all about your work and Grindor's theories and I make excellent poached eggs."

"I see. You came prepared. Come in. Let me look over your papers."

McDonnell put the gun on the coffee table. Thomas quickly picked it up and aimed it at him.

"What are you doing?" Muggs growled but then seemed to sense something and stopped.

"I'm trying to save you, Dr. McDonnell. I know all about you. Downstairs you have a time machine. You're planning to go back into the past to try to prevent your accident from occurring. But you can't do it. You can't go back. I tried to warn you before but you wouldn't listen. You refused to believe me. You had to see for yourself if your machine worked. You're a sad angry little man. What a waste of your genius. You could have made great contributions but instead you've built a monument to

87

suffering and now I have to put an end to it. You wouldn't listen to me before. I can't trust you now."

"Who are you? What do you want? What's your interest in this?"

"I'm trying to stop this storm you created. When you went back in time, you created a paradox and that's when the storms began. Eventually they will grow to the point of destroying the entire planet. I have to put an end to it. You've left me no choice. In order to save the world, I have to destroy you."

"Wait! You don't have to kill me. If you think you know so much about it, why don't you just go downstairs and destroy my machine? I'm a crippled man. I can't stop you. Just go ahead and destroy my life's work if you think you have to and be gone."

"I can't destroy it because I needed it to get here. If I destroyed it I would disappear and you would continue."

"And they say I'm crazy. Sounds like you're the nutcase."

"Dr. McDonnell, what became of your brother?"

"My brother? I have no idea. Haven't seen him in years. How do you know about my brother?"

"Because your brother was my great grandfather. I was named after him."

"Your great grandfather? How is that possible?"

"Because your machine works. I did my Master's Thesis on your theories. I inherited this old house. It was abandoned when you disappeared. I found your laboratory. It took a long time to get it working but I succeeded. Much of the technology downstairs is out of date in my time but I was able to improvise and get it running. My wife and I came back here to try to stop you, just as you are trying to go back to try to stop your accident."

"If what you say is true, your being here is just as much a paradox. What makes you think you can stop the storm? You probably created one yourself?"

"That might be true. But you haven't seen the future. We have nothing to lose. There isn't much time left."

"That's a very interesting story but I don't believe you."

"How else could I know about your brother? Can't you see the truth when it stands in front of you?"

"All I see is a crazy man with a gun."

"I had a feeling when I failed the last time that I would have only one option. You're a stubborn man who knows nothing but suffering. I can't save you but maybe I can save a boy from the past and maybe I can save the children of the future. Please forgive me Uncle Wilson. Your choices leave me no other choice. I just pray I'm making the right one." With that, Thomas pulled the trigger and killed McDonnell. Muggs put his head down and cried.

Thomas called Carla who joined him in the living room of the McDonnell house. She tried to reassure Thomas that he had taken the only option available.

"What happens now?" she asked.

"I suppose it depends on what happens in the past, whether anything has changed or not. For all we know the accident happens anyway. If that's the case, McDonnell still grows up to build his time machine, creates another paradox and it starts all over again. Maybe things just have to unfold as they do. Maybe things are destined to happen and can't be changed, even if that means the destruction of whole planets. I think we just have to wait and see.

Wilson McDonnell awoke on the morning of his sixteenth birthday. It looked like it was going to be a beautiful clear day with a blue sky and the sun shining.

When he and his brother Tommy went down for breakfast he saw his mother making his favorite poached eggs and bacon for breakfast. Tommy asked where his father was.

"He had to go into town to run an errand."

"Early on a Saturday morning? What kind of errand?" asked Wilson.

"Oh, just something." Wilson wondered if there wasn't maybe a birthday surprise awaiting him. When his father came home, he wasn't disappointed. His father had bought him a puppy for his birthday. Soon Wilson and Tommy were rolling on the floor with the little bundle of furry energy. The puppy yelped and licked them and jumped all over them. They giggled and squealed, playing on the floor.

"What are you going to call him?" asked his father.

"Muggs," said Wilson.

"Muggs? That's a stupid name," said Tommy.

"That's not a stupid name. It's his name. He's my dog so I get to name him."

"Enough playing," said Mrs. McDonnell. "We have to clean up for your party. Wilson, you're going to have to spread newspapers around your room until the dog is trained. It's a big responsibility having a dog. You think you're up to it?"

"Yes, Mom."

Later that morning the postman rang the bell. Wilson answered the door, eager to see if there were any birthday cards. Muggs shot out the door. Wilson ran after him. An ambulance came careening down the street with its siren blaring. Muggs ran out into the street in front of the ambulance. Wilson ran after him. At the last second, the driver slammed on the brakes and screeched to a halt. Wilson picked up Muggs and carried him back into the house. The ambulance driver wiped the sweat off his forehead and yelled to Wilson to be more careful in the future.

And in that future, Thomas and Carla noticed something change. The storm was quieting. The air was clearing. The sun came out to shine. The newspaper on the coffee table dissolved, disappearing into thin air. And then so did they.

Thomas and Carla returned to the future. They were in the basement of Wilson McDonnell's house, assuming it was still his house, and they seemed to be the same ages they were when they first left. The basement was different though. Gone were the machinery, reactor, computers, and generators. Instead there were pieces of old furniture. In one corner, there was a desk and some file cabinets as though that part of the basement was used as an office. Outside, the night sky was clear and full of stars. A half moon shone brightly. The storm was over. They both let it sink in for a few moments and then started jumping up and down hugging each other and yelling for joy. "We did it! We did it!"

They were interrupted by the sound of a door opening. A man wearing a uniform was coming down the basement stairs holding a flashlight. "What's going on? Who's down there? Show yourself!"

"Uh, er."

"Oh, it's you Mr. Windon. And Mrs. Windon. What are you doing here at this hour?"

Thomas and Carla looked at each other, puzzled. They had no idea who the man was. He appeared to be some kind of guard or night watchman who obviously knew them.

"Working late?" the watchman asked.

"Yes, we had to catch up on some things. But we're done now. We were just leaving."

They followed the guard up the stairs. When they reached the top, the house looked just like Wilson McDonnell's house except that the furniture was all in good condition, almost pristine and there were ropes blocking off sections of the rooms. When they exited the house, Thomas looked back. There was a sign in front of the house. It said:

Wilson McDonnell's Home and Museum,
Dedicated to the man who eradicated cancer in 2012.
United States National Landmark

Thomas and Carla looked at each other and hugged with tears in their eyes.

The Trial

or

The further adventures of Jonathan and Harvey as previously chronicled in "The Funeral" appearing in "A Drawer Full of Dreams"

You may wonder why I am sitting in a courtroom waiting for the trial of Mary Spencer to begin. Funny, I was wondering the same thing myself. It all goes back to my best and oldest friend, Harvey, whom I met in high school. At the time of our meeting, Harvey was about to get beaten up by the class bully, Rocco Morelli. I happened on the scene quite by accident and bumped into Rocco, sending him sprawling. As he struggled to his feet he couldn't see clearly and thought there were five of me and that I was the leader of a gang come to rescue poor Harvey. Rocco fled and never bothered either of us again. If I had known then what I know now, I would surely have joined forces with Rocco and helped him beat the crap out of Harvey.

Harvey was always trying to help me out, especially in the area of meeting women. One time Harvey decided I should enroll in an art class. He thought the girls who studied art were particularly exotic and would be interested in me. Unfortunately, Harvey messed up and signed me up to be a nude model. On the cold winter night that I showed up, the heating system in the art school was malfunctioning. Harvey was correct. The girls in the class showed a very intense interest in me for several hours, right down to my goose bumps and chattering teeth. I nearly caught pneumonia that night.

Another time, Harvey was convinced that I should take up scuba diving. He had found an ad for a one day course in diving and promised to meet me there. As usual, he didn't show up and as usual he screwed up. The class turned out to be, not scuba diving, but skydiving. The next thing I knew, I found myself on an airplane 14,000 feet above the ground, staring out of a gaping hole where a door should have been. I was pushed out at that dizzying height screaming, "Damn you Harvey!" all the way down.

I don't even want to talk about the fiasco of only a week ago when Harvey convinced me to attend a funeral in order to partner up with the deceased's granddaughter. And how does Harvey keep convincing me to go through with his insane plans? If only I knew. I once watched a performing hypnotist forcing hapless volunteers from the audience to do all kinds of extremely embarrassing things. They would wake up, dazed and confused, wondering how they got on stage. They didn't remember any of it. My life was very much like that with the exception of being cursed with the ability to remember every excruciating detail.

The latest scheme Harvey presented to me was to attend the trial of Mary Spencer who was accused of murdering her husband. "She didn't murder him," Harvey had said. "She just killed him. She accidentally ran over him a couple of times." Mary had gone to college with us and Harvey was convinced that if she spotted me in the courtroom I would have her undying gratitude for my show of loyalty and support, assuming of course that she would be acquitted and wasn't actually a murderer. I distinctly remember saying no to him. I remember thinking what a stupid idea it was. And yet here I was sitting in the courtroom. Harvey promised several times that he would meet me there but of course he was nowhere to be found. He'd done it again.

Once I entered the courtroom, I wasn't allowed to leave until there was an official recess. The courtroom was hot, stuffy, and crowded. I imagined to myself that the next time I entered a courtroom I would have a comfortable chair all to myself as I would be the defendant, on trial for murdering Harvey.

I dozed off for I don't know how long. When I awoke, the judge was hammering down his gavel announcing a recess. I couldn't believe it. I was actually going to get out of there without some impossible embarrassing consequences. Maybe my luck was finally going to change. Maybe the next time, I might even be able to resist the twisted logic that always allowed Harvey to convince me to do these things.

At that moment my cell phone rang and I knew it was Harvey calling me. I knew it because every few weeks he would take my phone and download a new ring tone that he would set for only his calls. Harvey was a fanatic for old movies. Invariably his ring tones were segments of dialogue from his favorite films. I had forgotten to silence the phone. At the moment the judge was about to bring down his gavel for the second time a voice emanated from my pocket so loud that everyone in the courtroom could hear it. It said, "I'm gonna git you, sucka!"

The judge looked up, shocked. The court officers immediately took me into custody and as they were dragging me through a side door, Mary Spencer smiled at me and waved. The guards hustled me into an office, surrounded me, and began grilling me about my threat to kill the judge. For the next several hours my life was once again a horror thanks to my dear friend Harvey.

"I don't think we're going to get anything out of this one," said the guard called Blinky.

"What do you think we should do with him," said the other one named Pinky. I started to laugh out loud thinking to myself that they had the names of the Pac Man characters.

"He's laughing at us. He's a cold blooded one for sure. We better lock him up for the night."

I was allowed one phone call so I called Harvey. He assured me he would be right there with bail money as soon as *The Mole People* was over.

"Harvey, I'm in jail! Can't *The Mole People* wait? You have it recorded. You can see it any time you want."

"It's John Agar, Johnny. Have some respect."

"I don't care about John Agar. Get down here and get me out."

"Not if you disrespect John Agar. The man was a genius. He was married to Shirley Temple for God's sake. That's practically sacred."

"Harvey, I'm in jail."

"Hey man, if you can't do the time, don't do the crime."

"I didn't do any crime. It was your stupid ring tone. They thought I was threatening the judge."

"Wow man, threatening a judge is pretty serious. Why'd you do that?"

"I didn't do that. I just told you . . . ."

"Oh man, they just discovered the 5000 year old Sumerian civilization living under the glacier in Mesopotamia. Wait 'til ole' Ward Cleaver meets up with the albinos."

"Ward Cleaver? What are you talking about?"

"Hugh Beaumont man, before he was the Beaver's father; one of the great underrated actors of all time in my humble opinion."

"Harvey, get me out of here!"

"Okay, chill out buddy. I'll be right down. But only because you're my best and oldest friend. I wouldn't interrupt *The Mole People* for just anyone, you know. I just hope you understand the sacrifice I'm making here."

"Harvey, get your ass down here."

"He sounds pretty dangerous, this one," said Blinky.

"You're right," said Pinky. "Harvey must be his accomplice. We're going to have to be very careful around these guys."

How I managed to drag myself to work the next day I'll never know. Harvey had already briefed Lorraine, the woman who works with us, on the gory details of the previous night.

"Oh, you poor thing," she said. "It must have been horrible. Does this mean you're gay now?"

"What?"

"I read in Reader's Digest that a lot of guys who go to prison become gay."

"I wasn't in prison, I was in jail and only for a few hours waiting for this moron to finish watching *The Mole People* and bail me out."

"*The Mole People*? That's my favorite movie," said Lorraine. "That John Agar is really cute."

"Yeah, but Beaumont really steals the show," said Harvey.

"I just never thought it was fair that the albinos were forced to be slaves to the mole people. It always made me cry."

"Oh yeah. Me too."

For once I didn't mind the insane conversation between Lorraine and Harvey. At least they weren't bothering me. I thought maybe I could take a nap but that was interrupted by Harvey shouting at me as he opened the morning newspaper.

"Johnny, why didn't you tell me?"

"Tell you what?"

"That you're engaged to Mary Spencer."

"Congratulations!" said Lorraine. "You sly devil. You sure work fast."

"What are you two talking about?"

"It's right here on the front page of the newspaper."

"Ooh, that's a nice picture of you," said Lorraine.

"Picture? Front page? Please tell me I'm dreaming."

But there it was, a picture of the bailiffs dragging me out of the courtroom with Mary Spencer smiling and waving at me. The article reported that I was engaged to Mary Spencer and that we had been carrying on for several years. This was the big breakthrough the prosecutors had been waiting for.

As I left work that afternoon I was besieged by reporters and photographers all wanting to know about my long standing affair with Mary Spencer. Suddenly a hand reached out to rescue me from the nightmare.

"Come with me. I'll get you out of this." I went with the man who led me to a nearby police car. "We just want to ask you a few questions."

The next thing I knew I was back in the small office with Blinky and Pinky.

"So you think you can outsmart us," said Blinky. I thought to myself that that probably wouldn't be too hard to do but kept my mouth shut. "Tell us, where were you last Saturday at about one in the afternoon at the time Mary Spencer murdered her husband?"

"Last Saturday? Let's see." Terror washed over me as I remembered. "I was attending a funeral."

"Whose funeral?"

"Myra Drake's. That is, I started out going to Myra Drake's funeral but I ended up at Agnes Woolsey's funeral."

"Check it out, Pinky. Ask around and see if anyone remembers a Jonathan Cooper attending that funeral."

"Uh, well, you won't find anyone because I attended it as Stanley Woolsey."

"You used an alias?"

"No. Well you see it's because I panicked and gave a fake name because I really was trying to meet Sheila Drake because Harvey thought I'd have a chance with her but I wound up being Stanley Woolsey. You can ask them about Stanley Woolsey. Ask Uncle Shirley or even Cousin Jeremy. They'd remember me."

"How do you know Rocco Morelli?"

"Rocco Morelli? What's he got to do with this? He was a bully in high school."

"And we understand you had an altercation with him. We understand that you and your gang beat him up."

"No, that never happened. He fell down. What's that got to do with any of this?"

"Rocco Morelli was Mary Spencer's husband as if you didn't know. You work for the General Insurance Company?"

"Yes."

"And I suppose you didn't know that your company had insured the life of Rocco Morelli and that you served as the actuary who approved the policy?"

"I didn't approve anything. Once a week I sign some papers. I don't even know what an actuary is."

"Hey Blinky," said Pinky. "I just checked out his story. Stanley Woolsey lives in New Jersey. I think we've got this punk dead to rights."

"So," said Blinky, "you were having a secret affair with Mary Spencer, you had a longstanding grudge against her husband whom you helped get life insurance, and you have no alibi."

"I didn't do anything. Ask Harvey."

"You mean your accomplice?"

"He's not an accomplice. He's an idiot."

They explained to me that under a new law enacted to save costs, I would be included as a defendant for Rocco's murder even though Mary Spencer's trial had already started. Harvey and Lorraine came to visit me in jail that night.

"I baked you a cake," said Lorraine. "I was going to hide a file inside so you could escape like they do in the movies but I figured it wouldn't pass the metal detectors so I just painted one on the top with icing instead."

"This is great," said Harvey. "I can't believe your good fortune."

"Good fortune? I'm being tried for murder."

"Yes, but you'll be sitting next to Mary Spencer every day of the trial. Have you forgotten what your mission was to begin with?"

"What mission?"

"To meet Mary Spencer. This is perfect. I'm so proud of you, man."

"Harvey, I'm on trial for murder."

"I just can't believe they caught you," said Lorraine. "You sure had us fooled, working with you every day and not realizing you were a cold blooded killer. You just never know, you know?"

"Lorraine, I never killed anyone. But if you don't get this moron out of here, I may just begin."

"We'd better go, Harvey. He could be dangerous. You'd think he'd have more gratitude that we took the time to come visit him. Hmmph! Some people are so rude. And here I even baked a cake for him."

"Listen buddy," said Harvey, "don't worry about a thing. I've got everything under control. I'm not going to let them send you to the bug house."

"Isn't that the big house?" asked Lorraine.

"No, I think it's the bug house."

"But I read in Reader's Digest . . . ."

"Stop it, both of you!" I shouted.

"Remember Johnny, ole buddy. I've got everything under control. There's nothing to worry about."

The next day I was taken to the courtroom and was seated next to Mary Spencer. She smiled at me and tried to hold my hand. I slapped it away. I didn't want anyone thinking I had anything to do with her. She walked her fingers up my arm and I shooed her hand away again. For most of the morning she was trying to flirt with me. I could see the members of the jury giving me looks of disgust, pointing at me, and talking amongst themselves.

There was a commotion in the back of the courtroom. I looked back and there was Harvey arguing with the guards. He was undoubtedly trying to get a seat but the courtroom was already filled. To my dismay, the guard allowed him to enter. To my horror, he proceeded down the aisle and sat next to me.

"What are you doing?" I asked.

"Don't worry," he said. "I've got everything under control."

When the judge entered the court, Harvey stood up and announced

101

that he was my new lawyer.

"Have you passed the bar?" asked the judge.

"Are you kidding me?" he replied. "I've been to every bar on Sixth Street."

"No, I don't mean that. I mean, are you a lawyer?"

"No your highness, but I've seen every episode of Perry Mason and I watch Judge Judy every chance I get."

"Very well, you may proceed."

"Wait a minute," I said, jumping out of my seat. "I want to change my plea. I'm guilty. I'm guilty of everything. I killed Rocco Morelli. I killed Jimmy Hoffa. I'm a spy. I'm a terrorist. Give me the electric chair. Please. Anything's better than letting this idiot defend me."

"Please sit down, sir. I do not find your outburst amusing."

They called the coroner to testify as to the state of the deceased when they found him. In graphic detail, the coroner listed the injuries including a crushed skull and tire tracks across the man's face. Harvey got up to cross examine him. "Now, you say the deceased was actually dead when you found him?"

"Yes."

"And how do you know that?"

"His heart wasn't beating."

"Did you examine his heart?"

"I examined him with a stethoscope."

"But you didn't actually remove the heart from the body to determine for sure that it wasn't beating."

"No, I didn't."

"Then for all you know with your haphazard examination, the

deceased might have actually still been alive."

"I don't think so."

"You don't think so. But you don't know for sure."

"He'd been lying there for an hour before I got there."

"How do you know that?"

"Because we know what time the killing took place and the time the first officers arrived."

"You mean the alleged traffic accident. Did you examine the watches of the other policemen to make sure they gave you an accurate reading of the time?"

"Well, no."

"I didn't think so. You didn't examine the heart of the deceased. You didn't test the watches of the policemen. It seems to me you made a very superficial examination. Did you test the deceased for rabies?"

"Rabies? No."

"No, I thought not. You just assumed the man had died from being run over."

"His skull was crushed."

"And how do you know that was a result of being run over? Couldn't a piano have fallen out of a window, landed on his head, and caused the same injuries?"

"There was no piano present."

"Maybe not by the time you arrived but you haven't answered the question. Couldn't a falling piano have caused the same injuries, yes or no?"

"Well, yes I guess so."

"You guess so. What about a falling anvil, or a jet airplane falling from the sky, or a lawn mower, or an exploding hot water heater? Did you check the area for any clues to see if there had been any exploding hot water heaters?"

"Well, no."

"I didn't think so. You just assumed because there was a body present and there was a car present that the car had caused the injuries. You jumped to conclusions. You used amateur guesswork instead of scientific testing."

"The man had tire tracks on his face."

"Yes, of course he did, but he could have been run over after the exploding hot water heater had landed on him."

At that point I took out a pen and grabbed the pad of paper on the table in front of me and began writing out my will.

The next person to testify was an eye witness to the event. She walked slowly to the front of the court, tapping a white cane on the floor in front of her. She sat down on the jury foreman's lap, realized her mistake and jumped up again. She bumped into the bailiff and knocked over the court reporter's desk. Finally she was led to the witness chair.

She testified that she saw Mary Spencer run over the man and that I was also present. When she was asked to identify Mary, she pointed to a window. When the prosecutor finished examining the witness, Harvey was invited to cross examine.

"No questions for this witness, your highness."

"It's 'your honor'."

"Yes, your highness. I realize it's my honor to cross examine this witness but I don't have any questions for her."

"Harvey, why don't you question her?" I asked. "She's blind."

"Because she has the jury's sympathy. It'll look bad on you if I give her a hard time. Don't worry. I've got everything under control."

"Harvey, she identified me as being there. You've got to destroy her testimony."

"Hey, who's the lawyer here, you or me?"

"Neither of us is the lawyer! You're an idiot and I'm a dead man."

The defense rested its case on the third day. Harvey had one witness to call. It was Lorraine.

"Lorraine? Why are you calling Lorraine? She has nothing to do with this."

"She's a character witness."

Lorraine took the stand and was sworn in. Harvey approached her.

"Now Lorraine, how long have you known Johnny Cooper?"

"About three years. We work together at General Insurance Company. You know that, you big silly. You work there too."

"And what kind of person would you say Johnny is?"

"Oh, I think he's very cute." She blushed. "Don't tell him I said so though. He'd be embarrassed."

"What I mean is, do you think Johnny is capable of being a killer?"

"Well, he did kill that wasp that was flying around the office that day. You remember? I was standing up on the desk screaming and you had already knocked a lamp down trying to swat it. But then Johnny came to the rescue. He was cold and calculating. He stalked that wasp and smashed it to smithereens. I couldn't believe his steely nerves, his single-minded purpose."

"But what I mean is, do you think he's capable of killing another person?"

"Oh heavens no. Not a chance. No way."

"And what makes you say that?"

"Because I read an article in Reader's Digest once that said that killers all have beady eyes. Johnny doesn't have beady eyes, well excepting of course all those times when he gets angry at you and says he's going to murder you, but otherwise no. He's as gentle as a lamb."

"Thank you. No more questions."

When Harvey returned to the table he said to me, "You see? I told you there's nothing to worry about."

"Oh, I'm not worried," I replied. "I'm absolutely certain they're going to give me the electric chair inside a gas chamber with a lethal injection added just for good measure."

The prosecutor gave his final arguments, relating once again in disgusting detail the extent of the injuries. He depicted me as a cold blooded mastermind who had tricked and seduced the innocent, naïve, and gullible Mary Spencer and turned her into a killer like I was. I could see the members of the jury looking at me with utter contempt. Some were gagging.

Harvey got up to make his speech. "Ladies and gentlemen of the jury and your highness, the judge, there is more here than meets the eye. Oh, I know you have a man with a crushed head and tire tracks on his face. You have Mary Spencer sitting in her car with the motor still running. You have fifteen eye witnesses who all saw her in the car. You would think that you'd have an open and shut case here. But you don't because there's one thing you don't have and that is absolute certainty. As long as there is reasonable doubt, you cannot convict my dear and oldest friend, Johnny Cooper. To have reasonable doubt, all you need is a plausible alternative explanation of the events at hand.

"So here's what I think really happened. Suppose Rocco Morelli had a twin brother, let's say his name was Herman, and he died of a heart attack. Mary and Rocco saw an opportunity. They put Rocco's brother in the freezer next to the chocolate ice cream until the following day when they knew there would be witnesses. Rocco and Mary staged a loud argument on the driveway. Mary pushed Rocco to the ground and then when nobody was looking, Rocco crawled away on his hands and knees and laid his brother on the ground in his place. And then, after the exploding hot water heater landed on his head, Mary took her car and ran over the man who was already dead, thus faking the death of Rocco Morelli so they could collect his insurance money. They found my poor friend Johnny here and placed the blame on him so he would get sent to the bug house and Mary would be acquitted and join her husband who is still alive and waiting for her somewhere in the Bahamas. That's what really happened. It's obvious."

I put my head down on the table. After Harvey's speech I figured they would just shoot me right there on the spot.

"It wasn't my fault!" shouted Mary Spencer suddenly. "Rocco made me do it. He promised we could get away with it. He didn't think anyone knew about his twin brother. He said nobody would suspect the hot water heater."

The next thing I knew, they were escorting Mary out of the courtroom and I was being released. You would think I would have been relieved but the thought of being indebted to Harvey for saving my life made me consider that I might have been better off with the electric chair.

The next day at work, things were back to normal, which was no real comfort. "You see," said Harvey. "I told you you didn't have anything to worry about."

"Lorraine, please tell that moron that I'm not talking to him."

"Well, I would think you'd have a little more gratitude than that," said Lorraine. "I certainly would if my friend helped me get away with murder."

"Lorraine, I didn't murder anyone . . . . yet."

"Oh my goodness," said Harvey, glancing at his newspaper. "I can't believe it."

"You can't believe what?" I asked before I could stop myself.

"Ginger Cassidy."

"What about her?"

"She's getting married."

"That's very nice. I'm very happy for her."

"You should go."

"I should go where?"

"To the wedding."

"Why would I want to go to the wedding? I wasn't invited."

"Of course you weren't invited. That doesn't matter."

"What do you mean that doesn't matter?"

"Johnny, you think too small. You've got to start thinking big. Thank goodness you have me around to watch out for you. So here's the plan. You dress up as an altar boy. You stand in the back of the church just before she walks out and you convince her that she should go out with you."

"You mean two minutes before she's about to get married."

"Hey, a lot can happen in two minutes."

"You should do it," said Lorraine. "It's a good plan."

"Lorraine, would you please open the window?"

"Why, is it hot in here?"

"No, I just figured I'd save myself a lot of trouble by just jumping out now."

"You have such a negative attitude," said Lorraine. "That's why things never work out for you. Just because a girl's getting married in two minutes you think you don't have a chance with her. Have some confidence in yourself for goodness sake."

"Come on, Johnny. I'll go with you. What's the worst thing that could happen?"

"You'll go too? No, I didn't ask that. I didn't say that." And once again I could feel myself falling into the black hole of Harvey's persuasive insanity. I suppose though when all is said and done, it's better to have a friend like Harvey than to have no friends at all.

No, definitely not.

Do Over

Denny Dugan ran as fast as his legs could carry him along the surf, the cool salty air blowing in his face. He shrieked with joy as he headed into the ocean and dove under the waves. He swam further and further, deeper into the quiet dark blue underwater world. There he could relax as the fish swam around him, curious at this intruder into their world. They spoke about it in hushed tones. Denny could hear their voices.

"He's doing better today, Mrs. Dugan."

"He looks a bit more comfortable. I was worried about him all night."

Denny slowly opened his eyes and was once again old and immobile and dying. He tried to focus on the faces surrounding the hospital bed. There was Nurse Korngold, the gentle pleasant woman from hospice care. There was his wife, Nora. The ordeal seemed to be aging her rapidly. He didn't remember the last time he saw her smile. There was his sister Phyllis sitting comfortably in a chair in the corner knitting something. There was a small skinny but muscular Mexican man jumping up and down waving his arms over his head with a huge smile on his face. He wore a white tee shirt and tight jeans. And there was Dr. Bleed. How could he have gotten stuck with a doctor named Bleed? Who was that Mexican guy? And where did he go? He didn't seem to be there anymore.

Denny allowed the quiet murmurings around him to fade into soft noise. He drifted off to the rhythm of the breathing machine. He didn't fall back asleep. He went to memory time. He watched the scenes of his life unfold. He'd been a conductor on the old Grandview commuter line. The days of his work life had dragged on in endless monotony, back and forth,

111

back and forth, punching tickets, holding doors open, calling out stops, waking up commuters, punching tickets, calling out stops, holding doors open. He thought it would never end. But it did. And now that his life was nearly over, it seemed that it had zipped by and was finished before he'd ever taken hold of it.

Was he ever young? Was there ever a time before the dying, before the railroad? Oh yes. Now he remembered. Baseball. It had consumed his childhood. He was the best player at the nightly choose-up games. He was the best player on his high school team, taking them twice to the state championship. He never understood why the game was so difficult for everyone else. He could see it all so clearly. Even in college where they threw mostly fast balls it was like slow motion to him. He knew where the ball was going. He just knew it. He knew when and where to swing the bat as if his arms took over and he didn't have to think about it. What did the coach need? An opposite field base hit to drive in some runs? A bunt? A home run? It didn't matter. Whatever was needed, he could do it. An impossible leaping catch near the wall? A stolen base? The coaches loved him. No matter what the situation, if it was his turn at bat they could relax with relief. Whatever was needed, he could do it. Under his photo in the school yearbook was the inscription: "He leaped up and the horsehide nestled in his glove".

He was drafted by the Yankees. He rose quickly through the minor leagues. As expected, he was called up to the majors in record time. In a close game against the Orioles, he was called on to pinch hit. It was so natural to him. It was the most natural thing in the world for him to be standing where Babe Ruth had once stood.

The pitcher wound up to deliver the first pitch. And then the world ended. He woke up three days later in a hospital. His skull was cracked from the pitch. He spent the next several months recovering as the team and the season continued without him. At first there were crowds of visitors, cards, well wishers, and promises but that soon drifted to apologies and unreturned phone calls. Soon he was old news, especially when it was obvious he would never play baseball again. At the age of twenty-five, he was an old man, never to fully recover. The headaches plagued him for the rest of his life. His vision was blurry, and his legs ached.

The team paid for all the medical bills, even for his wife's miscarriage. He had no idea what he was going to do with the rest of his life. He'd never given it a thought. There was only one road for him. He'd never considered any other. And now he was knocked off of it. His father-in-law got him a job on the railroad. Denny Dugan spent the rest of his working life punching tickets and opening doors, going back and forth, back and forth on an endless track to nowhere. The commuters sat, reading the sports pages and discussing the scores as Denny walked up and down the aisles all but invisible, punching their tickets and opening the doors. They had no idea who he had once been, who he was supposed to have been.

And now there was nothing left but to wait for death and even that seemed to have eluded him. He'd spent his whole life on the wrong track and now he was shoved off on a spur, watching the people watching him die. They stood or sat around him with somber expressions and muffled conversation. Except for that Mexican guy who was all smiles and giving Denny a thumbs up. Nobody else seemed to notice the strange man.

It was shortly after Denny's sixty-fifth birthday that he retired from the railroad after forty years of service. He got up that morning as he did every morning, groaning with back pain. His feet hurt. His head ached. He had sharp pains in his shoulder. He dragged himself to the bathroom where a small bowl of pills awaited him. Every night Denny's wife put out his pills for him and set up his coffee in the kitchen, helping to jump start him and send him on his way. Every morning there would be a sandwich in a plastic bag waiting for him in the refrigerator for his lunch.

Nora probably had as many aches and pains as Denny did but he didn't know about them. They rarely spoke to each other anymore beyond the passing of phone messages or reminders about doctor appointments. Occasionally they watched television together in silence. Sometimes they talked about the weather. He didn't remember what her laugh sounded like.

They met in college. She was a few years younger than he was and was his sister's roommate. Nora was very shy around the handsome muscular baseball star. She could barely look at him and was afraid to talk. Denny pursued her for weeks, calling her on the phone but she wouldn't go out with him. She desperately wanted to but she was terrified. Finally she relented and Denny proposed to her on their third date.

She was a dutiful baseball wife, easing into the lifestyle of late nights, long absences, and no complaints. She celebrated his successes and stayed out of his way on bad nights. When he was on the road she worried about him. She never told him how lonely and scared she was. When he came home, her life continued again.

Just about the same time Denny got called up to the majors they learned there was a baby on the way. A single pitch and their lives were over. She lost her husband. She lost her baby. She lost everything. For forty years she went through the motions of being his wife. They stopped talking. They stopped being intimate with each other. She was wracked with grief over the losses but couldn't talk to him about them. She felt guilty and lonely. He was filled with self pity. And that was that.

The day of his retirement was like any other. He punched the tickets and walked the aisles. He opened and closed the doors and announced the stops. He wondered if anyone would notice on Monday that he wasn't there anymore. He wondered if anyone would care. When he stepped off the train for the last time there was a small gathering waiting for him. His supervisor and a few other officials from the company were there to greet him. His heart lifted slightly thinking they were going to have a little ceremony in his honor until he realized they were only there to deliver his final check and to collect his badge and other company equipment.

Denny opened his eyes. The small group keeping vigil over his dying body stood around crying and comforting each other. Denny was confused. If anything, he felt a bit better but they were acting as if he'd gotten worse. In fact, Denny felt better than he had in years. He tried to move and was astonished that he could. He felt full of energy. He got out of bed but nobody seemed to notice. They didn't react when he spoke to them either, except for the Mexican man who came and put his arm around Denny's shoulders.

"How you doin' Bro?" he asked.

"What's going on here? How come you're the only one who can see me? I feel great and everyone's crying."

"That's why," he answered pointing back at the bed.

Denny gasped as he saw himself still lying there, white and not moving.

"You kicked the bucket, Bro," said the Mexican.

"Well who are you? How come you can see me and hear me?"

"You don't recognize me? I'm your guardian angel, man. Ernesto

Gonzalez at your service."

"My guardian angel?"

"Yeah man. I've been taking care of you your whole life. You know, pulling strings, making things happen."

"Making things happen? Making what things happen?"

"All of it, Bro."

"You son of a bitch!" Denny grabbed him by the throat and wrestled him to the ground trying to strangle him. They would have knocked things over if they had been solid but instead fell through the table and chairs in the room. Nora sniffled quietly into a Kleenex as Phyllis put her arm around her. Denny and Ernesto flew past them as Ernesto fled his attacker, running through the wall with Denny in hot pursuit.

"Come back here, you son of a bitch! I'm not finished with you."

A tall figure dressed in a white robe stood in the hallway outside the hospital room. Ernesto hid behind him. "Get him away from me, Joseph. He's trying to kill me."

"Let me at him," yelled Denny. Joseph held up his hand and suddenly Denny couldn't move. He slowed down as if encased in a marshmallow.

"Now let's all calm down," said Joseph.

"Did you see that?" asked Ernesto. "He's crazy, man. He's trying to kill me."

"He can't kill you, Ernesto. You're an angel, remember?"

"Oh yeah, I forgot. Nyah nyah, you can't kill me."

"Mmff. Fllrbrr," said Denny. Joseph pointed at Denny and released whatever was stopping him from talking although he still couldn't move. He found it particularly unnerving when nurses and hospital visitors walked

116

right through him.

"Let me at him," said Denny. "Who are you?" he asked Joseph. "Are you in charge around here? I want to lodge a complaint."

"Mr. Dugan, this is highly irregular. I have to ask you to calm down. Can we all just go into this lounge and talk things over?"

"There's nothing to discuss. This guy ruined my life. I want him fired. I want my money back. I want a refund."

"Please, let's just go into this lounge." Joseph released Denny who scowled at Ernesto. Ernesto stayed on the opposite side of Joseph where Denny couldn't get at him.

Joseph opened the door to the lounge. There were a few people inside. Joseph waved his hand in a circle and suddenly the people looked at their watches or remembered something and they all left the room. Joseph traced an outline around the door after they'd gone to make sure nobody else would enter. He pointed to a table where they could all sit down together. Denny took a swipe at Ernesto but he dodged it. Joseph pointed a finger at Denny and gave him a reproving look.

"Now what's all this about? Ernesto, why haven't you accompanied Mr. Dugan to heaven yet?"

"I tried but he wouldn't go. When I told him I was his guardian angel, he attacked me. I told you you should have assigned me to that accountant in Yonkers. This guy's crazy. And after all I've done for him."

"After all you did for me? What did you do for me?"

"Are you kidding me?" Ernesto pulled from his back pocket a pad of paper. "Let's see. I kept you from getting sick on twenty three occasions, there were five muggers I kept out of your way, and I pulled a few strings and made you win the lottery that time."

"The lottery? That was only a hundred dollars!"

"Hey man. What are you complaining about? That's good money. Besides, you had a pretty good life. You had a good job and a good wife. You almost never got sick. I got you that neat little house with the apple tree in the backyard. I think I did pretty good by you."

"You think you did good by me? What about getting hit in the head with a baseball? What about when my skull cracked and my life ended? What about that? Did you make that happen too?"

"Oh that. Are you still sore about that?"

"Did you make that happen?"

"Well yeah, of course." Denny rose again to attack him but Joseph stopped him. Denny sat down again.

"Why? Just tell me that. I've asked myself that question almost every day of my life. Why? Why did you have to do that to me? Why did you ruin my life?"

"It wasn't ruined. It was just different."

"It was ruined. You remember that stray dog we had?"

"Oh yeah, I forgot about him. I did that too. Little Snuffles. He was so cute. I found him walking down an alley and sent him to you. I figured you guys would be real good for each other."

"That cute dog destroyed all my furniture the first time we left him alone."

"Oh man, Joseph, you should have seen that. That poor little doggie just panicked. He ran around in circles and scratched and chewed up everything. It was hysterical."

"Why didn't you stop him?" asked Denny.

"I couldn't stop him. I wasn't his guardian angel, I was yours."

118

"But what was your point?" asked Joseph. "Why did you mention the dog?"

"After he trashed the house we got a cage for him. And every time we left him alone, we had to put him in the cage. We couldn't trust him. We had to contain him. That's what my whole life felt like. I worked and paid the bills. I punched the tickets and opened the doors. I watched little petty people, far smaller and stupider than I was, going off to their high paying important jobs while I went back and forth on that stupid train. Is that all I could be trusted with? Is that the best you could do for me? Was I no better than that dog, that I couldn't have been trusted with a better life? With just a little more freedom?

"I was supposed to be a baseball player, not a conductor. And I'm not even talking about the money. It wasn't the money. It wasn't the fame. When I played baseball I was alive. I was in control. My body could do anything I needed it to do. Do you have any idea what it's like running as fast as your legs can carry you, feeling the wind blowing in your face, and arriving at the exact spot to meet the ball in your glove? Can you understand that frozen moment in time when you're staring down a pitcher and he's trying to psych you out as well? It wasn't the roar of the crowd I missed. It was the crack of the bat, when you hit the ball on the sweet spot and you could barely feel it and you knew it was going over the fence before you took a single step. Why did that have to end? Why did you cheat me out of that?"

"You would have had to stop sometime anyway," said Joseph. "There still would have been a time when you would have had to retire."

"Yeah, of course, but it would have been my choice at my time. Why couldn't I have had the life I wanted?"

"That's a good question," answered Joseph. "Ernesto?"

"It was the best possible option. I looked at all the potentials and measured all the probabilities. It was the best choice."

"But why?" asked Denny. "I need to know why."

"Hey boss," said Ernesto. "Why don't we show him?"

"What do you mean?"

"Well, he's a good guy. He's got a few people praying for him and he made a lot more friends on that train that he thinks he did. Why don't we give him a do over?"

"A do over?"

"Yeah, you know, when kids are playing and like if there's a close play at third and they can't decide if the guy was safe or out so they do the play over. You see, man?" he said to Denny, "I was paying attention. And I made sure you didn't get busted that time when you stole that chewing gum too. You owe me for that."

"Come over here and I'll give you what I owe you."

"That's a good idea," said Joseph.

"What? You gonna let him hit me again?"

"No, I mean about the do over. Let's give him the life he thinks he should have had."

"You can do that?" asked Denny.

"Absolutely. How about if we start at the point where you got hit in the head?"

"That would be great. It's all I ever wanted. You see?" he said to Ernesto. "I knew I was right. You messed up on me and now I get to make it right. And if we do this over again, I don't want any guardian angels interfering with me and messing me up again."

"You want to do the honors?" asked Joseph.

Ernesto reached into his back pocket and pulled out a huge board with a lever on it that couldn't possibly have fit in his pocket. "You ready?" asked Ernesto.

"Yeah, I'm ready."

Ernesto pulled the lever and a trap door opened under Denny. With arms flailing, he fell through it, landing at home plate at Yankee Stadium. The crowd roundly booed the pitcher. The Yankee manager came out to see if Denny was okay. Denny brushed himself off and said he was fine although he looked a bit disoriented. The manager then turned to the umpire. "That son of a bitch was aiming right at his head!"

"Get back to the dugout," answered the umpire. "I'll handle things our here."

"Okay, rookie," said the manager to Denny, "get back in there and let's see what you can do."

The next pitch was low and outside for a ball. Then came a fastball over the middle and Denny smacked it to the wall for a double knocking in two runs. Standing on second base, Denny looked around for the first time and took it all in. He was in the majors. He was a Yankee. And he'd gotten his first hit. This was what he'd dreamed of his whole life. This was what he was born to do. Two pitches later, Denny stole third and later scored on a wild pitch.

He was still a bit disoriented as he sat back in the dugout. He would try to remember things, little things like where he lived. His mind seemed a blank but then a second later the details would fill in as though being painted at the moment. A picture of an apartment in Brooklyn would suddenly be there. Nora would be home waiting for him. No, the team was traveling to Chicago after the game. Nora had helped him pack that morning. He kissed her goodbye and wait, there was something else. Oh yeah, he rubbed her belly and said goodbye to Baby Dugan inside.

It wasn't long before Denny made the starting lineup. He continued to hit consistently and fielded his position with a lot of flair and few errors. He became a big favorite with the fans. Even on road trips there were crowds of people at the hotels trying to get autographs.

Back at home Nora was having a difficult pregnancy not made any easier by having to fend for herself during Denny's long absences. She was exhausted and depressed. Her phone calls were particularly difficult for Denny. He wanted to be sympathetic but he had to concentrate on baseball. Her problems distracted him and scared him. He was afraid for her and the baby. He didn't like being afraid or being powerless to do anything to help her. What kind of advice did she expect from him? He would tell her to call her doctor or his sister Phyllis. She would cry and tell him she missed him and wished he was home. The combination of guilt and helplessness wore on him and he started dreading the sound of the phone ringing.

It was in Cleveland that he noticed a particularly beautiful young lady in the crowd in the hotel lobby. She had a sunny smile and a cheerful laugh. After giving her an autograph, he asked her to go to dinner with him. The star struck young lady jumped at the chance. She had gone to the hotel hoping to get some autographs for her younger brother for his birthday. But she was also an avid baseball fan herself and an insecure young woman. She was flattered by Denny's attention to her and captivated by his sheer power. After dinner Denny invited her up to his room. He was lonely and genuinely enjoyed her company and she was very attracted to him. The next morning when she left his room, he rationalized it all to himself until he was exhausted and then put the whole thing out of his mind.

Having already crossed the line however, it was easier to continue taking advantage of the endless opportunities on the road. He convinced himself that he deserved the pleasure because of the sacrifices he had to make, leaving his wife behind and working such a strenuous lifestyle. Most of the guys did it. They assured him that it didn't count somehow, kind of like soldiers in a war. It was easier for him to deal with Nora and her aches and pains when he wasn't singularly dependent on her. The outside dalliances were good for his marriage, he told himself. It didn't matter what he did as long as she didn't know about it. The deeds themselves wouldn't hurt her, only finding out about them would.

But then she did find out. There was a picture in the newspaper. It was late in the season and the team was fighting for first place. The pressure was on. That led Denny to take more chances and be less careful about them. It also led to a complete reluctance to deal with Nora on any level. It was a horrible scene that night. She threw the newspaper in his face and screamed at him and cried. He yelled back, denying everything and actually accusing her of being disloyal and mistrusting. Then Nora doubled over in pain and Denny was truly terrified. He called an ambulance and she was rushed to the hospital.

Denny missed the next two games while Nora recovered in the hospital. She had lost the baby and went into a deep depression. Denny couldn't face her. When he returned to the team, his performance began to falter. He couldn't focus and before he knew it he was sitting on the bench. When Nora came home from the hospital, she packed her bags and went home to her parents.

Denny's life soon spiraled out of control. He no longer sought out women on the road. Now he just went to bars and got drunk and stayed out late. The few times the manager penciled him in the lineup he struck out at the plate and made errors in the field. Upper management was talking about sending him back down to the minors or even trading him. When you're doing well everyone is your friend. But when you go into an extended slump, especially as a rookie, they treat you as if you have some contagious disease. Then it's just, "What have you done for me lately?"

One night, even Eddie the bartender was getting nervous. Denny had almost gotten into a fight with another guy in the bar who was jeering at him, calling him a flash in the pan. Denny yelled back at the guy, slurring his words and took a swing at him but missed and fell down. Eddie pleaded with Denny to take a taxi home but he insisted he was okay to drive. Pouring rain pelted the windshield. It would have been difficult seeing through it even if he was sober. Denny kept dozing off and jerking himself back awake. At some point he hit a pot hole or something and that jarred him awake until he got home.

The next morning he was awakened by a knock on the door. Denny, groggy and with a terrific headache, opened it. At first he thought he saw four policemen but when he squinted and refocused, he realized there were only two of them. They wanted him to come downtown to answer some questions about the previous night. Denny laughed it off telling them that the other guy in the bar was taunting him and he didn't even take a swing at him, at least he didn't remember doing so, so if the guy was trying to make trouble and threatening a lawsuit or something he wasn't going to get anywhere.

It wasn't the guy in the bar. The policemen informed him he had hit and killed a pedestrian the night before. A companion of the deceased had taken down his license number. Denny was arrested for leaving the scene of an accident, driving while intoxicated, and manslaughter. He turned pale. His knees buckled.

The next several months were a blur of a nightmare. The team released him outright. Nora, at the insistence of her father, filed for divorce. Her father pointed a finger at Denny's chest threatening that they would sue him for everything he had. Then he threw an opened envelope at Denny's face. After they left, Denny picked it up. It was from the parents of the young lady he had gotten involved with in Cleveland. She had gotten pregnant and tried to kill herself. She survived but lost the baby. They were suing him as well.

Aside from those lawsuits he had his criminal trial to contend with. It dragged on for several weeks making the headlines every day. When the foreman read the verdict of guilty on all charges, Denny just shut down completely. He was not heading to the World Series. He was heading to prison.

Denny was placed in a special wing of the prison. As depressed as he'd become, they were concerned that he might be a suicide threat. He wasn't. He didn't have the will or energy even for that. He numbly walked from his cell to the dining room and back to his cell again. He would eat and sleep and eat and sleep, back and forth, back and forth.

The monotony one day was broken by a noise at his cell door. He had a visitor. That was strange. Visitors were never allowed in the cell blocks. What was he doing there? And who was he?

"Ernesto Gonzalez at your service," he said.

"Go away," said Denny.

"You don't remember me?"

"Go away."

"I'm your guardian angel. Denny my friend, haven't you had enough of this?"

"My what? Oh yeah! Now I remember. This was supposed to be my do over. But this was worse than the other life."

"That's what I was trying to tell you. Come on, let's get out of here." Ernesto opened the cell door and led Denny out. They went through another door and wound up back in the original hospital lounge where they had talked before and where Joseph was waiting for them.

"What happened?" Denny asked.

Joseph answered. "You were given a chance to see what your life would have been like if you hadn't gotten hit by that baseball. That's the life we saved you from. Do you understand now? All that time you were grieving for your lost baseball career but now you know how it would have turned out. It wasn't the dream you envisioned. You understand now Denny? We only get to experience the road we're on. Any other life is just a made up might have been. When things go wrong in our lives, we can indulge in regrets but they're only fantasies about a road not taken. You were angry at the world your whole life for depriving you of what you thought should have been; for stealing what you thought was rightfully yours."

"I tried to tell you, man," said Ernesto. "That's why I got you on the railroad. I was trying to show you that you were on the right track. I thought that was pretty clever of me. Didn't you get it?"

"So that's why I was hit in the head? That's why I had the life I had, to save me from the other one?"

"That's the ticket, bro," said Ernesto. "We calculated all the probabilities. We gave you the best life we could under the circumstances."

"But why did it have to be so horrible? I had such a dull boring job and a terrible marriage. Why did it have to be like that?"

"It didn't have to be like that," said Joseph. "That was your doing. Those were your choices. You were supposed to have a son. He would have fulfilled all your dreams for you. He would have been a natural athlete and have a professional career, taking care of you in retirement. But you stopped being intimate with your wife so that couldn't happen. You were supposed to have gotten a great coaching job in a university. A man who rode your train every day would have hired you. But you ignored all the people on your train. You never spoke to them. He never got the chance to get to know you. As for the rest of it, you can't hold us responsible for a lifetime of self pity and anger. You got dealt a bad hand, that's true, but it was up to you to play it, instead of just resenting it."

"I blew it," said Denny. "I blew it. I was so angry at what was taken from me that I never paid attention to what I had. How could I have been so blind? Nora put up with me all those years anyway. She stayed with me all those years and I never even thanked her. I never appreciated her. Hey, wait a minute! What about another do over? Can I have another chance? Can I have another chance at the life I had? I'll do it right this time. I will. I'll talk to the riders on the train. I'll devote myself to Nora and our family. I will. I promise. Can I get another chance?"

"I'm sorry," said Joseph. "You can't. We ran that demonstration for your benefit, so you could see for yourself what would have been. This life is over now."

"Then it was all for nothing."

"Nothing is for nothing, Denny," said Joseph. "Hopefully you've learned something and you've grown from this experience. And maybe you'll get another chance at another time. But for now, we have to move on."

"Wait. Before we go, can I talk to Nora? I need to talk to her."

"She won't be able to hear you," said Ernesto.

"I know. But I need to anyway."

Denny went back into the hospital room where his lifeless body still lay in the bed. The hospital orderlies were getting ready to move it. They were waiting for a doctor to examine the body and sign the papers. Nora sat in a corner. Her eyes were red from crying."

"Please don't be sad, Nora. We'll be together again. I'll make it all up to you. I promise I will. I know you can't hear me and I don't know if it matters or not but I really loved you. I just wanted you to know that."

At that moment there was a tapping at the window. Nora looked up to see a bird pecking at the window.

"Phyllis, look at that!"

"Yeah, it's a bird. What about it?"

"It's an oriole! There aren't any orioles around here. Don't you understand? It's a sign. Denny hated the Orioles. It's Denny. He's come to tell me he's all right and at peace. He made it to heaven. I'll be okay now. He's safe at home."

Phyllis thought it was a bit of a stretch but she wasn't about to argue the point. As long as Nora thought she was going to be okay, that was good enough for her.

"Goodbye Denny," said Nora. "Save a seat in the bleachers for me."

End of Cycle

Of the four in their study group, it was Illuminara who was pushing the most to once again return to the physical life of Earth. Illuminara, like her name, was a shimmering glow of white light. She had golden hair and bright blue eyes the color of turquoise. When she walked anywhere on Haven, and she usually preferred to walk rather than to "pop" somewhere, she was often accompanied by small furry animals that followed her around and ate out of her hand. Her closest friend and mate, Martin, would rather pop to a destination, especially now that they were going to be late for the Guild concert. But Illuminara was not to be dissuaded. Greeting the flowers along the way, and she seemed to know each one by name, was just as important to her as reaching her destination.

"You see?" said Martin. "This is why I don't want to be physical again. This is just like you," he said as she stooped down to talk to a chipmunk.

"He's lost," she said. She mumbled some strange noises back at the chipmunk. It hopped out of her hand and scurried off again. "He didn't remember the way to the crystal pools. It's very hard for them, Martin. They have such a narrow scope. They have a hard time seeing the big picture." Martin knew what she was trying to do. She often spoke like this in meta-messages trying to convey a point to him.

"But I think I am looking at the bigger picture," he said. "That's just the point. I don't want to stay at this level for eons. I want to move on. I want to go higher and try the next level. Can you imagine how much fun it'll be when we shed these bodies altogether and become pure light?"

"Yes I'm sure it would be great but once we move on, we wouldn't

129

be able to come back again. Earth is so exciting with all its drama and chaos. You have to admit it's great fun what with eating, and gravity, families, and uh, other Earthly delights."

"Yeah I remember. I also remember work, money, pain, hunger, and old age. And worst of all is the curse of amnesia. It takes half a lifetime just to remember what we're trying to do down there, assuming we figure it out at all. I don't like groping in the dark."

"It's not a curse, it's a blessing. It's what makes it all so exciting."

"It's just as exciting to move upward and Isabella agrees with me."

Isabella was also in their group. She was a colorful being with bright orange hair and glowing green eyes. The fourth in their group was Isabella's mate Theo, a comparatively darker brooding young man. Their advisor and teacher was Master Azar. As the End of Cycle was approaching they would have to make a decision about what they wanted to do next and while it wasn't mandatory that they decide as a group, they almost always did, as these four were bonded together in love and friendship.

The last time they were all in the physical, they had failed to find each other. Theo especially had had a difficult time as he fell in with a rough bunch of friends and wound up spending some time in prison. Master Azar had acted as their guardian angel, trying to whisper hints in their minds when they were quiet enough to hear him. He was able to manipulate events to a degree to put them in better position to find their paths, but it was up to them to recognize those opportunities when he presented them and they still had to make the right critical choices.

Their discussion would have to wait as Martin and Illuminara had reached the concert area. There were thousands of souls congregated in the open field. They took positions lying on their backs in concentric circles on the soft mossy ground with their heads pointing toward the outer edge. Arriving early would have afforded Martin and Illuminara a place nearer the center of the circle where the full impact of light and sound could be better experienced, and it would have given them more time to meditate before the concert began. As it happened however, they were not the last to arrive and it wouldn't have mattered anyway as they found Isabella halfway toward the center and she had saved places for them.

As the sun set with a glorious panoply of dazzling colors, the Guild flew in above them toward the center of the circle and floated upward forming a star pattern. There were nearly fifty artists performing at this gathering. They positioned themselves above the crowd and issued beams of light to interconnect themselves into an intricate pattern. Then they started chanting their haunting harmonies. Sprinkles of colored light fell to the crowd below like a rainbow of snow. When the beads of light landed on the people, they penetrated deep within, giving them surges and waves of blissful energy.

The three friends locked hands together as the entire audience lifted off the ground. They hovered just above it, and began very slowly to turn like a huge wheel. The music filled each soul with a deep personal transcendence. It wasn't just a concert, it was a healing, a lifting, it was a tiny glimpse of the infinite.

When the performance came to an end, the audience was lowered gently back to exactly the same spot they had started from. The lights connecting the Guild members faded. They joined together at the center, hovered lower to the mass of blissed out souls below, and then floated away, each in a different direction while sprinkling a final dusting of warmth onto the people below as they left.

Later when they had fully revived and were walking back to their home units, Illuminara said to Isabella, "You can do that, you know. You should be up there with them."

"I'm working on it. You know it's my deepest aspiration and Mistress Alleya says I'm almost ready. My light work is pretty much there but my voice still needs improvement."

"Your voice is beautiful. It's just as good as any of theirs."

"Thank you. I appreciate what you're saying but to combine the voice and the color together to produce the shimmerings, that's where I need more work. Mistress Alleya suggested another lifetime on Earth as a singer. She thinks if I can perfect my voice there amidst all that noise, it would be that much more improved when I return."

This news all but negated the healing effects of the concert for Martin. It meant that Isabella was moving back in the direction of wanting to incarnate to Earth at End of Cycle. There was still the question of what Theo would do, though. Clearly of the four of them, Theo most needed several more lives in the physical. On the other hand he was also the one who least wanted to go back. Theo wasn't anywhere near ready to move on to the next level so the choices for him were either to stay where he was and take an assignment at Haven or opt for another lifetime on Earth.

Isabella left the other two to pop back to her home unit. As usual, Illuminara insisted on walking and Martin had little choice but to stay with her. And as usual they were visited along the way by all the night creatures that stopped by to chat with her.

When they returned to their cottage, they sat together in silence, holding hands and facing each other before going off to sleep. The sleeping chamber could best be described as a room completely filled with warm soothing water. When they opened the door to it, the water stayed in. They dove in and closed the door behind them floating up toward the center of the room. Breathing in the crystal waters, they relaxed and drifted off to sleep initially holding hands but eventually letting go and occasionally gently bumping into each other during the night as they drifted in the room, weightless.

The next day in class, Master Azar tried to quell their doubts and fears about going back to Earth. "Remember my children, the best shortcut to a happy and successful life is love. That is always the best choice. When you reach difficult junctures in your lives, just take the path that is the way toward love. It isn't that difficult."

"It's easy to talk about all that up here but it's hard to see that down there," said Theo. "It's very confusing sometimes. It gets so loud and chaotic. Is the correct choice to take care of myself at the expense of the needs of my friends? Or should I remain loyal to them even if they're leading me astray? Which is the loving thing to do? Wouldn't it be easier if we could just remember who we are?"

"Well of course it would be easier but then what would be the point of the experience? You might just as well stay here. The whole point of being down there is to challenge yourselves, to test yourselves, but ultimately, to enjoy the experience. That's why roller coasters are so popular down there. They are a hint. The game is not played without hints. You just have to learn to pay attention."

"But how do we know what to pay attention to?" asked Theo.

"If nothing else, just pay attention to my voice inside you. I am always with you, guiding your steps and helping you along the way."

"You haven't been down there in a long time, have you?" asked

Martin. "The mind can be a pretty noisy place sometimes you know."

"Yes of course, but that's why you practice meditation here. The more you learn here, the more you take with you. The more you take with you, the more you remember who you are. When you get to the point that you go down there with almost complete memory. . . ."

"You don't have to go anymore?" asked Theo.

"You don't want to go anymore. The challenge is gone. The game is no fun if it's too easy. At that point you move on to the next level."

"It still doesn't make sense to me. It doesn't seem fair," said Theo.

"In what way is it not fair?" asked Azar.

"Martin, Illuminara, and Isabella are further along than I am so they're entitled to better options and choices to start with down there. But I'm the one who needs the head start, not them. Why shouldn't I have an advantageous birth situation? Why shouldn't I have a healthy, prosperous, loving, and spiritually awakened family to be born into? It wouldn't be so hard then."

"You're assuming that that would be an advantage. Do you think a ten year old boy should be allowed to drive a car just because it would get him to his destination faster?"

"Am I just a ten year old boy then? Is that what you're saying?"

"It's not a judgment, Theo, it's a fact. You are allowed a birth opportunity just ahead of your present level so you can grow into it and grow beyond it. You're not being punished. You're being protected. You don't want to lose ground. Don't forget the ultimate goal. It's what you learn down there that counts. It's how you grow down there. You may not start with the same advantages but you still start with the same tools and gifts and potentials. It's not what you have that matters, it's what you do with it. God's light shines on everyone equally, regardless of any other apparent inequalities. Now, that's enough for today. Let's meet here again in a couple of days and we'll continue the discussion."

After class they returned to the common area between their two houses to discuss their plans.

"Well it's obvious that Isabella has the greatest need," said Illuminara. "She needs to be a singer. We should let her choose first and then make our choices to accommodate her."

"I don't agree," said Isabella. "I think Theo has the greatest need. If he doesn't have our help and guidance down there he could fail even to find his way back here. He almost got lost the last time. We need to support him."

"I think you should just concentrate on your own needs and let me fend for myself," said Theo.

The other three reluctantly saw the logic in that but still refused to accept it. "No, I for one can't do that," said Martin.

"What are you talking about?" said Theo. "You don't even want to go back. The only reason you're going back is to be with Illuminara. What would be the point of wasting a lifetime you don't even want, just to take care of me?"

"My friend," said Martin, "helping you could never be a waste of anything."

"But why?" asked Theo.

"Because we love you," said Illuminara.

"That doesn't make any logical sense at all," said Theo.

"We know," said Isabella. "That's the whole point of it. Didn't you hear what Master Azar was saying today? It's true here as much as it's true down there. Love makes no logical sense. There's no rational reason for it. But it does make a lot of emotional and spiritual sense. That's why love is the proof of God."

"I don't understand," said Theo.

"But that's the point," said Martin. "With our help, you will."

The next day was a free day. Illuminara and Isabella went off to play in the crystal pools. Martin headed to the Great Library where he knew he would find Theo.

From the outside, the library appeared to be only a three story high structure with tall marble columns adorning the front steps. Many museums on Earth were designed subconsciously to look like the Great Library. Although the building appeared small from the outside, once inside, the space was infinite. Even Fredricks, the ancient librarian, occasionally found rooms and stairways he'd never seen before, and he had worked there for eons.

Martin found Theo in a room full of books that contained ancient secrets of the physical universe. Only the most advanced souls who were training to be Creators usually frequented that part of the Library.

"Hey friend, what are you studying?"

"The structure of the physical grid."

"Really? Isn't that a bit thick?"

"It's something I'm interested in."

"You have the strangest interests. What was that stuff you were reading a year ago?"

"Sound frequencies and their effects on bio-molecular structure. I was attempting to analyze the effects of sound as I had noticed that Isabella's singing always seems to have a soothing effect on me."

"She just has a beautiful voice, that's all."

"Yes, but I was interested in determining why that is."

"Theo, my friend, I think sometimes you're supposed to just let the experience happen. You have to allow it to be and just feel it."

"Yes, I suppose that's true, but sometimes I need to understand things. These are things The Creator knows, as it was He who created sound and light and their effects. Do you realize that if you took all the knowledge in this library, it would comprise only a fraction of what The Creator knows?"

"Yes, but there are other dimensions to The Creator than just knowledge."

"Yes, of course I know that, and there are other abilities I must master but it is the thirst for knowledge that burns my soul."

"Well, yeah, but if you could develop some of those other areas, maybe you'd have better options and you could be born to better circumstances. Maybe you could become a professor or researcher or something and progress faster. If you stay so limited and one dimensional you'll keep getting stuck with limited options and then you could lose your way again. You have to give yourself a leg up."

"I'm becoming a burden to the group, aren't I? I'm holding you all back."

"I didn't say that."

"No, but it's true nevertheless. I have the least number of options on Earth. If we are to try to stay together down there, you will all have to accommodate me. Without me in the group, you three could pretty much go wherever you want."

"Don't talk that way."

"Whether I say it out loud or not, the truth of it remains. And it will be up to me to make the decision because none of you will."

"What decision?"

"The decision about what we're going to do for the next cycle."

"What are you thinking? What have you got in mind?"

"Don't trouble yourself, Martin. It'll all work out. I'll see to it. This is very fascinating material I'm reading. Did you know that the grid is maintained through the minds of seven million souls? Each of them is connected to five others through points of light and they meditate in place for a hundred years until another comes to take his place."

"No, I didn't know that. I thought it all just kind of held together by itself."

"You should study more. There is much to learn."

"I'm sure that's true but that stuff doesn't really interest me."

The next day in class, Master Benjamin, the Keeper of Records was present to answer the group's questions. It was he who could tell the group what their options were and it was he who would approve the final decisions.

Isabella could have her choice of several different families. A few of them would afford her a mother who was a voice teacher. There were two potential fathers who were popular professional singers, and several others who had a great deal of talent but mostly just sang as a hobby. Isabella narrowed it down to two choices. One was a couple in Rome who sang opera professionally. The other couple lived in a small town in Iowa and sang in the church choir.

On a large screen in the front of the classroom, Master Benjamin showed Isabella the two couples. The pair in Rome were singing together.

They looked very happy. They were holding hands and were deeply connected to their music and to each other. Then she viewed the couple in Iowa. They were very sad. The woman had recently suffered a miscarriage and they were praying together for God to give them another chance at a child to love. It was an easy choice for Isabella.

Illuminara and Martin could pretty much have their pick of any available family and only needed to be born in reasonable proximity to each other.

The problem was Theo. Having the least experience on Earth of the four, he had the fewest options. There were several loving, healthy, and spiritual families he could choose from but they were all in obscure places on Earth in rather backward tribal lands. There were virtually no options anywhere near Isabella. The closest families available near her were several hundred miles away and were broken families with many obstacles and hardships.

"I'm sorry sir but that doesn't make sense," said Martin.

Benjamin raised his eyebrows. He was not used to being addressed in such a confrontive manner.

"Theo's right," Martin continued. "It doesn't make sense and it isn't fair. You'd think it would be the opposite. Theo should have his choice of the best families, not the most struggling ones. Why make it hardest on those who need the most help?"

"Are you questioning The Plan? Are you ready to take over the judgments of The Creator?"

"With respect sir, yes, I am questioning. And rather than trying to make me feel ashamed for asking the question, I'd prefer you simply answer it."

"Martin, please!" said Master Azar. "Have some respect."

"Since when is it disrespectful to ask questions?"

Master Azar was about to reproach Martin again but Master Benjamin stopped him. "Your impetuous young student is quite right. I stand corrected and I thank you for pointing out that even I still have much to learn. It is, of course, always proper to ask questions.

"As to the answer to your question, it really comes down to a matter of energy frequency. The soul of the applicant and the families that would receive him or her must match according to a similar level and quality of energy vibration as you no doubt already know. Your question presumes that the lighter energy of a more advanced family would have a positive effect upon a younger soul. However as we've seen in the past, the opposite is more often the case, that the denser darker energy of the younger soul has a deleterious effect on the rest of the family which places an unfair burden on them. I mean no disrespect to young Theo here. He is a fine and wonderful soul who is destined for greatness, but that progression must be earned slowly just as it was for the rest of you. These are not meant to be judgments nor should they be taken as such. Like any school, there is a logical progression. One doesn't jump from fifth grade directly to high school. The presence of difficult obstacles in one's lifetime is not meant to be a punishment. It is, in fact, a gift because the obstacles afford one the greatest opportunity to grow beyond them."

After the class, the four friends separated as they were required to do and spent the rest of the day in solitude to contemplate their options and choices. Illuminara headed to the crystal springs where she bathed under the warm colored waterfalls and slept among the flower beds. Isabella popped to the Hall of the Artist Guild so she could hear the golden strains of music coming from within. Martin soared to a mountain top where he could meditate among the clouds and listen to the plaintive cries of the eagles. Theo opted for a cool damp cave deep within a rock quarry.

The next day the four friends met again in the classroom with Master Benjamin. Isabella announced that she had changed her mind about the family in Iowa. She wanted instead to be born into the tribe of Aborigines in Australia where Theo would have the best family available to him and she could be with him and support him. Martin and Illuminara announced that they too wanted to be born into the tribe so they could be close to Theo and support him also.

"Well, Theo," said Benjamin, "the love and loyalty of your friends speaks well of you. Shall we sign the book and make it official?"

Theo stood up. "I cannot allow it. I will not be a burden to my friends. I have learned so much from them. Mostly I have learned about love. I have learned about making sacrifices for those one loves. They are more than willing to sacrifice their needs for my sake. But you see, I love them too. Master Benjamin, for the next cycle, I wish to volunteer to hold a position as a Keeper of the Grid."

An audible gasp was heard from Masters Benjamin and Azar. "No!" cried Isabella.

"Do you understand what you are saying?" asked Benjamin. "You would be completely isolated for a hundred years. Even I could not withstand the rigors and demands of such an assignment."

"I fully understand what I am volunteering for. But I don't see that it will be a hardship. I will have a hundred years to meditate on the love and loyalty of my friends. That way I will not hinder their plans for the next cycle. I do not wish to hold them back or be a burden to them. And by the end of my assignment, given the intensity of the spiritual cleansing I will go through, I will have caught up with them and we can move on from there together."

"Are you sure you want to do this? Many souls have sunk into madness even after a short time on the grid. Do you want some time to think this over?"

"I am ready to sign the book."

"Master Azar," said Benjamin, "I am humbled by the loyalty and love in this group. It speaks as well of you as it does of them. I will have much to contemplate in the coming months. Very well. Let us continue then with the assignments. Any volunteer for the grid is automatically approved. In light of that, I assume, Isabella, that you would like to request the couple in Iowa?"

Isabella could barely talk as she clutched Theo and wiped the tears from her eyes. "Yes, I would."

"Isabella, you are approved to be born to the couple in Iowa. They will raise you with love and respect and will cherish you. They will teach you with wisdom and they will encourage your love of music and your love of life. You will lead a good simple life. You will absorb the music of the wheat fields and of the clouds. You will absorb the music of the sunsets and of the flowers and the children. You will not marry but you will teach many children and touch their lives. When you return, you will be admitted to the Guild of Artists as an entry level apprentice."

"Thank you, Master Benjamin."

"In light of Theo's decision, there is no longer a need or possibility to keep the four of you together. Illuminara, if you agree to it, I have selected for you a family in Wyoming. You will have three older brothers who will guide and protect you. You will become a Park Ranger at Yellowstone Park. You will be where you most love to be, among nature and animals. You will help others to appreciate the beauty and wonder of Mother Earth at her purest. You will find you have a strange affinity with the animals, almost able to communicate with them."

"Thank you, Master Benjamin. It sounds wonderful. I accept."

"Martin, you are approved also to be born to a family in Wyoming. You will be the best friend of one of Illuminara's brothers. You and Illuminara will marry. Your choice of career will be open. You will have several options available to you and it will be a struggle for you to decide which path best suits you."

"Thank you, Master Benjamin. I accept."

"I think that ends the proceedings then. If you would each come up here and sign the book, it will be complete. I wish you all the best of luck in your journeys on Earth. I trust that Master Azar will find it easy guiding you as guardian spirit. And I trust you will have nothing to fear for the integrity of the physical grid with Theo as one of the Keepers. We'll meet again in about a hundred years at the next End of Cycle."

A week later the four friends arrived at the Hall of Entry where Martin presented his credentials to the gate keeper and was allowed entrance. The other three went to the visitor's area to witness the process. Martin was shown to his place in the great hall. Three attendants stood over him and laid hands on him. He could feel his vibration slowing down. He could feel himself getting heavy.

He found himself floating in a warm dark place. He could hear a loud rhythmic sound like turbine engines. He was very relaxed until he suddenly felt an intense squeezing pressure. It was very painful and frightening. He was being pushed through a very narrow opening that he could barely fit through. Again and again he could feel the intense pressure of being pushed through the opening. He feared he couldn't do it. The space wasn't big enough. Something was going wrong. He had to tell someone but he couldn't speak. He struggled helplessly and eventually he was through. Immediately he was blinded by bright lights and felt freezing cold air on his wet naked skin. All around him there was a rush of activity. He couldn't move or talk. He opened his mouth but all he could hear was a high pitched wailing sound. Suddenly at hearing the sound, everyone around him relaxed and the activity slowed down. It was only then that he realized that he had made it through successfully. He was scrunched into a tiny body that he couldn't control. When he was lifted toward a woman into whose deep eyes he stared, he knew he would be just fine.

A few days later, Isabella and Illuminara accompanied Theo to the Hall of Mysteries. They were not allowed to go in with him. They embraced him and wished him good luck. The door closed behind him.

Isabella and Illuminara spent many days together afterward at the crystal pools as they awaited their turn to enter the physical. Occasionally they would go to the Viewing Hall where they could peer into the physical world to look in on Martin. They laughed at his antics. He was a very cute little boy. After the equivalent of five Earth years had passed it was Illuminara's turn to enter the physical and soon afterward, Isabella followed.

Laura Ingram was not sad but just pensive as she sat on the swing on the front porch of her house in Cody, Wyoming. She had just returned from the funeral of her husband of sixty years. Sitting near her sipping a glass of water was another elderly woman she had met that day at the

144

funeral, a cousin of an old friend who happened to be in town from Iowa for a visit and had agreed to sing at the funeral.

"Thank you so much for your song this morning. You have such a lovely voice. Do you sing professionally?"

"No, I just sing in the choir back home in Iowa."

"Well I thank you very much. Marty would have loved it. *Ave Maria* was always one of his favorites."

"You two were married sixty years?"

"We were together even longer than that. He was my older brother's best friend. Gosh, it seems like I knew him forever. We were always good pals when we were children and then in high school it blossomed into something even more wonderful."

"How magnificent. I'm envious."

"Did you never marry?"

"No I never did. When I was a child, I dreamed of a tall dark handsome stranger who would carry me away in his arms but he never showed up. I guess it was just never meant to be. But I have no complaints. I have many friends and I taught music in the school back home so I feel like I had many children. They used to call me Auntie Isabel. Now they call me Grandma Isabel. They all grew up and then I taught their children and, heavens me, now I'm starting to teach their grandchildren."

"And now I'm envious of you. Marty and I never had children. I suppose that too just wasn't meant to be. But I always had my furry friends. I was a Park Ranger at Yellowstone for forty years. What a blessing that was. I still miss going to work each day. I haven't told too many people this. I wouldn't want them to think I've gone balmy but at our age, who cares anymore? I used to give names to all the animals. They were my friends, after all. Sometimes I could imagine they were trying to talk to me. I suppose they were my children. I watched them grow up and have families and watched their children and grandchildren so I suppose it was like your students only my children were elk and moose and even some bears."

"What kind of work did your husband do? Was he a Ranger as well?"

"No, Marty didn't have an affinity for it like I did. He tolerated my little insanities. He was a restless soul. It was as if he didn't really want to be here. I think he would have moved away to Cheyenne or Laramie or even a big city back east if it weren't for me. I wasn't about to move away so he was forced to make the best of it. He tried a whole bunch of things; farming, truck driving, we even had a small diner in town for a while. For a few years he moved down to the southern part of the state and worked the coal mines and only came home on weekends. I missed him terribly but he enjoyed the hard work and I couldn't begrudge him doing what he wanted. That's what I was doing, after all."

"It must be terribly hard for you now."

"Oh no. I don't think so. I'll just pretend he's back working the mines. I have a head full of memories and a heart full of love. That will have to carry me until we're together again."

"You have a wonderful attitude and a wonderful spirit. I feel as if I've known you for a long time even though we just met."

"I feel that as well. You're like a long lost sister who's come home. Say, I've got an idea. Have you ever been to Yellowstone?"

"No I never have."

"Tomorrow let's get in my jeep and go there. I'll show you around.

146

I have a lifetime free pass. It won't be good much longer. Might as well use it while I can."

"Are you up to it? Your nurse seems to be hovering over you as if she thinks you might keel over at any moment."

"Oh, hang the nurse. What's there to worry about, that we'll get eaten by bears? No bear in his right mind's going to be interested in us. We're just bone and gristle now. Come on, we're not so old that we've run out of adventures, are we? I'll pick you up in the morning."

"Yes of course. I'd love to go with you. It'll be great fun."

"Damn right it will be."

"See? I told you I could bring them together," said Master Azar to Master Benjamin. They were sitting comfortably in the Viewing Hall, watching the screen and eating popcorn.

"Yeah, but you had to kill me to do it," said Martin.

"Aw, quit complaining," said Azar. "Next time you'll have an even better time down there,"

"Next time? I'm not going back there again. No way. Uh uh. That's final."

"We'll see what Illuminara has to say about it. She'll be back here in a few months."

Illuminara was the next to pass over to Haven. Martin was there to ease her transition and help her recover. The two of them were present a few years later to welcome Isabella back. And eventually Theo returned as well, none the worse for wear. After a few weeks with the Healers, he was fully recovered.

"I think we should all be brothers and sisters next time," said

Illuminara.

"Give me a break," said Martin. "We're barely back here and you're already planning our next trip? I don't want to go back there again, especially as your little brother."

"Would you rather be my sister?"

"I don't think so."

"Okay, I have a better idea. You can be my son. I'll be married to Theo next time."

"Great idea," said Isabella. "I'll be your sister."

"I'm not doing it," said Martin.

"He's right," said Theo. "I wouldn't want to have him for a son. Let's make him our daughter instead."

"Ain't gonna happen," said Martin.

The four friends were back together again, laughing and joking, basking in the warmth of their deep and devoted love for one another. And so it went . . . on and on . . . forever.

How Darnell and Crazy Joe Saved Earth from Annihilation

Darnell was startled when his office communicator buzzed. Nobody ever called him and that was the way he liked it. He was a timid man whose only ambition was to remain anonymous. His office was tucked away in the bowels of the huge Klaxorian government headquarters. Darnell was an expert on the subject of Earth, a small insignificant planet several quorejumps away, circling the star called Bubla. Darnell was teased and laughed at his whole life because of his interest in Earth. As everyone on Klaxor knew, Earth was populated by small-minded antlike people. They scurried around staking out territories and fought amongst themselves trying to make bigger territories. The activities on Earth were generally laughed at and mostly just tolerated by the Klaxorians. Until this particular morning. Darnell's communicator buzzed again. Convinced now that it wasn't buzzing by mistake, he pressed the answer button to see who was calling.

Darnell jumped to attention when he heard the Foreign Minister's voice booming over the communicator. As he leaped up, he banged his knee on his desk and without thinking, shouted a Klaxorian obscenity.

"What did you say?" asked the Foreign Minister.

"Uh, n–n–n–nothing, sir."

"Come to my office at once."

"Y-y-yes sir."

Darnell had never been to the Foreign Minister's office before. He'd never been to any office before. His communicator had never buzzed before. Prior to this assignment he'd worked in the mailroom quietly sorting mail. That position had been arranged by his brother-in-law soon after he'd married Keela. A few years later when Claymore disappeared, Darnell was promoted to the Earth Affairs office. Five years later, his communicator buzzed for the first time.

Darnell timidly knocked on the door to the Foreign Minister's office. He had to knock twice more before he was finally heard.

"Come in," said the Foreign Minister, Mr. Umlaut.

Darnell was shocked to see the Prime Minister, Mr. Superius, there as well, pacing back and forth, agitated. He had only ever seen the Prime Minister on Viewscreen at home during news reports. Darnell tripped entering the room and sprawled on the floor. The Prime Minister himself helped Darnell to his feet and offered him a chair. Then the Prime Minister deferred to the Foreign Minister to lead the meeting.

"There's been an incident," began Umlaut but he was immediately interrupted by Superius.

"It's a crisis I tell you, a crisis," he said.

"Yes, as I was saying," said Umlaut, "there is a crisis."

"An attack would be more like it," said Superius.

"Would you like to continue?" asked Umlaut.

"No, no, you're doing fine. Please proceed." Darnell turned from one to the other trying to understand what they were talking about and what part he could possibly have in it.

"As I was saying," said Umlaut, "we've been attacked."

"It's an act of war," said Superius. "This can't be tolerated. We must respond. We'll obliterate those hooligans. We'll wipe them from the universe. We'll, . . . sorry. Please proceed."

"Yes, as I was saying, we've been attacked." He looked to Superius expecting to be interrupted again. Superius impatiently asked him what he was waiting for and told him to continue. "We've been attacked," he repeated. At this point both of them looked at Darnell expectantly.

"Well, aren't you going to say anything?" Umlaut asked Darnell. "This is your department, Darren."

"It's Darnell, sir, but I don't understand. How does this concern me?"

"We've been attacked by Earth!"

"Really? That's very unusual. I thought they only attacked each other."

"This isn't the first time it's happened," said Superius. "How could you not know that? I thought you were supposed to be the expert on Earth. You're supposed to know these things."

"Um, that was classified information, sir," said Umlaut.

"Ah, yes, of course. I knew that. I was just testing him. In times of war we can't trust anyone you know. He could be a spy. He might even be an Earthling."

"Now really, Superius," said Umlaut, "there's no reason to insult the man. I can personally vouch for him. Why his own brother-in-law is the Assistant Minister of Sewers. Now I think what we should do first is to go to the crash site and see if Darnell can enlighten us on what we found there."

They rode in the Prime Minister's personal space car. Darnell was reeling, disoriented. He'd never traveled outside the capital city before, let alone doing so in the presence of the Prime Minister. They headed for the Eastern Desert which seemed to stretch on forever. At last they arrived at the site. What was left of a huge rocket and the debris it was carrying was scattered for miles. There were scorch marks everywhere.

Superius directed Darnell to a section of the rocket that was still intact. On it was a rectangle with red and white stripes and a blue patch in the upper left corner that was full of stars. Below that it said, *Interstellar Garbage Disposal Company, United States of America.*

"What do you make of that?" asked Superius. "We figure it must be the name of their army. It's just a good thing the warhead didn't explode."

"Yes sir, but what makes you think this was an attack?" asked Darnell. "It might have just been an accidental crash."

"This," said Superius. He held up a small section of cardboard. On it were the words, *Grade A Eggs.* Darnell gasped when he saw it. In the Klaxorian language, Grade A Eggs happened to be the most flagrant threatening and insulting obscenity one could utter.

"Maybe it's a misunderstanding," said Darnell.

"But this isn't the first time it's happened," said Umlaut. "Five years ago we had a similar occurrence."

"I told you we should have attacked them back then," said Superius. "Now there can be no doubt about their intentions. We must fight back."

"You're right of course. There can be no doubt this time. We'll have to ready the Space Force and send enough nuclear weapons to destroy Earth. This kind of aggressive and insulting act cannot be ignored."

"It might just be a misunderstanding," said Darnell.

That night when he returned home, Darnell's apartment was darkened except for several candles lit around a picture frame. The picture held a central place on the mantelpiece in the living room. It was a photo of a young handsome Space Force officer, the first husband of Darnell's wife Keela. He was killed in the Battle of Zumnog. Every night she sat beneath the picture with her eyes closed. Darnell tiptoed across the room but accidentally kicked a table and startled her.

"Do you have to come clomping around here like a giant Soomsloth while I'm mourning?"

"I'm sorry dearest. I didn't mean to interrupt you."

"Well it's done and over with now. Hurry up and fix me supper. I'm starving."

"Yes dearest. Did you have a good day today?" Darnell didn't really want to ask that question. The answer was never a good one but if he didn't ask, it was worse. Then she would yell at him that much more for being inconsiderate and self centered in not asking.

"I had a terrible day. I visited Mrs. Gloregum and it took over an hour to get there through the busy traffic. By the time I got there my hair was a mess and I had to return to fix it. I was certainly not going to present myself to someone like Mrs. Goreglum with messy hair. That might be okay for the likes of you but I have my reputation to uphold. If you could afford to buy a better space car I wouldn't have to endure such insults but I don't really expect you to get any promotions. You're lucky enough my brother was able to get you a job at all."

"Yes, dearest. Shall I make you supper now?"

"What's that supposed to mean? Are you trying to insult me?"

"No dearest. Of course not."

"And how was your day, Darnell," he imagined her asking. "Oh fairly routine. I rode with the Prime Minister in his private space car and we discussed the destruction of Earth but other than that, nothing really unusual happened." But of course Keela never asked and Darnell never told her.

The next day there was a big summit meeting at the Foreign Minister's office. The Prime Minister was there as were all the Generals of

153

the Space Force, and Darnell. A heated discussion ensued about how quickly they could attack and how exactly they would go about destroying Earth; whether they should break it up into small pieces or vaporize it completely. There were differing opinions about what would happen to the oceans after the destruction; whether they would evaporate or freeze.

"Maybe it was just a misunderstanding," said a small voice that nobody heard. Darnell tried again. "Maybe it was a misunderstanding," he said. Suddenly all eyes were on him as if he had just smoodged or something. "I mean, maybe we should talk to them first."

"You can't talk to Earthlings," said one of the Generals. "They're barbaric and ignorant."

"But that's my point," persisted Darnell. "This isn't like them. Why would they make an unprovoked attack on us? I don't think they even know we're here. It might have just been an accident."

"But they sent a message," said Superius. "They said Grade A you know whats."

"But what about Section 3-6, paragraph five in the Codes of War?" asked Darnell.

Everyone groaned as Darnell lifted the heavy book to the table.

"It clearly says," continued Darnell undaunted, "that planets cannot be destroyed without first attempting a peaceful settlement and giving fair warning."

"But we gave them fair warning," said Umlaut. "We sent Claymore five years ago."

"Claymore?" said Darnell. "Is that what happened to him?"

"We don't know what happened to him. He never returned. We never heard from him again."

"Then you don't know for sure if the warning was given," answered Darnell. "We have to send someone else."

"Okay," said Superius. "Fine. I volunteer you."

"M-m-m-m-me?" asked Darnell.

"Yes, you. Be prepared to leave in the morning."

That night Darnell once again tiptoed around Keela as she was mourning her first husband. At supper, Keela gave the sign that he was allowed to speak.

"I'm leaving in the morning," he said.

"Okay."

"I'm going to Earth. It could be a very dangerous mission. I might never return."

"Oh bother! You mean I'll have to find myself another husband? Oh well, if I must I must but I think it's very inconsiderate of you to put me in a position like this."

"Are you, are you going to mourn me as well if I don't come back?"

"Don't be ridiculous. You're not a hero. You're just a clerk."

The next morning Darnell went through numerous briefings and orientations. It would take him approximately a week to arrive on Earth at superauric speed. He would land roughly at the same coordinates that Claymore had landed. He was to find the White House and speak to the head of the government that sent the rocket. "I think they call him the President," said Darnell.

"Yes, the President," said General Clux. "Take this with you. It is a communicator that will broadcast through space. Let us know how you're progressing. If the President does not listen to reason, tell us and we'll have you out of there in no time. Then we'll dice up that planet like chopped moogums."

Meanwhile, back on Earth

Crazy Joe sat out on his front porch watching the bright orange leaves fall to the front lawn. "Gettin' close to Halloween," he said to his roommate, Hank.

"So, are we going to do it or not?" asked Hank.

"Yeah, what the hell, let's do it. Send out the invitations. We'll have the best Halloween party ever. So what if Chloe broke up with me. Let's do it anyway. Maybe it'll cheer me up."

"Well all right then," said Hank. "What are you going to be?"

"I don't know. I'll think of something. What about you?"

"Maybe I'll dress up as an undertaker again. Are you going to look for a job today?"

"No, I don't think so. Maybe tomorrow. This is a bad time of year to be looking. Maybe I should wait until Spring."

Crazy Joe was a waiter when he bothered to work at all. His record for holding a job was six months. He'd worked in twenty different restaurants in the past three years and got fired from all of them. On one occasion he was fired before he was even hired. While filling out the application he was told he had to take a multiple choice exam that had a hundred questions about wines, sauces, and desserts.

"That's BULLSHIT!!" he yelled in the middle of the lunchtime crowd. He was quickly herded out. His last job he'd actually enjoyed because the food was pretty good and he was able to eat as much of it as he wanted. But one night a family of eight arrived and the head of the family was particularly annoying and demanding. He wanted water refills, clean napkins, different spoons and even asked for a different menu when he found a smudge on the one he had. He had Crazy Joe running back and forth every two minutes. In the meantime the people at Joe's other five tables were waiting for him impatiently. Finally the man summoned Crazy Joe over to his table and berated him, telling him that his soup was cold. Joe stuck his middle finger in the man's soup, pulled it out and held it up in front of the man and said, "No it's not," and walked away. Even though the man's family applauded, Crazy Joe was fired.

That incident was the last straw for Crazy Joe's girlfriend Chloe. Chloe had met him at Joe's third costume party years ago. She was invited by a co-worker of hers. Every year about five to ten new people got invited by previous guests and then became regulars themselves and invited their friends the following year. At their first meeting, Chloe was dressed as a cowgirl, and Crazy Joe was dressed as a hippy. Chloe had cap guns in her holsters and was shooting the guns every chance she got. She found Crazy Joe meditating on the floor and drew her gun on him. Staying in character, he said, "Make love, not war." Later that night she took him up on it and they were together ever since, at least until Joe stuck his finger in the man's soup.

Crazy Joe's roommate Hank owned the house they lived in. One night Hank was eating at one of the restaurants Joe got fired from. A man was complaining that Joe had forgotten to bring him dinner rolls. It was a very busy night. Joe told him he'd get to him as soon as he could but the man persisted in a loud voice demanding a dinner roll that instant. Joe picked up a roll from the table where he was and flung it to the boisterous guest, knocking the man's toupee off, which fell into his salad. Hank was the guy whose roll got thrown. He admired the roll toss so much that he invited Joe to join him for dinner after the manager came out and fired him. When he heard that Joe was also looking for a place to live, Hank invited him to stay with him.

As always, Hank and Crazy Joe spent weeks preparing for the party. The least of their concerns was the food and drink. What they meticulously focused on were the decorations. By the night of the party there were skeletons and cobwebs everywhere. They had rubber body parts oozing with blood sticking out from under various pieces of furniture. The bottles of alcohol had labels on them like "Bat's Blood" and "Essence of Spleen". Even the bathrooms were decorated so anyone who imbibed too much beer and needed to relieve himself, was stared at by dozens of skulls all laughing and making crude remarks.

The big night finally arrived and the guests began showing up. There were cats and clowns, pirates and pixies, night creatures and ninjas. The beer started flowing and everyone was having a great time. The stereo was cranked and the party soon spilled into the spacious backyard.

Crazy Joe's friend Jake showed up dressed as a gangster and his girlfriend, Sheila was dressed as a flapper. As usual, they were arguing before they even got to the party. Jake had taken issue with Sheila's costume complaining that it revealed too much of parts of her that he felt belonged only to his eyes.

"Where's Crazy Joe?" people asked Hank.

"He's still upstairs getting his costume together."

"What's he going to be?"

"I don't know. He wouldn't tell me."

At that moment the entire house shook.

"What the hell was that?" someone asked.

"I don't know. Felt like an earthquake."

After landing, Darnell quickly went through the sequence to close up the spaceship and render it invisible. He staggered to the ground finding it difficult to walk since Earth had a much greater gravitational pull then did Klaxor. He stumbled around the ground where he had landed. There were strange people milling around nearby. He went up to one of them and asked where the White House was.

"It's right over there," the man answered, pointing to Crazy Joe's house. "Great costume!"

Darnell trudged to the back door of the house. He kept his hand on his laser gun while sifting through the crowd. This was the strangest assortment of beings he'd ever seen, especially for a government building but then again, he knew Earthlings were strange.

"Hey! Look at the alien!" they all yelled. "Great costume." They all patted his back and welcomed him in.

The monotone speaker on his space helmet broadcasted his words. "Take me to your leader. I must see the President." Everyone applauded the stunning details of his elaborate costume. To Darnell, the clapping of hands was startling and incomprehensible.

It was about that time that Crazy Joe came down the stairs and as you might have anticipated by now, he was dressed as the President. Everyone told him that an alien was looking for him. Crazy Joe made his way through the crowd toward the back door. When Darnell saw him he asked, "Are you the President?"

"Yes I surely am, Mr. Spaceman, what can I do you for?"

From the monotone speaker, Joe heard, "I have come to warn you that we must destroy your planet because of your aggressive attack on us."

"Well, that sounds reasonable," said Joe. "Got time for a beer first?"

"What is beer?"

"Oh that's right. You're an alien. You don't know about beer. Well why don't you take off that helmet and I'll show you what beer is."

"Can't take off helmet. Hostile atmosphere. Dangerous to Klaxorian lungs."

"Yeah, I'll bet it is. Must be gettin' kind of hot in there though. Let me help you off with that."

Darnell pulled out his gun. "Do not touch helmet. Earth atmosphere dangerous to Klaxorian lungs."

"All right. Suit yourself. Great costume though. Where did you get it?"

"Issued by Minister of Space Force."

"Oh yeah. Of course. I should have known. Hey everyone, where's Hank? He's gotta see this."

But Hank was inexplicably nowhere to be found.

It was about this time that Jake and Sheila, having had a goodly amount of said beer, took their bickering to a higher level. Jake was yelling at her and calling her names. Darnell didn't know the meaning of the words but there was no mistaking the tone. Jake slapped Sheila. Darnell was shocked to see that and he stepped in to intervene before she could get slapped again.

"That is not a proper way to treat females," he said.

"Oh yeah? Well why don't you just butt out?" answered Jake.

160

"You want me to stick my butt out? Why?"

"Hey spaceman, you want to go to the moon?"

"No thank you, I just came from there."

"Hey, you think you're a wise guy or something?"

"Wise? Oh yes, intelligent, knowledgeable. Yes, I believe I am."

"Well why don't you take off that helmet so I can punch you in the nose?"

"Cannot remove helmet. Earth atmosphere dangerous to Klaxorian lungs."

"Oh that's too bad. I guess I'll have to punch you in the stomach then."

Darnell pulled out his gun. "Please do not attempt to harm me. I will have to defend myself."

"Oh, isn't that cute. Where did you get that, at a toy store?" Jake then made a move to punch Darnell. Darnell fired his gun which sent out a thin green laser light beam that knocked Jake off his feet. Jake scratched his head and noticed his hair was singed. He jumped up to attack again. Darnell fired again and the blast knocked Jake out cold.

Before he knew what was happening, Sheila pulled off Darnell's helmet to give him a kiss. Darnell grasped at it desperately, holding his breath. Sheila kissed him.

"It's about time someone stood up to that jerk," she said. "I've been taking his crap way too long."

Darnell turned blue trying desperately to retrieve the helmet and return it to his head. He fumbled with it and dropped it. He couldn't hold out any longer. He blew the air out of his lungs and took a deep breath, closing his eyes and waiting to die. But nothing happened. He opened one eye. Then the other. He took another deep breath. The air tasted strangely sweet. He was puzzled. He'd always been told that Earth air was poisonous to Klaxorians and to breathe it would mean instant death. Could they have been wrong, or were Klaxorians being lied to? He spent the next several moments taking short breaths and tasting the air. He was greatly relieved to still be alive.

"Mr. President, I would like to try some of that liquid now. What did you call it, Burr?"

"Beer, spaceman. Best thing we've got here on Earth. Well, second best anyway. So tell me, who the hell are you?"

"I am Darnell from Klaxor. I have come to speak to the President."

"Well come on out to the backyard where it's a little quieter and we'll have ourselves a little parley." He led Darnell out the back door. "Ah, that's better. Okay now, if you insist on staying in character I guess I have to also. So as President of these here United States, what can I do for you, spaceman?"

"You have attacked us without provocation. This must desist or we will be forced to destroy Earth."

"Okay, no problem. Anything else you need?"

"Uh, no. You agree to terms?"

"Sure, why not? How's that beer?"

"It is interesting. It makes bubbles in my mouth and makes my head dizzy."

"Yep, that's what it's supposed to do. So are we all square now? Have we headed off a war? Shall we shake on it?"

"Is that the custom here?"

"Oh sure. When you make an agreement, you have to shake on it."

"Very well." Darnell began shaking all over as though seized by a sudden case of the shivers. Then he suddenly stopped. "Aren't you going to shake too?"

"Well generally we just shake hands."

"Oh I see. Forgive my mistake." Then Darnell began shaking his hands vigorously. "Is this the way it's done?"

"Yeah, that'll do just fine. So you'll call off your army now?"

"If you agree to terms and sign this paper, we will not attack."

"No problem. I'll just put my John Henry on that and then it's a done deal."

"Thank you, President John Henry. I will use my communicator to inform the Prime Minister that you have agreed to terms. I am much relieved and thankful to you sir. You Earthlings are not nearly as barbaric as we had all heard."

Darnell walked to a secluded spot near some trees in Crazy Joe's backyard. He pulled out his communicator and pressed the button to speak. "Hello Prime Minister? This is Darnell. Can you hear me?" Darnell heard nothing but static. He tried a few times more. Then suddenly he could hear voices. The Prime Minister and the Foreign Minister were talking among themselves. Darnell tried a few more times to get their attention but it seemed he could only receive and not send. He assumed there must have been interference because of the dense Earth atmosphere. He made a mental note to try to contact them again once he was free of the atmosphere and on his way back. Just as he was about to return the communicator back to his pocket the words of the Prime Minister caught his attention.

"Are the plans ready for the attack?" he asked.

"Yes, all is ready."

"Good. If we don't hear from that idiot in another week we can go ahead with our plans. We've sent two messengers and heard nothing back. According to the statutes we are free to attack. Darren isn't the only one who reads the law."

"But what happens if we do hear from him? We'd have to call the whole thing off. The Cretorians wouldn't like that. They've been waiting five years already for us to sell them the remains of Earth."

"We won't hear from him. We gave him a defective communicator. We've got nothing to worry about."

"Oh there you are," said Sheila. "I've been looking all over for you." Darnell jumped when he heard Sheila's voice. "What's the matter? Are you all right?"

"What? No, it's not good. We haven't much time. I'm not sure what to do."

"Hey Sheila, have you seen Hank?" asked Crazy Joe.

"Nope. Haven't seen him all night."

"I better go look for him."

"I wanted to thank you again," said Sheila to Darnell.

"Is that the way Earth females always dress?" he asked somewhat bug-eyed.

"Are you going to give me a hard time about this costume too?"

"Oh no, I think it is very attractive. On Klaxor the females are much more modest but they have less reason to be. You're the most beautiful female I've ever seen."

"Well, thank you. And you're the bravest spaceman I've ever met too."

"Oh, I'm not brave. I'm just an unimportant clerk."

164

"Well, I don't know about what you do in your private life, but tonight you're a brave spaceman and I love you for it."

"You love me?"

"I think you're kind of cute. So, are you married or anything?"

"I have a mate back on Klaxor."

"Oh, well she must be a very lucky lady."

"Actually she hates me."

"Sometimes I think Jake hates me too. I think I've had about enough of him. Maybe you and I can be friends."

"I would be greatly honored to be friends with you. Back on Klaxor I don't have any friends."

"Listen, can we just drop all this Klaxor stuff for a while? I know you're all dressed up as a spaceman and all but I want to know who you really are."

"Oh, sure. Well, let's see. Back on Klaxor I work for the Ministry of Foreign Affairs and I am an expert on Earth."

"Yeah, I know all that but what do you down here on Earth?"

"Oh, yes I understand. My mission. I was to seek the President and try to head off an intergalactic war. But I seem to have failed in my mission. They will attack anyway and there's nothing I can do about it. I'm very worried."

"Okay, I guess you don't really want to talk to me. I'm sorry. I must say I'm a bit disappointed. I guess nobody's who they seem to be whether it's a costume party or not. Well, nice to meet you. Goodbye."

"But, I don't understand. What did I say to offend you?" But she was gone.

Back in the house Crazy Joe finally found Hank upstairs watching a movie. "Hey pal, what are you doing up here? You're not even in costume."

"I just got a little tired of all the noise."

"Listen, there's this guy downstairs you gotta see. He's got this crazy spaceman costume on and he's absolutely relentless about staying in character. It's hysterical. You gotta see it."

"Maybe later."

"Hey, what's going on with you? I'm the one who broke up with my girlfriend. What are you so depressed about."

"I'm not depressed. I'm just not in the mood for a party."

"Well if you're not going to come downstairs, I'll just have to bring him up here."

"No don't!"

"What's going on with you?"

"Okay, never mind. It had to happen sooner or later. I'll come down with you."

Crazy Joe found Darnell still wandering around the backyard. "Hey Spaceman, I want to introduce you to my roommate, Hank Claymore."

"Claymore, is that you?"

"Yes it's me. You found me. What are you going to do, tie me up and haul me back?"

"We thought you died."

"You guys know each other?" asked Joe.

"Yeah, sort of," answered Hank. "You mean you weren't sent here to bring me back? I wish I'd known. I've been hiding from you all night."

"No, I came to talk to your President to head off a war. They attacked again."

"Uh, I think I'm gettin' out of here," said Crazy Joe. "This is gettin' too weird even for me."

"That wasn't an attack. It was just garbage. They don't even do that anymore."

"But why haven't we heard from you? Why didn't you return?"

"I like it here. They have great females and beer and stuff. It's much more fun than back at home. Oh yeah, I know they're still a bit backward and all but they've got some great things here too. They have parties, and this stuff called ice cream, you gotta try ice cream. And pizza! Man that's living. And they have these crazy games that thousands of people pay to watch, where they fight over a ball for a few hours and then they all shake hands and go home. There's nothing back home for us. You gotta stay here."

"It does seem a lot friendlier than we thought it would be. Too bad it will all be destroyed."

"Destroyed? What are you talking about?"

"They've been lying to us, Claymore. Superius wants a war so he can sell off the debris to the Cretonians and make a fat profit. They sabotaged my communicator. I wasn't able to send any transmissions to head off the war but I've been listening. If they don't hear from me within a week, they'll attack. There's nothing I can do about it. I have to go back. It's the only way. I'm not sure if I could get used to it here anyway. I already made Sheila angry at me and I don't even know what I said wrong."

"You see? That's what I'm talking about. We certainly don't have any females back home like Sheila. Come with me. Let's see if I can help patch it up."

They found Sheila in tears talking to Crazy Joe. When she saw

Darnell she froze up and turned her back to him.

"Tell her you're sorry," said Hank. "That almost always works."

"But what am I sorry for?"

"It doesn't matter. Just tell her you're sorry and uh, take her for a ride. You have your ship nearby?"

"Well I suppose it's worth a try." He tapped Sheila on the shoulder. "Sheila, I'm sorry. Can we talk it over? Would you like to go for a ride?"

"Okay, but no more space stuff."

"Well, how about just one more space thing? There's something in the backyard I want to show you."

"You think it's that easy?" Joe asked Hank. "You just apologize and everything's better?"

"Why don't you find out for yourself? Look who just came through the front door."

Darnell took the control box out of his pocket and made the ship appear. He took the hand of a very shocked Sheila and led her up the steps. A few hours later, they were drifting together near the moon, holding hands by Earthlight.

"Now what was that thing you did to my lips earlier?"

"You mean kissing? Yes, I can teach you kissing. And a lot of other Earth stuff too."

After they landed back at the party Darnell was very quiet. Hank noticed and asked him what the matter was.

"I have to go back. I don't want to. I have nothing to go home to. Back there I'm nothing. My boss is using me. My wife is using me. And now I have all these wonderful memories and friends I can only dream about the rest of my life."

"Don't go back. Stay here with us. You can live here with Joe and me."

"Oh no you don't," said Sheila. "You come and live with me. I don't care what anyone thinks of you back home. To me, you're a hero."

"I'm not a hero. I've never done anything brave in my life."

"You came here," said Sheila. "You stood up to Jake and zapped him. But that's not why you're my hero. You're my hero because you're a decent and honest man and that takes more courage than anything. Please stay here with me."

"But if I don't go back, they'll attack. I have to send them word that I've made contact or else they'll be here with their super nuclear hyper bombs. I have to leave you, Sheila. It's the only way I can save you."

"Then come back when you're done."

"I'm sure that would be impossible."

"Wait a minute," said Hank. "You don't have to go. You just have to send word."

"But the communicator is broken. They saw to that. I have to go back."

"No you don't. Just send the rocket with the treaty Joe signed."

"You think that would be enough?"

"According to sub-paragraph 3C it's enough."

"You read those books too?"

"Sometimes I get a little homesick. They sent copies with me. Sometimes I read them to remind myself why I don't want to go back there."

"Okay, let's do it." Darnell placed the peace treaty back in the space ship and set the controls to return it to Klaxor. The Prime Minister would not be able to attack Earth. Darnell also left one other item on the ship addressed to the Prime Minister himself. It was a box of Grade A Eggs.

The Healing

Fred Lang considered himself to be a reasonable man. He was successful in business, having risen to a vice-presidency in a moderate sized corporation. He was a respected member of the community, attended church faithfully every Sunday, was a member of the local Chamber of Commerce, and was a member of the school board. He prided himself on having a well ordered life. He liked things neat and understandable. He was intelligent and rational. Except when it came to his son, whom he had always adored but never understood.

Young Tommy Lang had all the outward appearances of being normal until around the time he began walking and talking. Where Fred was a fairly private person, Tommy talked to everyone. He would go up to strangers and introduce himself and ask them to be his best friend; checkout clerks in the grocery store, waitresses, homeless people, policemen, even others just waiting alongside for a light to change green. "Hi. My name is Tommy. Do you want to be my best friend?" When the family bought a new sleeper sofa, Tommy went up to everyone he saw and said, "We have a new couch. It's magic. It turns into a bed. Do you want to sleep over at our house on our new magic bed?"

Fred bought his son a baseball glove when Tommy was only three, expecting him to grow into it. When Tommy was seven, Fred signed him up for T-Ball. Fred was encouraged when he saw how excited Tommy was to put on his new uniform. But when Tommy took his position in the field, he only watched the clouds roll by, picked dandelions, and asked the umpire if he wanted to be his best friend.

When Fred took Tommy to see his first major league baseball game,

171

Tommy was only interested in eating popcorn, hot dogs, pretzels, and cotton candy, and asking the beer vendor if he wanted to be his best friend.

Tommy became the subject of many arguments between his parents. Fred blamed his wife, Mary, for babying him. "The kid's not normal," he would say. "He doesn't like sports or anything. All he ever does is play with his toys."

"He's different," she would answer. "He's just a dreamer. The world needs dreamers."

And what kind of toys did Tommy play with? Not cars or trucks. Not toy soldiers or fire engines. He played with dragons and unicorns, wizards and mermaids. Fred had a particularly difficult time accepting the mermaids. They were practically dolls for heaven's sake.

Fred had hoped that when Tommy started school, things would improve. Surely the other boys would have an influence on him and straighten him out. But things only got worse for young Tommy. The teachers all loved him. He was very bright and was eager to answer questions when called upon. But as a result, he quickly became an object of ridicule for the other boys. He was teased and bullied and sometimes came home crying. Fred was regularly exasperated.

"You shouldn't take any of that crap from them," he would tell his son. "You have to fight back. Pick the biggest guy and punch him in the nose. The more blood the better."

"But that would hurt them," Tommy would answer. "I don't want to hurt anyone."

"But they're hurting you!"

"That's their choice. They're just angry people and when I'm around them, their anger spills onto me. They're scared of me because they

172

don't understand me. I don't want to be like them. I don't want to get angry and start hitting like they do."

"You're not being like them. They're bullies. It's different. You have to fight back to defend yourself. You can't let people walk all over you. Have some pride, damn it. What the hell's the matter with you, anyway?"

"I don't think there's anything wrong with me. Do you?"

"Yeah, I do. You're a freak. You go around all the time in a dream world. You've got to face reality. This is the real world. There are no dragons or unicorns or all that other crap. There are bullies and bad guys and you have to learn to be alert and defend yourself."

"But it doesn't have to be that way. I'm in the world too and I'm not a bad guy. And I do have pride. I'm proud of who I am. Aren't you proud of me?"

"No Tommy, I'm not. I don't have any respect for cowards and sissies. Just go to your room."

A tear rolled down Tommy's face as he shuffled away from his father, his head down and his shoulders drooping.

"That was not called for, Fred," said Mary.

"Don't start defending him. Don't you start defending that behavior. How's he going to survive in the world if he doesn't get a thicker skin? When's he going to learn how to deal with bullies?"

"As far as I'm concerned, you're the only bully he has to worry about. How dare you call him names like that? Did you see the look on his face just now? He adores you. He looks up to you. He doesn't need to learn to fight and give other boys bloody noses. The only thing he needs is your respect. If he doesn't get that, he'll never survive in the world no matter how thick his skin is."

"Mary, you don't understand. You don't know what it's like out there. You're not in the real world either. I'm out there every day, trying to survive surrounded by backstabbers and sharks. You've got to be tough in this world."

"You mean to tell me you think all that fighting and scrambling for the almighty dollar is the real world? I don't think so. I don't think the Garden of Eden was a stock market. I don't think fighting and competing is what we're here for."

"Aw, what's the use of trying to argue with you? You're just as much in a dream world as he is. All of sudden you don't like money? You don't like your washer and dryer? You don't like our house in the suburbs? You want to give all this up and live in the city? You want to get a tiny apartment like we had when we first got married?"

"No I don't want the apartment we had when we first got married. But I'd give all this up in a second to have the relationship we had when we first got married. Sure, I love all our comforts. But I don't like what they're doing to you, working to get them. I don't like what's happened to you."

They were interrupted by a door slamming upstairs. They realized that Tommy had heard everything. "Oh dear, I have to go to him," said Mary.

"I'm not finished talking to you," said Fred.

"I'm sorry, Fred, but for the time being, I'm finished listening. Our son needs me."

"Yeah, go ahead and run to him. That's why he's such a baby you know."

Mary knocked gently on Tommy's door. "Go away," he said from inside.

"Tommy, I want to talk to you."

"I don't want to talk." Mary opened the door anyway. Tommy was busy clearing off the top of his dresser, putting his little toys into a box.

"What are you doing?"

"I'm throwing these things away," he said tearfully.

"Why?"

"Because they're baby toys."

"Tommy, he didn't mean those things he said."

"Yes he did."

"Well maybe he did, but he's wrong."

"No he's not. He's right. I'm a freak. Everyone thinks so and now he thinks so too."

"He does not think you're a freak."

"Yes, he does."

"Well so what if he does? Tommy, sit down for minute."

"I don't want to."

"Put that box down and sit down and look at me. After I'm done talking to you, if you still need to throw that stuff away, I'll help you."

"Okay."

"Tommy, you remember what you told me about the bullies at school? You remember what you said about why they're bullies?"

"Yeah."

"What did you say?"

"I said they're scared of me because I'm different."

"That's right. And you feel sorry for them, don't you?"

"A little."

"Then you need to feel sorry for your father too. He's just being a big bully too. And the reason is because he's scared."

"Dad isn't scared of anything."

"Oh yes he is. He's terrified."

"Of what?"

"Of you."

"That's crazy. How can he be scared of me?"

"Same reason the other bullies are, because you're different. He doesn't understand you. He's afraid you won't be strong enough to make it on your own. He loves you, Tommy. He loves you more than anything in the world. That's why you drive him crazy."

"But you understand me. Why can't he?"

"I'll tell you the truth, Tommy, I don't understand you either. But I do love you and I trust you and I know that you have some kind of magic in you. You'll survive somehow. I don't know how but you will. You'll do it your way. You can't be Dad. You have to be you. And he's going to have to understand that too. And some day he will. Now you still want to throw away all your toy dragons?"

"No," he said tearfully.

"Good. I don't want to either. Now you come over here and let Mommy give you a big hug."

Things didn't really improve after that. The flames died down but the embers continued to glow and never really went out. Fred was at odds with his son and Mary continued to run interference between them. Fred saw Mary as taking Tommy's side and contributing to his continued weakness. It wasn't as though there were daily battles or constant tension. They went on vacations together, watched movies some evenings, ordered pizza on Friday nights, celebrated birthdays and Christmas with lavish gifts. Fred occasionally was even able to buy a book for Tommy about wizards or dragons. But at any moment, an incident or wrong word could fan the flames again.

Over the summer before he started high school, Tommy visited his grandfather in Santa Fe and developed an interest in Native American culture. He visited a reservation and participated in a sweat lodge. When he returned, he spent hours in his room drawing pictures of animals and beating drums. He read every book he could get his hands on about animal totems and spirit guides. He decided he wanted to be a Shaman or healer.

When Tommy started high school, things began to tense up again. He was no longer bullied at school, having shot up to nearly six feet in height and having gained a muscular body that he didn't have to work for, but he still didn't have any friends. There were many different cliques at the school but none of them were interested in dragons and wizards let alone animal spirit guides. He was also quickly losing interest in geography, math and science. He didn't think he needed any of that stuff anymore.

It was the advent of Tommy's learning how to drive that brought things to a head. Physically grown up, Tommy was nevertheless still very much a dreamer and Fred was afraid that he couldn't pay enough attention to the road to be safe. On the few times he took his son driving, Tommy would sometimes get distracted and almost hit another vehicle. Once he ran through a stop sign, not noticing it, and nearly hit a woman crossing the street. When they got home after that incident, Fred raged at him. When grades came around, things did not improve. Tommy was lost and lonely and hated school and one day during one of their driving lessons, he brought up the subject of dropping out.

"Are you nuts?" said his father. "You're not dropping out of school. That's just not an option. Now I've bent over backwards trying to be tolerant of all this fantasy shit, but you've about reached your limit, buddy. What do you think you're going to do? How are you going to survive?"

"I want to be a healer. I thought I could go back to a reservation or maybe to South America and learn from a real Shaman or something. Why should I stay in school? It's too hard. It's not fair that I should have to go through all that."

"Hey buddy, sometimes life isn't fair. You just have to suck it up and make the most of it. You have to be tough."

"I'm going to be a healer. I want to help people."

"You are going to finish school first. And I don't mean just high school. You're going to college too. You get yourself an education first. Then if you want to throw it all away and follow some stupid pipe dream, you go ahead. Where did you think you were going to get the money to do all this traveling? You think I'm going to pay for it? You're nuts if you think so. You're going to get an education. If you drop out, you're on your own. I'm not going to support someone who's on his way to becoming a lifelong loser. That's where I draw the line. You're just a lazy dreamer who's trying to avoid life and I won't have it."

Tommy looked over at his father, hurt and shocked at what he'd said.

"Hey, watch the road. Keep your eye on the road! LOOK OUT FOR THAT BUS!!!"

Fred didn't hear the smash of metal on metal. Everything just kind of slowed down as they crashed into the back of the bus. Fred slowly floated up out of the car and hovered peacefully over the mangled metal and broken glass. He watched as people with shocked faces ran toward the crash, whipping out their cell phones as they ran. He saw his son slumped over the steering wheel, blood dripping from cuts on his face. He saw himself next to his son, slumped over and lifeless. He took it all in, feeling very peaceful somehow. In the far distance he was vaguely aware of sirens and red flashing lights as ambulances and police cars descended upon the scene.

Fred floated off, drawn to a bright light beckoning him as though inviting him home to safety and peace. He floated toward it, picking up speed and suddenly rushing through a tunnel. He came to a stop in a soft fuzzy white place that exuded love and tranquility. He saw two men walking toward him. They wore white robes and somehow glowed. One was an older man with a full beard, a gentle face, and a twinkle in his eye. The other was a younger man who was a bit more serious.

"Hey, where am I?" asked Fred. "Am I dead?"

"That hasn't been decided yet," answered the older man. "Why don't you sit down so we can talk about it?" And suddenly the cloudlike substance that surrounded them rose up to form comfortable cushiony seats for the three of them.

"Is my son okay?"

"He will be okay. He suffered some bad cuts but he's being treated and he will make a full recovery."

"Thank heaven for that," answered Fred. The two men looked at each other and chuckled.

"What about the bus? Was anyone hurt?"

"The bus was empty. The driver was only a little shaken up. He'll be fine."

"But what about me? What do you mean it hasn't been decided yet?"

"There are things we need to discuss. The choice will be yours."

"I don't understand."

"You will. My name is Joseph. This is Thomas. We have things to discuss and to show you."

"Okay, let's get on with it then. Whoa, I'm still a bit woozy. That was some accident."

"There are no accidents, Fred. That's one of the things you'll learn here. You brought that upon yourself because of your anger and your fears. Everything is for a reason even when the reason is not clear and things look awful at close distance. It's all part of the great plan, but within that plan we still have free choice. Nothing is set in stone. It's a bit much to go into at this point. If you decide to stay, you will learn all of it. For now I want to show you some things. Thomas, will you please assist?"

Thomas stood up and put his hand on Fred's forehead. Suddenly Fred was transported back to the city from which he'd come. He was in a seedy section of town, full of drunks and homeless people. One man drew his attention. He sat on the sidewalk, dirty and smelly, with old clothes that had holes in them. He had matted hair and a full beard. His eyes were empty of life. They just stared vacantly ahead. Fred was aware that Thomas was still standing next to him.

"Who is that? Why are we here? Why does he look familiar?"

"That's your son Tommy about fifteen years from now. The guilt from your death consumed him. He never got over it. He never earned your respect. He still hears all the things you said to him about being a dreamer

180

and being a loser. He has clothed himself in those images. They have become his identity. He will not recover."

"It's all my fault. Is that what I'm supposed to see? But I didn't mean it. I was only trying to do the best I could. I love that boy. I swear I do. Surely you must know that. Surely you must believe that."

"Of course I do. That's why you have a chance to go back and make things right."

"Yes, of course. Send me back right now."

"There's more to see first and there's more to know."

They were suddenly transported to another place. They were standing in the back of a long line in front of a large bookstore. All the people in front of them seemed eager and excited to be meeting the famous author they had come to see.

"What is this place?" asked Fred. Before he could get an answer, they were interrupted by loud shouts.

"There he is!"

"He's here!"

A limousine had pulled to a stop at the curb and a handsome young man exited, waving to the crowd of people who had come to see him. Fred couldn't get a good look at his face.

"I don't get this," said Fred. "What are we doing here?" His question was answered as the line snaked around toward the door of the store. Above the door was a large banner that said, "Appearing at noon today only. World famous author and healer, Tom Lang."

"Tommy? They're all here waiting to see Tommy? Is that who he becomes if I go back?"

"This is who he becomes if you go back and make the right

choices."

"Well that's great. Send me back. This is great. He's going to be very successful."

"There's something more you need to know."

"What's that?"

The store and the line of people disappeared before Thomas answered Fred's question. "If you decide to go back, you will be paralyzed from the waist down. It will be a very difficult life for you. Because of the time and expense to recover and your inability to work, you will lose your house and have to move back to the city. It will be very hard for you."

"Won't he have just as much guilt in that case?"

"Yes, he will. But with your love and respect, he can channel it to good instead of turning it in against himself."

"I . . .I'm not sure I can do that. I'm not sure if I can deal with being crippled."

"There is no blame if you decide not to."

"Well what kind of a choice is that? Is that supposed to be fair?"

"Hey, buddy. Sometimes life isn't fair. You just have to suck it up and make the most of it."

"What?"

"Your words, not mine. Maybe it'll help if I show you one more picture."

They were transported to an intensive care unit in a hospital. There was Fred hooked up to a breathing machine, being fed by tubes. And there was Tommy huddled over him holding his hand, tears running down his face.

"He's been here every day since he recovered. He hasn't left your side. He goes back and forth between praying for you and apologizing to you and begging you to come back to him. It is his prayers that have brought me to you. It is his prayers that have given you a second chance. If not for him, the cord would already have been severed and you'd be gone."

Tears rolled down Fred's face watching his son watching over him. "He really is a healer, isn't he?"

"That's why he came to you, to heal you."

"Then I can't let him down. Send me back. I don't care about the consequences. I don't care about anything. Send me back. For his sake."

"Very well. When you get back, you won't remember any of this." Thomas removed his hand from Fred's forehead.

As Thomas's image began to fade, Fred called out to him. "Do I know you from somewhere? You look awfully familiar."

"Some people call me Tommy."

The hand in Tommy's moved. He jumped up, startled. Was it real? Did he imagine it? Another squeeze. Tommy ran for the doctors. There was a bustle of activity as doctors and nurses converged on the room. Tommy called his mother and told her the news amid sobs of joy.

In a few days, Fred recovered enough to be able to talk, at first barely in a whisper. Tommy bent over to hear what his father tried to say.

"Hey Tommy, will you be my best friend?"

"I'm so sorry, Dad. It was all my fault."

"Wasn't your fault."

"I was so scared I was going to lose you."

"You'll never lose me, son."

The doctors did a thorough examination and ran several tests before revealing the bad news that Fred would never walk again. Tommy was

183

crushed. Mary did her best to keep their spirits up while crying herself to sleep every night.

But Fred would not accept the news. He was determined to walk again.

"Dad, I don't know. You heard what the doctors said."

"Nothing is set in stone," he said. "You got any of that animal medicine stuff for me?"

"Are you serious?"

"Yeah, I'm serious. You think I can do this alone? I need your help, son. What have you got for me?"

"Salmon! I was just reading about it. They're about overcoming obstacles. You see, they have to swim upstream. They're the energy of single minded determination. They persevere when others can't. They do the impossible."

"Sounds like what I need. Let's get started. I'll do physical therapy every day and I'll work with you every night. And we'll eat plenty of salmon."

By the end of the year, Tommy had made the honor roll at school. By the time he graduated, Fred was able to walk down the aisle to attend the graduation ceremony and shake his son's hand. The newspapers heard about Fred's amazing recovery and printed several articles about the local "miracle man". A publisher offered Tommy a generous advance to write a book about the healing work he'd done with his father. Tommy wrote the book that summer. In the fall, Tommy took off to South America to study with the Shamans. He returned after a few years, a rich celebrity. His book was a best seller. There was talk about making it into a movie.

"You must be very proud of your son," said a reporter to Fred one day.

"Yes, I am very proud of him," he said.   "And he knows it."

Tech Support

Having survived the attack of the golden worms, Cody Mingus retrieved the pieces of gold that the dead worms transformed into. He then used the gold in the market to buy the magic flint from the sorcerer. He progressed to the Sacred Caves where he started a fire to attract the Rainbow Bird sitting on its nest. Having lured the bird off its nest, Cody raced to steal one of the painted eggs that gave him the power to fly. He then flew up to the top of Mt. Pisgar to fight the fire breathing dragon and rescue Lady Annabel. When he returned her to the castle he was rewarded with his weight in gold, was commissioned to be the Protector of the Realm, and was given the hand of Lady Annabel in marriage. Having completed the quest, Cody shut off his computer and headed for bed. It was 3:00 AM.

He was very groggy when he arrived at work the next morning. Cody had come to New York from his home town of Gilman, Illinois, with dreams of creating exciting and dramatic new computer games. Unfortunately he had neither the programming skills nor any artistic talent necessary for the job. So in order to survive, he had taken a job as a tech support agent for Deltronics, a national internet service provider. He worked in an office three floors below street level. The office was filled with long tables upon which stood loud ringing telephones. Overhead were buzzing blinking fluorescent lights that made the room appear like a mausoleum with strobe lights.

Four people worked at the New York City call center. When Cody first started there, the office was run by a strict disciplinarian, Miss Poot, a controlled woman with a pinched face. She squinted at everyone when she spoke as if she had a mouth full of sour lemon juice and had chronic

187

diarrhea, keeping both her mouth and her sphincter under tight control lest anything embarrassing escape from either end.

All incoming calls at the office were recorded. The agents were restricted to a number of scripts they were allowed to read to the customers when answering questions or fielding complaints. Any deviations from the scripts resulted in disciplinary points. A buildup of disciplinary points led to a private meeting with Miss Poot, whom everyone called "Pooty" behind her back. Nobody cared much if they had to meet with her. In fact since it meant time away from having to answer the telephones, they looked forward to it. On the other hand she did have that odd odor about her, a mixture of mustard, flowers, and mothballs, so invariably anyone who had to meet with her in the morning usually skipped lunch that day.

When Kelvin Bohannon came on board, things began to change rapidly. Kelvin became known as the Computer Whisperer. He had an innate sense about the machines. After Kelvin was working only a few weeks Miss Poot was gone. After his first meeting with Miss Poot, Kelvin hacked into the server and began creating records of bogus calls in which Miss Poot supposedly invited callers to participate in bizarre obscene behaviors that were physically impossible even for a seasoned contortionist.

After Miss Poot was fired, Cody and Kelvin became the de facto heads of the office. They hired Angie Twillaby who was a master of the *Bone Mystery Game*, and Irving Chan, who was part Chinese and part Jewish.

"How can you be part Chinese and part Jewish," they asked him when he applied for the job.

"My parents met at a Chinese restaurant. My mother wasn't very good with chopsticks. Her egg roll flew across the room and landed in my father's lap. Very symbolic, that. So that's how they met. Now at parties we have Egg Drop Soup with Matzo Balls in it."

"Your mother's Jewish? How could she not know how to use chopsticks?"

"Yeah, I know. She faked it. Dad didn't have a chance once she set her sights on him."

Cody couldn't wait for the others to arrive the morning after he completed level nine of the *Protector of the Realm* game. Cody kept silent until they all arrived.

"Hey, what's up with you?" Irving asked.

"I made it to the end of level nine last night," announced Cody. "I won the hand of Lady Annabel."

"Bet you did it the hard way," said Irving. "You got the flint from the sorcerer in the market?"

"That's the only way you can start the fire in the Sacred Cave."

"There's a shortcut. Two stalls down from the sorcerer is a book salesman. You ask him for the golden book and. . ."

"Yeah, I know about that. I read about it in *Cheats Monthly*. I tried it but the salesman turns you away telling you he doesn't have the book."

"Stop interrupting me. *Cheats* doesn't know what they're talking about. I can't believe you still subscribe to it. You have to ask the book salesman three times. Then you walk away and come back and ask for the blue book and then the golden book again. You take that to the fireworks stall. You turn around three times counterclockwise and two times clockwise. Then you get this green glow around your character and you have ultimate power. You can go straight to Lady Annabel without having to face the dragon or anything."

"How do you get past the dragon when you get there?"

"If you do it my way, the dragon's sleeping when you get there."

"How do you find out these things?"

"Oh yeah, and there's a secret rock in the cave. If you hit it five times a door opens and you go into a room where all the programmers are sitting around eating pizza. It's hysterical. You gotta see it."

"There's another one," said Angie. "If you go up to the dragon, and hit Alt-Tab and then type 'Dragon Master', the dragon gets the face of Bill Gates for three seconds and then farts."

"I'll have to try that tonight," said Irving.

They were interrupted by a phone ringing. "Who left the phones on?" asked Cody.

"I think I did," said Angie. "Sorry. I called my parents last night. Forgot to switch it off."

"Whose turn is it?" asked Irving.

"I think it's mine," said Kelvin. The caller was placed in the voice mail system. It would be a few minutes before the caller meandered through all the options and selected his desire to speak with a human in English.

The phone rang again and Kelvin picked it up. "Yes, how can I help you?"

"My internet service is down."

"I'm sorry for the inconvenience. Let me check your connection." Kelvin put the phone on hold. "So, Cody, after you rescued Lady Annabel, did you try going to the next level?"

"No, I stopped. It was getting late. I figured I'd pick it up again tonight."

"You're in for a rude awakening, my friend."

"What do you mean?"

"You'll see." Kelvin clicked the phone back on. "Yes sir, how may I help you?"

"I just told you. My internet is down. You were going to check the connection."

"I'm sorry for the inconvenience. I see that you have lost your internet connection."

"Yes, I just told you that."

"Is your telephone working?"

"I'm on the damn telephone."

"I'm sorry. These are things I need to check."

"Can you fix my connection?"

"I'm sorry for the inconvenience."

"Stop apologizing! Just fix it, okay?"

"I apologize for my previous apology." The line went dead. "Oh, he hung up."

"You weren't even close," said Angie.

"What's the record?" asked Kelvin.

"Twenty five apologies in five minutes."

"I can't get to that if they hang up. That isn't fair."

The phone rang again. "Same guy," said Kelvin. "Come on, Cody, it's your turn."

"Yes sir, what seems to be the problem?"

"My internet service is down. I was talking to another agent but he didn't seem to be able to help me."

"I'm sorry for the inconvenience. Is your telephone working okay?"

"Yes, damn it! The phone is working fine. I'm on it!"

"I'm sorry for your frustration. Are there lights on your cable modem?"

"Now we're getting somewhere. Yes, there's one light."

"What color is it?"

"It's green."

"Is there a yellow light?"

"No, just the green one. The others are blank."

"What about a red light? Are there any red lights?"

"I just told you. There's only a single green light."

"I see. And the green light is still green?"

"Yes, it's still green. It hasn't turned purple."

"Just a moment while I put you on hold." Instead of putting him on hold, Cody hung up the phone. "I think we have a live one here. Whose turn is it next?"

"I'll take him," said Angie. Five minutes later he called again. Angie answered. "How can I help you?" she asked.

"My internet service is down. I need it fixed."

"I apologize for your inconvenience. Is your telephone working okay?"

The man was sizzling. "Yes," he spit out. "My phone is working. My internet isn't working. I have one green light. No red or yellow or purple lights, just a single green light."

"I apologize for your inconvenience."

"Listen, can I speak to a supervisor please?"

"Of course, can I put you on hold for a moment?"

"Yes." Angie hung up the phone and then turned the phones off.

"What did you do that for?" asked Irving. "I wanted to be the supervisor."

"I was getting bored. Now how do you get to the programmers eating pizza again?"

At the end of the day Cody crammed himself into a subway car, into a mass of comatose smelly bodies, many of whose lives were even worse than his. The people clung tightly to the hanger straps as the subway cars jostled back and forth but the people didn't move because there was no room to do so. They all wore the vacant stare of the living dead.

Cody pushed through the mass of people to get through the door at his stop. From the subway station, he trudged the last five blocks to his walkup apartment. After unlocking the six deadbolts on his door he entered and collapsed onto the sofa careful to avoid the exposed springs. He lay there staring at the patterns on the walls made by the chipping plaster, and listening to the scratching noises from within them. He chuckled to himself and sang out loud to a familiar tune:

"The walls are alive with the sound of roaches,

And small little mice scurrying up and down.

Uh, can't think of anything that rhymes with roaches. I gotta get some food."

He went into the kitchen and slapped together a liver sausage, onion and cheese sandwich on white bread and wolfed it down with a cold root beer. He was anxious to get back to his computer, especially after the dire warning that Kelvin had given him. Before launching the game he checked his email. There were a few spam messages, a warning about a virus attack he knew to be bogus, and a few inane jokes from friends. There was a deep spiritual message promising eternal salvation, a million dollars in cash, any wish wished for, and protection provided by a personal angel if he would forward the message to twenty of his friends. If he deleted it, he would immediately break out in terminal warts, get hit by a truck within three days, and be hounded by evil spirits. He deleted the message and closed his email program.

Then he launched *Protector of the Realm*. Yes, he wanted to continue a game in progress. He entered his username which was Lance Victorius. A message popped up on the screen reminding him that he had successfully completed level nine and asked if he want to continue to the next level. He answered yes.

Level ten began with a long script scrolling down the screen explaining that on the eve of the wedding to Lady Annabel, the evil dark knight Drackmore, with his outcast band of thieves, had broken into the castle and kidnapped Lady Annabel and was holding her captive somewhere in the Maze of Mizmore deep in the Forest of Doom. In order to capture her, he would have to find clues to locate the forest, get past the trolls, figure out how to span the Alban River where the bridge had been destroyed, and finally, get through the maze, fighting evil demons and monsters at every turn. Did he wish to proceed?

"Yes," Cody said out loud to the screen as he clicked his mouse button.

"Are you sure you want to proceed?"

"Yes, that's why I'm selecting the option saying I want to proceed."

"Are you absolutely sure you want to proceed?"

Once again Cody selected the button to proceed. A window opened with this announcement: "Congratulations! You have succeeded in mastering nine levels of Protector of the Realm. I can see you wish to proceed to Level Ten. I am excited to announce that Level Ten is available in *Protector of the Realm II*, available at a store near you wherever software is sold. Or you can click on this link to our website and order a copy immediately for only $89.99 plus shipping charges. Thank you for supporting Klaghorn Enterprises."

"What? Are you shittin' me? What kind of crap is that? You're going to leave me hanging in the middle of a game and charge me to continue it? Screw you, Klaghorn. I won't do it."

Immediately, Cody went to E-Bay to see if he could find the game there cheaper. When he put in the search for it, he found the following message: "In cooperation with Klaghorn Enterprises, E-Bay has agreed not to allow software from that company to be sold at E-Bay. Thank you for your understanding."

"Okay," said Cody to himself. "This calls for desperate measures." He then went to a site known to carry bootleg and beta versions of popular software for download. "Aha!" shouted Cody when he found it listed. "There's always a backdoor." He clicked the selection for download. At first it appeared to be downloading the game but then a window popped up showing Cody which files on his hard drive were being deleted. A virus! Cody panicked and did a cold shutdown from which he could not recover. When he tried to boot up his computer again he saw a red screen with a graphic of a table galloping in circles like a horse. A message across the top of the screen announced that he'd been hit by the Dirty Gremlin virus and told him to have a nice day.

Cody stared at the screen dumbfounded and pissed. The one thing he had, to sustain him through his miserable life, were the nightly adventures on his computer where he could slay dragons, rescue fair maidens, drive cars at manic speeds through city streets, or combat the evil

Quormunk through the swamps and marshes of the planet Heranimuck. In these games he was a winner, a hero, meeting every challenge and bravely fighting every foe. Never once in any video game he ever played did he get stuck in a smelly subway car with a bum drinking out of a paper bag and peeing on himself. Never once did he have to go to a meaningless job, turning off his mind to survive and getting yelled at by a fat man in a suit. That might happen during the day. But at night he was Lance Victorius.

He read the message over and over again hoping it would change or that it was a joke. He thought if he waited long enough, maybe the message would disappear. But it sat there on his desktop staring at him, mocking him. Cody thought he even heard it laughing at him. It looked like the letters were growing and turning red. He shut off the computer.

It would take him a couple of days to restore and rebuild his computer. And then he still had the problem of what to do about *Protector of the Realm*. He could start all over again as a new user but that wouldn't be fun or challenging. He already knew all the secrets. He could zip through half the levels in just a couple of hours. The thought of buying the upgrade was out of the question. It wasn't the money, it was the principle. Cody felt he had a moral right to be able to continue a game without having to pay more money to do so. It wasn't fair.

The next morning when Cody arrived at work, Kelvin didn't even have to ask. He could see Cody's hands shaking. He could see the pale face and the look of shock. Cody was going through full tilt withdrawal.

"Just pay the extra money," he said to him.

"Yeah, like Boris Klaghorn needs my money. He's a multi-gazillionaire. Why does he have to soak us poor little guys for more money just to continue a game?"

"Because that's how you get to be a multi-gazillionaire," said Angie.

"I won't do it," said Cody. "It's the principle of the thing, Kelvin. He's got a lock on E-Bay too and he's probably behind the virus attack I got. No, I don't need his game. I've got plenty of other games. I haven't even started *Master of the Dark Planets* yet."

"I'll give you three days," said Kelvin. "Four tops before you run out to Software Joe's and beg him for a copy of *Protector II*."

"Unless of course, you'd like to get a bit of revenge first," said Irving.

"What are you talking about?" asked Cody.

"He's one of our customers," said Irving.

"Who is?"

"Klaghorn."

"No way! Why would he have private internet? He can just remote into Klaghorn Enterprises. Why would he pay us for internet?"

"He doesn't pay us. We pay him. It's some deal they worked out years ago. He wrote the program for *Call Center*, the software we use to log our calls. He gets free internet from us and we buy his software. He's a customer, I tell you. So let's have some fun with him."

"What have you got in mind?"

"Well, for starters we cut off his service. Then he has to call here for tech support. We can run him around for weeks. Drive him crazy. See how he likes being toyed with."

"I don't know," said Cody. "Can it be traced?"

"Not a chance," said Irving. "I just log into his account and cut off his service."

"But that would leave a record. You still have to log in."

"Not if I log in as Jasper Gilhooly."

"Who the hell is Jasper Gilhooly?"

"Someone I created for just such a purpose. What do you say? Are you in or out?"

They all opted in. Irving made the necessary changes. Then they waited for the phone to ring. It took a couple of days until a personal assistant of Mr. Klaghorn's called in. They asked her so many questions "for security's sake" that Boris Klaghorn himself was eventually forced to call in.

"Hello, I'm calling because my internet service has been disrupted. I don't understand why you couldn't speak to my assistant and I had to take care of this myself. I'm a very busy man. I don't have time for such nonsense."

Cody couldn't believe he was actually talking to Boris Klaghorn himself. He panicked and handed the phone to Irving.

Irving spoke into the phone. "What's your name?"

"Boris Klaghorn."

"Yeah, right, and I'm Mickey Mouse," said Irving, and he hung up the phone.

Boris called again. They played their usual games and nonsense. Surprisingly, Boris was not getting overly annoyed. It made them nervous. Klaghorn was a man who could be surrounded by a hundred hostile enemies all pointing machine guns at him and he could still act as though he had the upper hand, and amazingly, he could convince them of it too. They soon tired of playing with him and were just a bit intimidated as well so they reinstated his internet service. They thought that would be the end of it.

198

A week later, with Cody's computer rebuilt, he again launched *Protector of the Realm,* having resigned himself to purchase the upgrade. He got to the screen where it asked if he wanted to upgrade. Reluctantly he hit the button that said "Yes" and his computer immediately shut down. It had been limping along since the rebuild, locking up and spontaneously rebooting. Cody was met with dead silence when he tried to power it up again. No lights. No fans. No beeps. Nothing. Cody desperately checked the cables and power supplies before admitting his worst fears to himself. He was stuck in the real world without an escape and with only a hundred and seventeen dollars to his name.

There was only one recourse. He combed through the deep pile of papers atop his desk. Somewhere in there was the user guide for his computer and somewhere in it was the phone number for tech support. At last he found it and punched in the numbers. He entered his serial number, hit number three for hardware problems, hit number two to signify that he had a tower machine, and hit ten other numbers as he wended his way through the voice mail system. At last a phone was ringing. At last he could speak to a human. "Good evening," said the voice on the other end. "Welcome to technical support for the Klaghorn Computer Company. How can I help you?"

"No!" screamed Cody into the phone and slammed down the receiver. Panic set in. It had to be a coincidence. But what if it wasn't? What if Klaghorn had found him and messed up his computer? Boris Klaghorn hadn't seemed particularly upset, even when they started asking him if his toaster was working properly. He wasn't even upset when they asked him if maybe he had an electric toothbrush running in the bathroom, telling him that they sometimes caused interference with computers. But why wasn't he upset? Did he know he held all the cards from the beginning? Had Cody told him his name? He couldn't remember. Surely he wouldn't have given his name. Surely Klaghorn couldn't have traced him and found him and somehow sabotaged his computer through the game. Could he?

Cody tried to remember the details of their conversations. Kelvin had fielded the early calls and then Cody had posed as the supervisor. He'd hung up on Klaghorn three times. He promised to call back four times and of course, didn't. Was there anything else? Had he missed anything? Suddenly a sick feeling engulfed him. Klaghorn had mentioned that the problem had cost him an important deal. But wasn't he laughing?

Cody called Kelvin. "I can't believe this," Kelvin said. "You have any idea what time it is? Don't you ever sleep? Listen, don't worry about it. You're being paranoid. Even I couldn't hack into a system and completely shut it down. Did you check the cables? You didn't have a power failure or anything, did you?"

"Stop talking like tech support and listen to me. Klaghorn did it. I just know it. He knows where I live. He had special code written into the game and shut me down because we hassled him."

"Cody, think about what you're saying. It just can't be. You said yourself you had an old computer. It just failed, that's all. It's just a coincidence. You could probably just replace the power supply and be up and running in no time."

"Yeah, I guess you're right. I'm being silly."

"You ought to just get yourself a new computer."

"That would be nice but I've only got a hundred and seventeen dollars to my name and I'm three months behind in the rent."

Later, as Cody was contemplating his sorry fate, he was jarred by the ringing of his telephone. A tape recorded telemarketer was selling, of all things, discounted computers starting at the low price of a hundred and seventeen dollars. An ad was promised to arrive in the morning mail. Sure enough when Cody checked his mailbox the next morning, amid the many overdue bills, there was an ad from a store out in New Jersey that sold secondhand computers. He called Irving to tell him he wasn't coming in to work and then set out to find the place.

This can't be right, he thought as he looked again at the directions on the flyer. He had been driving for two hours, meandering through neighborhoods, industrial parks, and even gravel roads. He'd seen most of Brooklyn and Queens He'd crossed Manhattan and burrowed through the Holland Tunnel. Now he was turned back and heading straight for the Hudson River with nothing ahead of him but a road that actually entered the water.

Just as he was about to turn around and abandon the search, he saw, in front of him, a small sign not three feet above the ground. He had to get out of his car to read it. There was an arrow pointing to the left and written barely legibly with cracked paint were the words, "Klaghorn's Computer Supplies". A cold chill ran up his spine. His stomach turned and his heart was beating loudly in his ears. He looked to the left and could see only a gravel road with some bushes lining it. He wanted to turn back but felt compelled to see it through. He imagined he would find Klaghorn himself in a small shack by the Hudson, waiting patiently for him to show up. Klaghorn would kill him and sink him to the bottom of the river never to be seen or heard from again. Cody pulled out his cell phone to inform Kelvin that in the event of his disappearance, Boris Klaghorn would be the prime suspect. But his phone was out of range. A dead zone. The symbolism was not lost on Cody. Klaghorn had planned the whole thing very carefully. Cody decided to proceed and meet his fate. He might as well get it over with. If he didn't, Klaghorn would hunt him down anyway.

About a half mile down the road he did indeed see a small shack with a sign on it that said, "Klaghorn's Computer Supplies". Cody parked the car and carefully opened the door of the shack. There were several tables inside the dimly lit room, upon which were several old computer boxes covered in cobwebs. In the corner was a large plush chair in which an old skinny bearded man dozed with a newspaper over his chest. Cody coughed and cleared his throat waking up the old man.

"Huh?" he said.

"Excuse me, I'm looking for Klaghorn's computers."

"You found it, Cody Mingus. Congratulations." Cody's body erupted in goose bumps.

"How did you know my name?"

"I mailed you a letter, didn't I?"

"I guess so."

"Well then."

"Are you Boris Klaghorn?"

"Yes I am, Cody. I want to tell you your little shenanigans cost me a lot of money."

"Are you going to kill me?"

"I should, shouldn't I?"

"Please don't. Please. I'll make it up to you. I'll do anything. Please don't kill me."

"How are you going to make it up to me? Do you have a couple of

202

million dollars lying around in your apartment? Maybe hidden in that ugly red sofa of yours with the springs hanging out?"

"No sir."

"No? I didn't think so. Or maybe you sent your fortune back home to your mother back in Gilman, Illinois. Is that what you did? Sent it to your mother at 1245 Main Street?"

"No sir."

"No I didn't think so. I'd guess you probably only have about a hundred and seventeen dollars to your name and you're probably about three months behind on your rent, so there's not much you can do to make this up to me, is there?"

"I guess not, sir."

"Well, I'm not going to kill you, so stop shaking and sit down. This has been a little demonstration of what can happen when a stray cat like you decides to play games with a man-eating lion like myself. So I'm willing to make you a little deal. You see we both have something to gain here. In lieu of killing you, I'm going to give you a new computer free of charge. In fact, I can offer you the Super Duper Special Deluxe Turbo X-33C Extra! What do you think of that? Have we got a deal?"

"Why would you do that? What's the catch? What do you get out of the deal?"

"I need new characters for my games. I want you to try out my new machine and see how it runs. I will even include a beta version of my new Super Sim Reality Game. I want you to test it. Use the extra turbo booster when you play it. After about four weeks you will come to work for me, helping me develop a new character for *Protector of the Realm*. That's what you've always wanted to do, isn't it?"

"Yes."

"Good. Then take this machine home with you and I'd say in about four weeks I will come for you and then I will own you. I mean, I will hire you. Oh, and one thing more. Tell your friends that if they mess with any more customers it won't be just their computers that crash."

"Yes sir, I will. Thank you for not killing me."

Cody took his new computer home, cabled it up and plugged it in. He took a deep breath and pushed the power button. The box began to hum and the colored lights danced around the edges. It booted up quickly and responded so well it seemed to anticipate his moves.

It took Cody a couple days to load all of his software. The new computer turned out to be a dream machine. The graphics on his games were almost three dimensional and lightning fast. He told the others what had happened and what Klaghorn had said. They were, of course, skeptical, that is, until messages began appearing on their screens from Boris Klaghorn telling them they'd better behave.

After using the new computer for about a week, Cody installed the *Super Sim Reality Game* and switched on the extra turbo booster. The game required him to create characters and set up a lifestyle for himself. He gave himself a million dollars to start with and deposited it into the virtual bank. Then he created a partner and named her Camille. He made her tall, very sexy, with jet black hair and green eyes. For personality type, he checked 'cat' and then hit Enter.

Suddenly he heard a loud cracking sound in the living room like a firecracker going off. He ran into the room to see what had caused it. He was shocked to see a woman lying on the sofa, curled up sleepy and seductive.

"Who? Who are you? How did you get in here?"

"I'm Camille. I'm here for you."

This can't be happening, he thought. A sudden knock on the door made Cody nearly jump out of his skin. It was the landlady asking for the rent and reminding him that he was already three months in arrears. If he didn't pay the balance by the end of the month they were going to evict him. The landlady eyed Camille suspiciously.

"I'll get the rent for you. I promise."

"Yeah, I've heard that before. I'm warning you Mr. Mingus. This is your last chance." Cody forced the door closed and nearly jumped again when he turned around and saw Camille making gestures with her hand inviting him to join her on the sofa.

"You just wait there," he said. "I have to figure out what to do about you. Oh my God. What am I going to do? What was I going to do? Oh yeah, the rent. The bank. Have to call the bank. Have to pay the rent. No! Put your dress back on!" he called to Camille. "Just stay put. Stay!"

Cody fumbled with the phone trying to find the number to the bank.

"Midtown Bank, this is Priscilla, how can I help you?"

"Priscilla? Yes, you see I have to pay the rent but I only have a hundred and seventeen dollars in my account but I'm three months behind and I need a loan. Stop that! What? No, I'm sorry I wasn't talking to you. I was talking to the strange woman who suddenly appeared in my living room but that's a whole different problem. I don't think you can help me with that problem but I need help. I have to pay the rent or I'll get kicked out of my apartment."

"Shall I look up your balance?"

"Well you needn't do that because I know how much . . . . ."

"Here it is, Mr. Mingus. Your current balance is one million one hundred and seventeen dollars."

"See I told you. . . What?"

"One million one hundred and seventeen dollars."

"That's impossible."

"You made a deposit of one million dollars just about a half hour ago."

"What? Oh no that was in the Sim game. I put a million into my account on the computer."

"Is there anything else I can help you with tonight?"

"It's real? I really have a million dollars?"

"One million one hundred and seventeen dollars. It's definitely real. Is there anything else I can help you with?"

"Uh. No."

"Thank you for calling Midtown Bank."

Cody hung up the phone and called Kelvin.

"Hey, buddy. Slow down. I can't understand what you're saying."

"I'm saying that Klaghorn gave me a magic computer. I put a million dollars in the Sim game and now I have a million dollars and there's a beautiful woman on the couch and she won't leave me alone and . . . Oh my God. Where did she go? I think she's taking a bath. Kelvin, what am I going to do?"

"Okay, so let's see if I've got this straight," said Kelvin. "You've got a million dollars in the bank and a gorgeous woman in the bathtub who will do anything you want and you're asking me for advice?"

"Uh, yeah."

"Well under the circumstances I have three words for you: Go for it!"

After much pacing back and forth and after he ran out of fingernails to bite, Cody decided he had little choice but to take Kelvin's advice. He didn't understand what was happening but as long as it was there, he might as well enjoy it. The first thing he did was to quit his job and pay off the rent. Then he bought a giant screen television. In the days that followed, Cody and Camille spent their afternoons in Central Park and their nights in bed. She was perfect. She responded to his every need. She was a great cook, loved all the things he loved, did everything only to please him. So why was he so miserable? He was lonely and bored. Camille was so completely devoted to him that she offered no challenge, no interaction. Conversations were meaningless. Camille agreed with whatever Cody said. So one night he snuck out to the den and launched *Super Sim Reality Game* and made some adjustments to her personality. He gave her opinions, preferences, choices, a personality and mind of her own.

Cody could sense subtle changes at first. She sometimes actually disagreed with him when they talked. He found it refreshing. They actually had things to talk about. She didn't just go along with anything he happened to say. And she started to want things for herself. Small things at first. As they strolled through Central Park she asked for a hot dog one day and later for an ice cream cone. In the afternoon, she looked up at the tall buildings and told Cody she wanted him to buy her an apartment in one of them. Then they'd be nearer to the park. Cody thought about it and decided it was a good idea. They purchased an apartment on Central Park West and moved in.

As soon as they settled in, Camille wanted new furniture so they went shopping. Then she decided to have the kitchen rebuilt more to her

207

liking. Soon she was tired of the new kitchen and decided to hire a maid. Then one day while she was watching a romantic movie on television she decided she wanted Cody to marry her. They went down to City Hall and got married a few days later. As the days and weeks followed, her demands grew as her activity diminished. Soon she failed even to get out of bed. She ordered both Cody and the maid around constantly. "Fix me a snack. Plump up my pillow. Rub my feet. Pull down the shades. Don't talk so loud."

One day when Cody tried to get her out of bed to take a walk in the park she railed on him, cursing him out with words not heard even in locker rooms. She threw at him anything she could reach, smashing several vases against the wall as Cody and the maid ducked and ran out of the room.

Cody slept on the sofa that night. The next morning Camille announced she wanted a divorce and that she was going to sue him for the apartment, the furniture, the car, and all his money. And the computer.

The computer! Cody had forgotten all about the computer. He fired it up and launched *Super Sim Reality Game* and with one push of the mouse button his troubles were over. He deleted her. Later, he spent a quiet restful evening watching television. The next day he strolled alone in Central Park watching the children play, feeding the pigeons, and eating hot dogs from the street vendors. All was peaceful and quiet.

Two days later there was a knock on the door. It was a police officer inquiring as to the whereabouts of one Camille Simulated. Cody laughed and explained to the officer that she no longer existed. The officer did not find the statement amusing, interpreting it to mean that she was dead. He arrested Cody on suspicion of murder.

Cody forgot that when he had created Camille, she came with a whole family. He had forgotten to delete them as well. They had called the police when they hadn't heard from her in two days. The more Cody tried to explain his innocence the crazier and guiltier he sounded. He also had no explanation for where all that money had come from. The Internal Revenue Service was called in to investigate as well. Cody's assets were now frozen. He had nothing and no way to defend himself. The maid was questioned by the police and verified that the couple had been fighting recently.

The evidence against Cody was mounting. The police retrieved Cody's computer and found an email message he'd sent to Kelvin telling him that things had gotten desperate and that he had gotten rid of Camille. It didn't take the jury long to decide that Cody was guilty and they sentenced him to life in prison.

The night before Cody was to be transferred from the county jail to the state prison, he was taken from his cell. He had a visitor. It was Boris Klaghorn.

"You! You're the guy who ruined my life! You're the one who gave me that computer."

"Yes, I gave you that computer. But I didn't ruin your life. You did that yourself. You were actually given a rare gift. You could have done anything with that computer. You could have saved the world, ended disease, eliminated poverty. But what did you choose instead? Pretty much what I expected. You chose your own selfish needs. I hope you've learned your lesson."

"Oh I have. I have. I promise to change my ways. I swear I'll be different from now on. Just get me out of here and I'll show you."

"What makes you think I can get you out of here?"

"What do you mean? You know as well as I do I didn't kill anyone.

You've got to help me."

"That's exactly what I came here to do. I promised you a job, didn't I? I will take custody of you now and you will belong to me."

"How can you do that? What do you mean belong to you?"

"I have the means. I can make you disappear. They'll never find you."

"Where will I be?"

"You will be a character in one of my games. Isn't that what you've always wanted? Isn't that when you really come alive, when you're playing *Protector of the Realm*? You don't really belong in this world, do you? Aren't you happiest when you're playing my computer games? Haven't you ever felt that that's where you really belong? How do you think I get such vivid characters? Now just sign this contract and you'll be one of them."

"How can that be possible?"

"I don't have time to explain it. Just tell me, do we have a deal or don't we? Would you rather be Sir Lance Victorius, a knight at the royal castle of Lady Annabel, or spend the rest of your life in prison."

"I'd be a knight?"

"Oh yes, of course."

"Okay, I'll sign."

"Very good. I'll go home and make the necessary arrangements. It's just a matter of programming. In a couple of hours you'll find the door to your cell unlocked. Open it and leave and you're free."

"You had this planned all along, didn't you?"

"Yes, but I couldn't have accomplished my goal without your help and cooperation." Cody signed the papers.

"Ah, that's wonderful," said Klaghorn. "Now give me a few hours and then just walk out the door of your cell. You'll find it unlocked."

Cody was returned to his cell. Every few minutes he tried the door but it wouldn't budge. Before turning in that night Cody gave the door one last try and to his amazement, it opened. On the other side was complete darkness. He inched his way forward and then found a clearing to the right. He was immediately beset by a swarm of giant golden worms. They attacked from all sides. Cody fought his way through, killing them with a sword he found lying against the wall. The dead worms turned into pieces of gold.

Cody pocketed the gold and exited the cave, finding himself at the opening of the public market. He found the Sorcerer. Cody used the gold to purchase the flint. He then found his way to the Sacred Caves and lit the fire luring the Rainbow Bird off its nest. He marveled at how much more beautiful the bird was in person. After stealing the egg, Cody flew to the top of Mt. Pisgar, slew the dragon and rescued Lady Annabel. The sight of her took his breath away. She hugged him, thanked him for saving her and praised his strength and courage.

When he returned her to the castle, the king made Cody a knight of the realm and instructed him to report to Sir Carlton. Carlton assigned Cody to be in charge of the royal stable and take care of the King's horses.

"No wait, there must be some mistake," said Cody. "I'm supposed to be a knight and fight battles and win the hearts of fair damsels. You can't stick me in the stable with a shovel. I won't do it."

"But according to Lord Klaghorn, the king's Minister of Internal Affairs, you signed a contract. If you don't fulfill it, he will send you back to your world."

"He tricked me."

"You'll get used to it. I was a corporate executive in the other world but I was caught embezzling money. Unfortunately the company was Klaghorn Enterprises. I've been here ever since. What about you? What's your story?"

"I was a tech support agent."

"Whew! You're lucky he didn't make you a horse like Nelly here."

"Nelly was a person too?"

"His ex-wife's divorce lawyer." The horse snorted and kicked up some straw.

Cody picked up the shovel and began cleaning out the stable, gagging at the smell.

"So, what do you think?" asked Boris.

"It's not bad," said Gerald McGrew, the head of programming, "but I don't know if anyone's going to believe it. *Tech Support* might make a good short story but it doesn't quite measure up as a video game. Kids these days are looking for action and bloodshed. Nobody even got killed in your game. You need to make Boris much more evil and you shouldn't use your own name for the bad guy. Overall, I think it's a bit too high brow for the general public but it definitely shows potential. Keep working on it and maybe soon you can quit your day job and come work for us.

Star Maker, Inc.

It was Tiffany Amber Crystal who put the monkey wrench in Billy Bellows's ordered life. Billy was the chief dishwasher at Hugo's Diner, a position he held with pride. Not having finished high school, he was grateful to have a good management position. He had started as a busboy and after only a couple of years, was promoted to dishwasher, Assistant Chief Dishwasher, and finally after eight years on the job, attained the rank of Chief Dishwasher.

Working at the diner almost as long was Mary Slossen. She was the kind of hard working, non-complaining woman that people tended to overlook and take for granted. Whenever she was around Billy, she became very nervous and tongue-tied. She admired the way he could stack the dinner plates onto the racks, his sweaty muscular arms bulging under the white uniform he wore. She loved to hear him giving orders to his subordinate dishwashers, keeping the process humming in machine-like precision. Every night, Billy walked Mary home. Every night, she wanted to invite him up to her apartment but instead shook his hand and thanked him for walking her home, afraid even to look into his eyes.

And then one day, Hugo hired Tiffany Amber Crystal. Tiffany made it clear that she was only biding her time working there until her acting and modeling career took off. While Mary and the other waitresses wore comfortable sensible sneakers to work, Tiffany insisted on wearing sparkling high heeled shoes. Her long fingernails were manicured with multicolored polish on each nail. She wore glittery makeup on her face making her look like smiling candy. When Billy first saw her, he dropped a dinner plate.

213

Mary's income soon plummeted as all the customers wanted to sit at Tiffany's tables. Tiffany flashed her smile and chewed her gum and told everyone how she was going to be a movie star someday. "You just wait and you'll see me up on that big screen and I'm not going to be in just anything, mind you. I'm going to be a serious actress like Marla Streep."

Tiffany's sudden presence at Hugo's diner had the effect of dropping an elephant on the deck of a small boat. Suddenly everything was off balance and rolling around. After having spent years in therapy, Mary was just getting to the point where she was going to draw up enough courage to tell Billy she liked him. And then Tiffany showed up and Billy's jaw dropped and had yet to close again. Everyone was falling all over themselves trying to get Tiffany's attention. Billy figured he had the best chance with her. After all, he was the Chief Dishwasher, a position of no small responsibility.

Billy began exercising in the evenings. Every morning he showered and slicked down his hair. He slathered himself in cologne. He saved up his money and bought an old used car. One day as they were closing up for the night, Billy sidled over to Tiffany and offered her a ride home.

"Thank you but I'm being picked up," she said.

"Well, actually I was thinking," said Billy. "I mean I was wondering. Well, would you like to go to a movie with me some time? Or out to dinner, or something? I figure we could probably hit it off real nice, you and me."

"Mr. Bellows, you're a dishwasher."

"I'm the Chief Dishwasher," he corrected her.

"I can't go out with a dishwasher. I'm going to be a serious actress someday. How would that look? I have to associate myself only with important people who can support and further my career and who are in keeping with my future status."

Billy was crushed. Mary felt bad for him but was glad Tiffany had turned him down. She wanted to go to him and comfort him. She wanted to tell him he shouldn't waste his time with superficial people like Tiffany Amber Crystal; that he needed a good woman who really cared about him and respected him. She wanted to tell him all that. But she didn't. And as if Tiffany's rejection wasn't bad enough, Billy's car wouldn't start. It banged and belched and wheezed and coughed and died.

As Billy walked home, depressed and desolate, a strong wind picked up and he began to get pelted with thick raindrops. Lightning cracked the sky and thunder rumbled the pavement. A newspaper blew in his face. He pulled it off and was about to throw it away when something caught his eye. It was an advertisement for a company called *Star Maker, Inc.*

"Are you tired of being a nobody?" the ad said. "Wouldn't you rather be a somebody? Make an appointment today for a full life makeover. No matter what your circumstance is, we can make you rich and famous. Results guaranteed." Billy folded up the soggy sheet of paper and decided to give them a try.

The next morning he called in sick and rode a slow hot crowded bus downtown. When he reached his stop, he elbowed his way to the exit door and started walking the three blocks to The Alton, a towering eighty story office building that made him dizzy to look up to the top of it. As he approached the guard station in the lobby, he almost changed his mind. All around him were men and women in expensive tailored suits, scurrying around, looking very serious and focused. Billy had worn his old mismatched suit with a wrinkled white shirt and gravy stains on his tie.

"Can I help you?" asked a guard. "Are you here to make a delivery?"

"I was looking for this place," said Billy, showing him the ad.

"You want that elevator over there," he said. He pointed to a single elevator apart from the rest of the elevators. It had a red door on it in contrast to the simple gray doors on the others. Above the door was a dial and an arrow. It appeared to go to only two stops, one marked Lobby and the other marked Stardom. Billy shrugged his shoulders and pushed the button. The door swung open and Billy entered. Inside were two buttons, Lobby and Stardom. He pushed Stardom. The door closed and the car lifted at a fast clip seeming to go to the top of the skyscraper.

When he exited the elevator he found himself in a hallway opposite a single door that had *Star Maker, Inc.* neatly printed on the glass window. Entering, he found a small man sitting behind a desk talking on two telephones at once and signaling Billy to sit in the chair in front of him. The man held a cigar in one hand. Ashes fell onto the expensive teak desk when he gestured to Billy. He didn't seem to care. There were several more telephones on the desk and ten television monitors on the walls to the side. Looking out the window behind the man, Billy noticed he couldn't have been any higher than the fourth or fifth floor. The man hung up the phones and pointed out the window as if reading Billy's mind. "It's all an illusion, kid. Eh? Eh? Eh? All smoke and mirrors. What's your name, kid?"

"Billy Bellows, sir."

"Do you have an appointment?"

"Well, no. I saw your ad."

"You don't have an appointment? What are you, crazy? You think

216

you can just barge in here without an appointment? Get out of here. Go on. Get out!"

Billy sheepishly made his way back to the door feeling embarrassed and stupid.

"Just a minute, kid. Come back here." Billy turned around to face him again. "That's what you've been getting your whole life, isn't it? Pushed around? Ignored? Standing around in the back of the line with your hands in your pockets looking stupid? Am I right? Am I right? Eh? Eh? Eh? Go back out the door. Go down the hall to your right and enter the next door you see."

Billy exited the office and headed down the hall to an unmarked door. He opened it and immediately jumped back as he was bombarded with light and noise. The door opened to a long corridor that came alive with bright blinding lights and blasting music and what sounded like thousands of people cheering him. There was a long red carpet on the floor. On the walls of the corridor were projected movies of people waving at him and cheering him. Flashbulbs popped from tiny holes in the walls. At the end of the corridor was another door that opened back into the office of *Star Maker, Inc.* The small man with the cigar was waiting for him.

"Mr. Bellows, an honor, sir. Please come in. Can I get you anything? Would you like a cigar? Please sit down here. I'm Sammy Staccato. Glad to meet you, sir."

Thoroughly confused, Billy sat back down in the same chair he had exited just a few moments earlier.

"Just a small demonstration of what lies in store for you Mr. Bellows. If you sign with us, you'll get the star treatment everywhere you go; first class travel, five star hotels, people asking for your autograph.

You'll be somebody. That's what you want, isn't it? Eh? Eh? Eh? That's what you've dreamed of. Let me guess. You're not appreciated at work, right?"

"Uh, not exactly."

"You want to travel. You want to see interesting places and people."

"Well, I .."

"No no, don't tell me. I have it. You've been spurned by a pretty girl."

"Yeah, I .."

"Don't worry about it, Bellows. They'll be eating out of your hand. Eh? Eh? Eh? Why I could probably guarantee you a date with Elizabeth DeVores."

"Elizabeth DeVores? The movie star?"

"Whatever you want, kid. Are you interested? Are you ready to sign up?"

"But how does it all work? What does it cost? I don't have a lot of money. I'm only a dishwasher. I didn't even finish high school."

"Doesn't cost a thing. Don't worry about it. Let me take care of everything."

"But how does it work?"

"That's what I like about you, Bellows. You have an inquisitive mind. Eh? Eh? Eh? You want to know the ins and outs, the nuts and bolts, how things work. That's why you're destined for stardom. Okay, here's the deal. It's a one year, three phase process. You don't pay me any upfront money but I get ten percent of everything you earn for as long as we're in business. If you opt out before the first year has completed, you owe me a penalty of a hundred thousand dollars. Now, does that sound like a bad deal? Huh? No upfront money? Doesn't cost you a thing out of pocket? Eh? Eh? Eh? What do you say? In or out?"

"Well, I don't know. I have to think about it."

"Sure. Sure. I can understand that. It's a lot to think about. Total change of lifestyle. No problem. You've got one minute to decide. No second chances on this, babe. In or out?"

"Okay, I'll do it." Billy was handed a thick wad of paper and instructed to sign on the back page which he did.

"Congratulations, Mr. Bellows. You're on your way. Now here's the first step. Take this key and go to the bus station. Find the locker this belongs to and bring me the contents. Don't look inside of what you find there."

"What's inside?"

"Your future, son."

"This isn't anything illegal, is it?"

"Absolutely not."

Later that day, Billy found his way to the bus station and located the locker. Inside, he found a small brown battered briefcase. As promised, he didn't open it. He returned to the office of Star Maker, Inc. and handed it over to Sammy Staccato. "Great job, kid," said Staccato. "I'll take it from here. Be sure to pick up tomorrow's newspaper."

"That's all?"

"That's all, kid."

"But I don't understand. What does this briefcase have to do with my getting famous? What's going on? When does it start?"

"Already started, kid. Ball's rolling. Eh? Eh? Eh? Remember to get a newspaper."

Billy went home to his apartment but didn't get any sleep that night. His mind was filled with worried thoughts. He should have looked in the briefcase. He should never have agreed to the whole thing. An office like that in a downtown skyscraper? He must have done something illegal. Maybe the briefcase had drugs in it or a bomb or something. In the morning he would read in the newspaper that he was about to be arrested. That would make him famous. Some joke that would be.

The next morning Billy went back to work. He was afraid to buy a newspaper but he didn't need one. Everyone at Hugo's diner already had one and they all pointed to him and started talking as soon as he entered. Completely bewildered, Billy grabbed Hugo's newspaper and was shocked to see his picture on the front page. Alarmed, he read the story. It said that he had found a briefcase containing a hundred thousand dollars in cash and had returned it to its owner and had asked for nothing in return. He was hailed as a Good Samaritan and was nicknamed, Boy Scout Billy.

For the rest of the morning the phone at Hugo's diner rang off the hook. The calls were mostly from reporters wanting interviews. All the customers wanted Billy to autograph their copy of the newspaper. Billy walked around in a daze. NBC called. They wanted Billy to appear on The Today Show. Before the day was up, he had also gotten calls from Jay Leno's people and David Letterman's staff. Billy pulled the gold leaf business card from his wallet and called Sammy Staccato.

"Did Leno call yet?" Sammy asked.

"Yes, but .. "

"You're on your way, kid."

"But I don't understand. It's not true. The newspaper said I found all this cash and returned it. It's a lie."

"No it ain't, kid. Eh? Eh? Eh? The briefcase was full of cash, just like they said. You found it at the bus station and returned it to me. It's all true."

"But."

"Listen, kid. It's how things work. You just drop a seed in the middle of the soup and it starts boiling. Enjoy the ride, kid."

A limousine picked Billy up that evening and took him to the airport where tickets awaited him for a first class flight to New York. Another limousine took him to the Park Plaza Hotel where he stayed in a huge three room suite. He was told he could order anything he wanted from room service courtesy of NBC. The next morning he was taken to Rockefeller Plaza. He was still in a daze as they led him to the makeup room. He caught glimpses of people he thought he should recognize. Then before he knew it, he was out on the set in front of bright blinding lights and the smiling face of Matt Lauer who was trying to put him at ease. No light was more daunting though, than the red light on the camera. When it came on he could feel it pierce through him. He could feel the millions of people watching his every move, listening to his every word.

The interview proceeded as though in a hazy dream. He could hear himself answering questions as though he were still in bed watching from his own television. Before he knew it, Lauer was shaking his hand. The red light on the camera went out and they broke for a commercial. After the show, the limousine driver offered to take him anywhere he wanted before heading to the Ed Sullivan Theater for the David Letterman taping later in the day.

Letterman was a gracious host but made several jokes at Billy's expense. Again that red camera light seized on him like an electric shock coursing through his body, making his mind numb and his body behave in slow motion. The laughter of the audience and the music from the band sounded like they were from a different room. Only when the red light turned off did life speed up again and his senses worked properly. He had no idea what he had said.

The next day he flew back home. Only when he returned to his tiny apartment did things feel normal again. He felt as though he'd awakened from a strange dream. But a dream that persisted. The next several days were a firestorm of activity. He thought things would settle down to normal in a couple of weeks but he was sadly mistaken. It was an election year, so all the candidates running for office now jumped on the bandwagon. Some of them exploited Billy's experience to point out the weaknesses in security at bus and train stations. What if the briefcase had contained something sinister instead of just cash?

Senator Westin, especially took up the cause. He introduced the Billy Bellows Bill into Congress to lock down security at bus and train stations. The bill would make it virtually impossible for anyone to do anything at any public transportation venue and would cost millions of tax dollars to implement. It would inconvenience everyone and not have any effect on making those places more secure but all the other politicians were afraid to oppose it lest they appear weak on the issue of security. "If it saves one life it's worth it," Westin proclaimed.

Within a few months, Billy's celebrity had taken on a life of its own. He was now famous for being famous and he was invited to every charity event taking place that summer. At each one, Sammy Staccato made sure there were photographers present to document the activities of his client. Soon Billy was appearing in People magazine. And he was getting dozens of calls from companies desperately wanting him to endorse their products. He was Boy Scout Billy, the symbol of safety, security and integrity. He endorsed safes, burglar alarm systems, and even briefcases; anything with even a remote tie-in to the briefcase at the bus station. It started getting just a little ridiculous when all boundaries broke and he was being asked to endorse bathing suits, hemorrhoid medicines, sports cars, and Tabasco Sauce. He had long since quit his job at Hugo's diner much to the disappointment of Mary Slossen, and was earning more money than he'd ever dreamed of.

And then the bubble burst. He picked up a newspaper one day and read, to his horror, a report claiming that he'd been arrested once a long time ago for petty theft. And there was more. Rumors were circulating that his finding and returning the briefcase full of money was a big hoax. Shocked, he headed for Sammy Staccato's office.

"Did you see this?" he asked. "How can they do this to me? I was never arrested for anything. I want you to find out who's responsible for this."

"Already found him, kid. It was me."

"What? You did this? Why?"

"Phase two, kid. It's in the contract."

"But why?"

"Don't worry, kid. Eh? Eh? Eh? Ride's gonna get a little bumpy for a bit. Pruning the flowers, that's all. It's all part of the deal. It's the American way. They build you up and then they knock you down again. I'll have a limo pick you up in the morning. I've got an empty apartment downtown. You stay there until this all blows over."

Billy was taken to the apartment. There wasn't much to do there except to watch television. Over the next few weeks, Billy heard one shocking story about himself after another. None of them were true, nor did they purport to be. They were reporting rumors, all fed to them by Sammy Staccato. After several weeks, there was a report that Billy had entered rehab for alcoholism and he would stay there for a month. In actuality, Bill just remained in the apartment. When the month was over, Sammy Staccato sent a limousine back to the apartment to pick up Billy.

"You okay, kid?"

"Yeah, I guess so. But I want out. I didn't bargain for any of this."

"Oh, it was fun when things were good but you can't take the heat, eh? Okay, give me a hundred thousand dollars and we'll call it quits, but you're still out there on the down side. Know what I mean, kid? Eh? Eh? Eh? I suggest you stay on the bus. I'm taking care of you."

"Taking care of me? You ruined me! Everyone thinks I'm a drunken ex-con or something."

"They'll forget it. You're entering phase three."

"What happens in phase three?"

"Redemption, kid. You go on the apology circuit. Same deal as before. You go on Leno and Letterman, maybe we can even get you Oprah. You get real contrite. You apologize for letting everyone down. You blame it all on alcohol and tell them you're rehabbed. Nothing like redemption to clear the air. People eat it up even more than heroism. A fall and then a recovery and you're the fair-haired boy again. Trust me, kid. Eh? Eh? Eh? I know what I'm talking about."

To his amazement, Billy found that Sammy was exactly correct. Not only was he welcomed back as a redeemed hero, but all the offers increased exponentially. There were even more invitations for charity parties, endorsements, and television appearances. And there was an added component. Now that he had fallen from grace and risen again, he was invited to be a motivational speaker. They asked him to give graduation speeches, pep talks before boards of directors, and he was invited to give a talk at the annual Motivational Speakers Forum with a dozen other famous motivational speakers.

The day before his Forum speech, Billy had to tape a television commercial for a hand cream product. He arrived at the studio and was introduced to all the technicians and talent. All of sudden his heart skipped a beat. The actress hired to show her dainty fresh hands to the camera and give her testimonial on the product was none other than Tiffany Amber Crystal. He'd almost completely forgotten about her. She was just as beautiful as ever with her candy smile and sparkling eyes. Finally, here was his chance. He was somebody now. This was the moment he'd been waiting for. It was why he had gone through the whole ordeal in the first place. Confidently, he sidled over to her as she was rehearsing her lines and casually asked her to go out to dinner with him. She turned to face him and blushed bright crimson.

"Oh, gosh, Mr. Bellows, I couldn't go out with you. You're so important and famous. I'm just a struggling actress. It wouldn't be right."

"But Tiffany it's me. I'm still me. You knew me when I was just a dishwasher. Come on. I did all this for you."

"You couldn't have been a dishwasher. Come on, Mr. Bellows. Don't kid me. You're an important person. I'm just a nobody. Please excuse me but I have to rehearse my lines. I really need this job." Billy was stunned.

He was still reeling the next day when his limo dropped him at the Motivational Speakers Forum. There were a few thousand people in the audience, all eager to drink in the wisdom of the successful important speakers. They all hoped that some of the greatness would rub off on them and maybe they would have a chance to be released and redeemed from their small meager lives and cross the threshold to freedom and happiness.

Billy was scheduled to be the first speaker after lunch on the first day of the Forum. He was introduced to a thunder of applause and walked out on the stage looking out at the mass of eager hungry people. As he looked out over the audience he saw, to his amazement, sitting in the third row, his old friend Mary Slossen. How she could have afforded the eight hundred dollar entrance fee, he couldn't imagine. She had the same look on her face as everyone else, waiting to hear his words of wisdom, waiting for him to reveal the secret that would free them all from their suffering and hardship forever.

Billy opened his mouth and everyone hunched forward to hear him. He raised his hand and everyone gasped. And then something happened. All at once scared, sad, and shocked, he couldn't go through with it. He walked off the stage, exited the auditorium, got into a cab and headed straight for the Alton Building to see Sammy Staccato.

"I want out," he said.

"You want out? Why, kid?"

"Because it's all a sham. It's phony. It's one thing to toy with the press or even the politicians, but those were real people at the auditorium. I just couldn't do it. I couldn't lie to them. I don't have anything to tell them. I'm not a hero."

"Sure you are, kid. You're a real honest to goodness hero."

"No I'm not. You made it all up. None of it was real."

"It was all real, kid. I told you not to look inside that briefcase and you didn't. You could have looked. You could have stolen that money. But you didn't. That shows you have integrity. You're an honest man. You're Boy Scout Billy Bellows, a national hero."

"Why does that make me a hero?"

"Because there are so damn few honest people left, that's why. Sad but true. Otherwise returning a bunch of money to its rightful owner wouldn't have been news in the first place. So you want out, huh? Are you sure?"

"Yeah, I'm sure."

"Okay, the year's up. The deal's done. So what have you learned from this experience?"

"I don't know. I don't know that I've learned anything except how gullible people are. It's pretty depressing really."

"Nope. That isn't what you learned. I'll tell you what you learned. You learned that you can light a million candles outside of a pumpkin and it's still just a pumpkin but if you light just one candle on the inside, you get a Jack-O-Lantern. You understand, kid?"

"I was somebody to begin with, wasn't I?"

"You sure were, kid. You just didn't know it. I'm proud of you. It's been nice doin' business with you."

As Billy rode the elevator back down to the lobby, he felt something lost but also something gained. Then he suddenly remembered that he'd forgotten to thank Sammy Staccato. He pushed the button to go back up to the office. When he exited the elevator the sign was gone from Sammy's office door. Puzzled, he opened the door and found himself looking into a tiny broom closet. He closed it and looked at it again to make sure he was in the right place. Then he went down the hall to the other door that had led to the red carpet. He opened it and it too was just a tiny broom closet.

The next morning he went to Hugo's diner hoping to get his old job back. He saw Hugo at the cash register and cautiously approached him.

"Are you feeling better today, Billy?"

"Uh, yeah. I was hoping to get my job back."

"What are you talking about? You didn't lose your job. You think you'd lose your job just because you took a sick day? Come on now, get back in the kitchen and get to work. Billy scratched his head completely bewildered. On a hunch he looked at the date on Hugo's newspaper. The paper was a year old.

"Is that a misprint, Hugo? It says it's last year's newspaper."

"Are you sure you're feeling okay, Billy? You need another day off or something?"

After work, Billy walked Mary home as he usually did. Just before he left her, she grabbed his arm and asked him if he might like to come up to her apartment and visit for a while. He took her hand. It was shaking. He looked into her frightened blue eyes. Yes, he would very much like to go up and visit with her. They had some pizza and spent the evening watching television. As they were watching the news, a story came on about a bellboy who had found a satchel full of cash in a locker at a bowling alley and was hailed as a hero for returning it to its rightful owner. Billy laughed so hard he almost choked on his pizza.

"What's so funny, Billy?"

"Life, Mary, life."

She frowned, puzzled, but took Billy's arm and nestled her head contentedly on his shoulder. Perhaps he was right.

Payback

They say the choices we make are sometimes like the tumblers of a combination lock. Each and all of them must fall into place before the vault will open and you can access the treasures within. When we experience the rare moments when those doors open up for us, the vast array of choices and events leading up to those moments reveal themselves like a glorious explosion of fireworks, lighting up the sky to the awe and wonder of the people gazing at it from below.

Last week at Garland's Restaurant was such a moment when my wife Sara and I had dinner with Mayor Gilmore and his wife. I'm a psychologist with a very small private practice just trying to survive, just like everyone else. I'm not in the habit of rubbing shoulders with men of power. The seeds of this get-together with the mayor were sown years ago when Sara was in the second grade and became best friends with Ellen Carson.

Ellen had just moved to Paxton City and had no friends. Being the new kid in town, she suffered the usual teasing in the schoolyard that new kids often go through. It didn't help any when in the midst of all the teasing, Ellen had a biological accident and subsequently fell to the ground crying. A hand reached out to her. It was the hand of my dear wife Sara.

The previous Sunday, Pastor Jones had given a lengthy sermon about reaching out to those in need. Although many in the congregation slept through his droning tedious sermons filled with biblical verses and flowery poems, Sara always sat riveted, listening to every word, intent on becoming the best possible person she could be and seeing the weekly sermons as lessons in personal enrichment. I'm usually happy and proud to

231

say that Sara hasn't changed much from when she was seven. I say "usually" because from the day we met, she decided to extend her ambitions of being a saintly person to me as well, and she would often instruct me on the ways and means of bettering myself. This has often been quite exasperating despite the fact that she is usually right. Please don't tell her I said that or she'll get that satisfied triumphant smile on her face that is so lovely to look at and so hard to take.

Sara and Ellen became best friends. Sara not only rescued Ellen that day but had the good grace never to mention the incident again. She insisted that all of her friends accept the new girl into their group as well, so in very short order it was as if Ellen had always lived in Paxton City. The two girls remained inseparable, helping each other with homework, taking art and drama classes together, rooming together in college, and consoling each other through bad relationships.

When Sara decided that I was to marry her, Ellen was our Maid of Honor. A few years later when Ellen married the handsome, romantic, dashing and ambitious Jack Gilmore (her description, not mine), Sara was Matron of Honor. We worked hard for Jack when he decided to run for Mayor and celebrated his victory. When Ellen learned she was pregnant, Sara was the first person to get the news, even before Ellen's own mother. Jack and Ellen invited us to a celebratory dinner at Garland's Restaurant which brings us back to last week.

Jack Gilmore is a strong and confident man. Although Paxton City isn't quite the metropolis of some of the larger eastern cities, Jack takes his responsibilities very seriously and there have been more than a few occasions when he's had to juggle special interest groups with tact and sometimes with force. I've never known him not to look a man in the eye when talking to him. I've never known him to be intimidated by anyone. But for some reason the thought of becoming a father for the first time left him nervous, trembling, and completely devoid of reason. He doted over Ellen as if she were in her ninth month instead of her second. He worried over her, making sure to pull her chair out for her and hold her hand when they were walking. When she perused the menu, he gave her advice about which entrees would be the most nutritious for their child. It was very sweet to watch. It was curious to see an otherwise reasonable and powerful man acting so endearingly stupid.

But this story is not just about how Sara and Ellen became friends. There were several other tumblers falling that night. If not for choices that I myself had made nearly five years before, Mayor Jack Gilmore would not have survived the evening.

As I mentioned earlier, Jack was quite nervous and not his usual calm and careful self. While we were eating dessert, Ellen choked slightly on her cherry pie a-la-mode and Jack jumped to her rescue. It was just a tiny cough that ordinarily would have escaped notice. Jack turned suddenly, alarmed for his wife and somehow caught his foot under a busboy walking by the table carrying several dishes.

Aside from just the dishes, the busboy carried a heavier than normal amount of life on his tired old shoulders. He had a few days' growth of beard and a glassy look in his eyes that spoke of too many fights and too many bottles of whiskey. He had tattoos on his muscular arms. I knew that the owner of the restaurant had a habit of trying to give jobs to guys who were down on their luck and this guy was clearly one of them. The busboy tangled on Jack's foot. He fell forward and the dishes came down with a crash.

An ignorant group at a large table nearby where too much alcohol had been flowing, erupted into applause and laughter. The busboy, embarrassed and angry, stood himself up glaring at Jack. His hand reached into his back pocket. I could clearly see he was pulling out a knife. I could see what was going to happen. I think I was the only one who noticed. And I was not in a position to stop it nor did I have time even to shout a warning. I stood up in great alarm and the distracted busboy's eyes met mine. Something shocked him back to his senses as he looked at me. There seemed to be some kind of recognition. His face softened. The knife returned to his pocket. He nodded at me and swiftly walked away and out of the restaurant.

A flurry of activity ensued as several other waiters and busboys hurried to clean the mess on the floor. Ellen pushed Jack away, chastising him for being so anxious. She and Sara had a big laugh over it. Only I was shaking and flushed, knowing what had almost just happened. Jack looked around wanting to apologize to the busboy but the man was long gone, probably never to return. The busboy's eyes haunted me the rest of the evening. He had looked at me as if he knew me. There was something vaguely familiar about him.

On the way home, my dear wife forced me to admit that I had had a good time and that I was glad I had decided to go. "Except for that strange busboy," she said. "Did you see the look in his eyes? I thought he was going to kill Jack. The whole thing was spooky." And then, suddenly, that one word unlocked the floodgates of memory and the images came pouring in. The Spook. I hadn't thought about him in years.

It was about five years before that night. I was a struggling psychologist with a small private practice. One day I received a phone call

234

regarding a colleague who had fallen ill and had to take a medical leave of absence. He was one of the staff psychologists at Stratton prison. I was asked to take his place for six months. I welcomed the opportunity. The thought of some steady income was a welcome relief despite the venue. I had worked in prisons before so I was a natural fit. Despite the potential dangers and depressing atmosphere, I had always found the prison population refreshing in a strange perverse way. The prisoners were often very interesting and charismatic characters with a strong sense of integrity even if it was directed toward a poor set of values. Gaining the respect of cons is not easy, but once gained, their loyalty is something to treasure.

It didn't take me long to get settled into a routine. I took over Andy's caseload and other duties without a problem. Around the second or third week, I first became aware of The Spook as everyone else in the institution did, as a vague entity just on the outskirts of consciousness. He was a dark skulking presence, shuffling along the sidewalks with his ever present broom, sweeping a path for himself as he walked. He had a ruddy complexion and dirty matted rust colored hair and a prematurely gray beard. Even the toughest cons gave him a wide berth, avoiding any contact with him.

I knew little about him except for the many rumors I'd heard swirling around the institution; that The Spook had killed ten people with his bare hands in a drunken rage, that he had nearly destroyed the prison mess hall one day when somebody bumped into him and spilled his coffee, that he had set fire to a gas station causing an explosion heard miles away with flames climbing several hundred feet in the air. So when I got a call from the warden himself asking me to see The Spook, I approached the situation with a great deal of trepidation. He was in a detention cell having tried to kill himself. It was my job to assess the situation and see what I could do for him.

I learned that his name was Joey McLean. Knowing his name made the situation a little more personal and less scary, but only slightly. The guards unlocked his cell and allowed me to enter, locking the door behind me. He sat on his cot hunched over with his arms wrapped around his knees. He did not look up when I entered.

I introduced myself and told him why I was there. No response. I began my standard monologue about how desperate he must have felt and that I was there to help him if I possibly could. Occasionally I would ask him a question but he might as well have been in a coma for all the response I got. And then I had one of those moments; one of those inspired moments off script and spontaneous. I looked at him, hunched over and closed off from the world, and asked him a question. "When exactly did you give up on yourself?" He grunted. It was a short quiet grunt almost like a laugh but a laugh forced from a place of profound sadness and loneliness. Contact had been made. I tried to dig a little deeper into the notch I'd made in his armor. I told him that I was available for him if he ever wanted to talk to me and that no matter how much he might have given up on himself, I would not give up on him. He turned his head at that point and looked at me. Then he put it down again.

It was about a week later that I heard he wanted to see me so I arranged an appointment. He came to the first session not much more animated than he was in the holding cell. I made a few attempts to start a conversation with him but he was mostly silent. I kept up as much of a monologue as I could but he seemed to be oblivious of it. But when I asked him if he wanted to return the following week he nodded yes.

And so began my work with The Spook. Word spread throughout the prison that I was working with him, if sitting in silence could be called work. But since just about everyone in the prison was terrified of him including the chaplains, I became something of a minor celebrity for having the courage just to sit in the same room with him.

One day he came into the office and asked me how many people I thought he could kill if he dropped a match down the gas pump at the physical plant.

"Only about two or three," I said, not missing a beat. "It wouldn't be nearly worth the effort. If you want to make a real impact you should bomb the administration building. Then you could take out about twenty or thirty people."

A slow smile appeared on his face. It was a gamble but I'd learned long ago that there was a big difference between carrying out a violent act and just talking about it. If he was going to do damage to anyone he would have done so with or without my input and he wouldn't tell me about it beforehand. I didn't ask myself why he wanted to blow up a building. I asked myself why he wanted to tell me about it. It was as if his comment was a question.

"Can I scare you?"

And my answer told him, "No, you can't."

"Good. Now let me tell you what's really going on in my mind, because it sure as hell is scaring me." It was a significant turning point. He knew he could trust me.

He started telling me about a frightening dream he'd had the night before. He was captured by a crowd of people who stripped him and then stood around pointing at him and laughing. He told me about his alcoholic mother who regularly beat him as a child when she wasn't passed out on the floor. He told me about his father who hadn't been heard from since Joey was five years old. Joey had completed only about six years of school and dropped out. He then began a life of petty burglaries and shoplifting sprees. He spent several years in group homes, reform schools, and juvenile prisons, working his way up the ladder to adult prison.

One time he came in to see me all excited. There had been an incident reported on all the news programs about a mass shooting in a fast food restaurant. "Someday I'm going to do something like that," he said. "Someday you'll read about me in the newspapers."

"Well, it's nice to have ambitions," I answered. "Why those ambitions?"

"It's big. He took out five people at one time. Now everyone knows who he is."

"Is that important? To be known?"

"Well sure it is. Nobody's going to mess with that guy."

I was beginning to understand him. I was beginning to suspect that not only were none of the rumors about him true, but that he'd probably started most of them himself. The measure of how terrified he was of other people was how dangerously he portrayed himself. If he could keep people away from him because they were afraid of him, he would be safe.

A couple of weeks before Christmas he decided he wanted to go home and he threatened to destroy the entire prison if he didn't get his way. I heard about it from just about everyone from the warden on down. "Do something about it," was the warden's demand.

When Joey showed up for his weekly session I saw that he was dead serious. For whatever reason, he had become obsessed with the idea of going home for Christmas and he didn't care how unlikely that possibility was. He was up for a parole hearing about a week before Christmas and he wanted out. I told him I would do what I could for him despite his threats, not because of them. I told him I would have to administer some psychological tests so the results could bolster whatever I would say on his behalf. He agreed to do anything I asked. He left the office and I wondered to myself how I was going to pull this off and what I had gotten myself into.

I gave him a screening test just to find out if he was literate enough to take the normal tests. Since he'd only gotten through sixth grade, I needed to know if he had the verbal and written skills to understand and answer the elaborate questionnaires I would have to give him. To my relief and amazement, he passed the screening test. On the day of testing, he worked for three hours to complete the written tests. Afterward I gave him some projective tests as well.

The next day I stared at the results and recalculated them several times. They could not possibly be accurate. The scores showed him to be in the normal range on every measure. Even normal people don't score in the normal range. I called him to the office and showed him the results and explained what they meant. A slow smile appeared on his face as though I'd discovered a secret.

The day of the parole hearing arrived. I was a little late and they'd already decided to deny him. When I rushed in and introduced myself, they allowed me to speak.

"Thank you for hearing me out," I said. I started by recounting all the rumors about The Spook and how dangerous and frightening a person he was believed to be. And then I dropped the bomb revealing that little of it was true; that as scary a person Joey was, that's how terrified he really was

239

of others. He made himself out to be dangerous to keep others away. It was all just an elaborate defense mechanism. In reality he was a fairly normal person, obviously very intelligent, and as long as there was no alcohol present, he was not likely to be dangerous. They glanced over to Joey who sat quietly listening. The Board conferred among themselves and decided to take a chance and parole him provided that he enter an alcohol prevention program. Joey did not jump for joy. He did not show any emotion at all. He didn't even look at the panel. He just stood up and left the room. I thanked them on his behalf.

Three days later, two days before Christmas, he was back in prison. I called him to my office. He was almost as depressed as the first time I'd seen him. He was ashamed and he had confirmed to himself once again that he was a hopeless loser without any chance of making it in normal society. He told me that on his very first night home, his mother had gotten drunk and berated him for hours about being stupid and lazy, a horrible burden, and a complete failure. Joe grabbed her whiskey bottle but rather than hitting her over the head with it which was his first impulse, he emptied it instead down his throat. Things quickly spiraled out of control and the police were eventually called in. Joey pulled a knife on one of the officers but miraculously was disarmed and subdued without anyone being hurt.

As had happened in many of our encounters, He hung his head expecting me to yell at him, to call him names, to at least be frustrated and angry with him. But I couldn't do any of those things even if I had thought to. He'd already done a complete job on himself. Instead, I told him I was proud of him. He looked up, startled and puzzled. "At least you got out there and tried," I said. "Nobody got hurt. Next time you'll do better."

He grunted as if to say, "Yeah, sure."

"Joey, I want to tell you something and I want you to look me in the eye so I'll know you're listening." He lifted his head and his eyes met mine. "Joey, if I had known then what I know now; if I had known that your parole would last all of about two days, I still would have done what I did for you. I still would have worked just as hard for your release. You deserved the chance and I'm glad I was able to help you. I have no regrets." Tears slowly rolled down his cheek.

A few weeks later, my friend Andy returned to his job and I left the prison. I made a point of introducing Andy to The Spook and briefed him on what had happened in his absence. When I said goodbye to Joey he couldn't look me in the eye. He mumbled a few things that sounded like a thank you. He told me maybe he'd try again and maybe some day he would be in a position to pay me back for the favor I'd done him.

Last week at Garland's Restaurant he paid me back. I suddenly got goose bumps remembering that it was Mayor Gilmore himself, who'd recommended me to fill in at the prison. The circle completed. The tumblers fell. The door opened. A life was saved.

Dear Santa

Under any other circumstance it might have been exciting for eight year old Bobby Quentin to ride in the front seat of an ambulance, speeding through the city streets, blasting through red lights as the siren blared and cars dashed out of the way. There was no less of a bustle of activity when they arrived at the hospital. His mother was carted to an operating room and his ragged red-eyed father tagged along behind her.

They all forgot about Bobby. He sat alone in the chair near the emergency entrance where they had planted him, tightly clutching Mr. Smith, his faithful teddy bear. Every time the outside doors opened, he felt the rush of frigid air chilling him to the bone. He saw the snowflakes rushing in and dying on the hospital floor. He didn't want to think of the hospital as a place where anyone or anything died. He watched as more carts came wheeling in followed by bewildered families wearing worried looks and red eyes. It was a horror movie endlessly repeating itself.

"Don't worry, Mr. Smith," he said to his companion, "They'll take care of Mommy. She'll be home in time for Christmas tomorrow. I know she will because that's what I prayed for and Mommy always says that God can do anything and all you have to do is ask Him so don't you worry."

But then far down the hallway, Bobby saw his father slumped over and shaking, a doctor had his arm around him and Bobby knew. He knew he'd lost his mother and his father and God and Christmas all in the same night and all he had left was Mr. Smith.

For several days afterward, the Christmas presents lay untouched under the tree. Strange people he didn't know came and left the house. They all wore dark clothing and dark expressions. They forced smiles at

243

Bobby and patted his head.

One morning the Christmas tree was gone. Bobby's father had taken it out to the backyard and set it on fire, lights, decorations and all. A charred angel lay there for weeks until it was covered with snow and forgotten about. Bobby spent hours hiding in his mother's closet, crying and smelling her clothes but soon they were gone too and by New Year's, so was he. Aunt Martha arrived one morning to announce that Bobby was to live with her from then on. She packed a few things and hustled him off to her car. His father was not there to say goodbye. When Bobby grabbed Mr. Smith, Aunt Martha insisted that he was too old for teddy bears. Bobby didn't cry. He had run out of tears.

Fifty years later

The alarm clock startled Robert Quentin out of his sleep. He didn't care. It wasn't as though he ever had any dreams. He opened one reluctant eye and surveyed his surroundings from the mattress on the floor where he slept. There wasn't much to see. He lived in a rented room in an old beaten down hotel that mostly sold rooms by the hour. A half empty bag of potato chips lay where he'd left it on the floor. When he picked it up, a mouse ran out of it and escaped into a crack between the refrigerator and the wall. He didn't have a kitchen to speak of, just a half-fridge, a sink, and a hot plate on a counter lining one wall. Robert identified the scratchy static noise that bothered his ears. The television was still turned on, the taped movie of the previous night having ended. He didn't remember what he had seen.

Robert picked up the empty whiskey bottle that was the source of his grogginess and lack of memory and tossed it in the brown paper bag that served as a garbage receptacle.

Robert entered the tiny closet that he had to go through to get to his bathroom. He turned on the bright light and immediately winced. An old man he barely recognized stared back at him from the mirror. Where had that face come from? Didn't he used to be young? No, he was never young. Youth like everything else had been taken from him.

He thought back over the years. There was little he really wanted to remember but he was too weak to resist the tide of the onrushing pictures that imprinted themselves relentlessly upon his mind, especially this time of year, just before Thanksgiving, when the chill wind began to creep up one's spine. It was right around this time of year when he got into his first fight.

He was nine years old. A year had passed since his mother had died having left him in emotional suspended animation. It was the day before Thanksgiving. The teacher asked each child to come to the front of the class to share with the rest of the children what they were thankful for. When it was Bobby's turn he said just one word, "Nothing!" After class some ill-advised boys teased him about it. They went home with bloody souvenirs of lessons learned. Until that day, Bobby had been withdrawn and rarely spoke. But something came alive that day and it wasn't good. From that time on, Bobby went out of his way to pick fights. There was something strangely satisfying about it. It gave him a sense of mastery, of control. But it didn't take long before the fighting put him in conflict with the school administration which then put him in conflict with Aunt Martha.

Bobby had a palatable relationship with Aunt Martha. She had little warmth or comfort to give him but by then he had little need of it. As long as he stayed out of her way and kept his part of the house clean, she didn't bother him. She didn't care if he did his homework or not or watched TV until late at night. But when he got into trouble at school, she was pulled into it and that she didn't like, all the more so since it involved fighting, which Aunt Martha considered barbaric and uncivilized as she considered most things that were masculine.

There followed a series of suspensions and even a short stint in reform school where Bobby's fighting skills were honed and refined. When at last he finished high school he was turned out into the world. He worked factory and construction jobs mostly and spent his money getting drunk and carousing with women. Until he met Sally.

Sally was the sister of one of the men Bobby worked with and drank with. Despite all his efforts to the contrary, Bobby's armor could not withstand Sally's relentless cheerfulness. She had decided that there was a decent kind man buried deep within his rough exterior and she was bound and determined to bring it out, clean it up, tame it, and marry it. There followed several years of stability and contentment that even Bobby could not deny or fail to appreciate. When their son, Eric was born, Bobby was almost convinced that the storm had ended and life could be good.

But every year around Thanksgiving, Bobby started drinking and didn't stop until New Year's. During that time he was a surly angry cynical man. One year he knocked down the Christmas tree in a drunken stupor and almost started the place on fire. Another year he gambled away money he was supposed to spend on Eric's Christmas presents, and every year, he managed to insult most of his in-laws. Sally tried her best to control him, rationalize his behavior, and make the best of the situation but exhaustion took over and she began to fear the holiday season. She tried to get him into counseling but it broke off early on and soon the holiday anger seeped more and more into the rest of the year and finally she gave up on him. She took Eric and moved out.

Bobby tried on the role of absent father but it was too difficult for him. When Eric turned ten, Bobby got drunk and failed to show up at his birthday party and pretty much never saw him again.

A sharp pain brought him back to the present. He didn't realize he'd been shaving and he'd nicked his chin which now had a small spot of blood that was growing larger.

Eventually Robert dragged himself off to work. He kept his head down as he rode the bus. Two days until Thanksgiving. A department store was the last place he wanted to be during the coming month. At least he could hide in the engine room in the basement where his small office was located. As general handyman for the store he was responsible for all problems mechanical, electrical, or plumbing. A lot of the repairs had to be done after hours which suited him just fine. The fewer people he had to deal with the better. Most of the other problems he could foist off on his assistant and kindred spirit Jerry, a survivor of the sixties and Vietnam. Many days they drank together after work and then stumbled to their respective homes.

"I'm only working a half day today, Chief. Remember?" said Jerry.

"Oh yeah, you're going home for Thanksgiving."

"Why don't you come with me? My sister won't mind another warm body."

"I don't do Thanksgiving. I have nothing to be thankful for."

"Everyone has something to be thankful for, even me."

"Not me. And especially not now. As far as I'm concerned I'd be real happy if they just cut out the last two months of the year and went straight from October to January."

"I hear you. Holidays can be a real challenge. The one I can't handle is the Fourth of July. I hear those fireworks going off and I think I'm back in Nam. Can't sleep. Get all jittery. I have to go off in the woods camping or something."

"Yeah, well, I guess we all have our battle scars, one way or another."

"I feel bad for you Chief, cooped up here in this dungeon all by yourself. Hey I've got a Christmas pres. ., er, I have something for you. I got it years ago from an old Indian Medicine Man or something. It's supposed to bring you luck. You see? On one side is an Eagle's head and on the other is the back of its head. It's supposed to help you turn your life around. Why don't you keep it? It might bring you luck."

"I don't believe in luck, at least I don't believe in good luck. I certainly know a lot about bad luck. It's followed me around all my life."

"Take it. You never know. I don't think I'll be needing it anymore and you've been a good friend. Oh hey, I forgot to tell you. The boss wants to see you."

"Yeah? Maybe I'm getting a bonus this year. Maybe my luck's changing already."

"I don't think so. I mean, well it's a damn shame is what it is. I've got to go. I just want to say it's been great working with you. Better days ahead, huh?"

"Yeah, better days." Robert left to go see the boss. He was puzzled by Jerry. Sounded like a farewell or something.

"Ah, Mr. Quentin, come on in. Take a chair," said the boss, Mr.

Garrett.

"What's this about?" asked Robert. "Some problem with the plumbing on the fourth floor again?"

"No, I'm afraid it's a bit more serious than that. You know times are difficult right now. We're getting hammered by all the malls in the suburbs and by the Internet. People just don't want to come downtown anymore. The big department store is a thing of the past. Used to be we had a whole floor of toys this time of year. Parents would bring their kids and leave them here all day to play. Now everything's electronic. You don't even have to come to the store to shop anymore. Well, what are you going to do?"

"What does that have to do with me?"

"Ah yes. Well I'm afraid I have some bad news for you. We're going to be outsourcing your position beginning next week. I'd hoped to be able to give you more notice but the decision didn't come from me. I have no control over this store anymore."

"Next week? That doesn't give me a lot of time to get anything else, especially during the holiday season. What about Jerry? Is he going too?"

"Yes, we told him earlier and asked him not to say anything to you. He's leaving for his sister's house but he won't be coming back again. They only approved one week's severance for each of you. I'm sorry I couldn't do more. You've been a good employee."

"Yeah, well, don't worry about it. I'll just go to the homeless shelter. I've been there before. I can handle it. Jerry said my luck was going to change. I guess it has, just not for the better. Don't worry about it. I know you did the best you could. You've always been fair to me. Have a good holiday, Mr. Garrett."

"Wait a minute! I just had an idea. How would you like to work here another month?"

"Well yeah. That would be great but how could you swing it?"

"We need to hire a Santa Claus. Why don't you be Santa Claus this year? You'd be great. Of course you'd have to, you know, lay off the drink and all."

"No. I don't think I could do that, I mean be Santa Claus. I don't even like Christmas. I'm not the guy for that. Sorry."

"C'mon Robert. Do it. It would be a personal favor to me. Stick it to the Advisory Board for wanting to get rid of you."

"No. I'm sorry Mr. Garrett. I can't do it. I won't do it." Robert put his hand in his pocket and felt the small round amulet Jerry had given him. Something tingled in his hand and vibrated up his arm. He pulled it from his pocket and looked at it. He saw a small girl where the eagle had been. She was sitting at a table writing a letter and talking out loud.

"Dear Santa, I know you'll help us because I believe in you real bad and because you're magic and . . . ." Her voice trailed off and the image disappeared.

"Hey Robert, are you okay?"

"What? Yeah, I'm fine."

"So, you'll do it? Can I count on you?"

"No, I'm sorry Mr. Garrett. I think it would be a mistake."

At lunchtime, Robert slipped out of the store and headed to the homeless shelter to make arrangements to stay there for a couple of months. He was already a few months behind in his rent at the hotel and the manager was anxious to get him out to make room for the more lucrative transient clientele so it was either sleep on the streets or at the homeless shelter. Miss Swanson, who ran the shelter, was glad to see Robert and invited him to stay for lunch but told him they were full up and they wouldn't be able to take him in. They were expecting a colder than usual winter season and the city was inspecting them very closely to make sure they didn't put any more cots in the place than were allowed by law.

"They're trying to shut us down," said Miss Swanson. "They want to tear this building down and put up offices."

"Seems to be the same story everywhere these days," said Robert. "People don't count. Just money. It's okay, I'll make do."

"Won't you stay for lunch?"

"No thanks. I'm not much hungry right now."

Robert headed back to the store. He figured he would just have to camp out at Albert's Alley, the nickname given to an alley where several homeless people find cardboard boxes to live in and build fires in garbage cans to keep warm. He kept his hands deep in his pockets trying to keep them warm when his hand again found the amulet. He pulled it out of his pocket and looked at it. Again there was the image of the little girl writing a letter. "Dear Santa, I know you'll help us . . . ." Alarmed, he stuffed it back in his pocket.

"What do you want from me?" he cried out to no one in particular. He heard the little girl's voice in his head.

"Please Santa. Please help us. Please Santa. We need you."

"Okay, I'll do it! Just shut up and leave me alone!"

And before he knew it, he was back in the office of Mr. Garrett who was shaking his hand and thanking him. He would start in two days.

Thanksgiving arrived the next day and along with it a bone chilling slushy snowfall.   In houses everywhere, families gathered together for massive feasts and did all the things families normally did on that day; ate too much, drank too much, laughed and argued.   Robert sludged through the snow to a nearly empty Chinese restaurant where he ate dinner alone.   He wasn't sad.   He wasn't lonely.   Those feelings had long ago left him.   A gaping empty numbness filled their place.

Next morning, Robert found himself in the employee locker room carefully becoming Santa Claus.   A padded vest filled out his belly.   He put on the familiar red pants and buckled the large brass buckle on the black belt.   The boots were a bit tight.   As the jacket went on, Robert began sweating and he hadn't even donned the beard, wig, and hat yet.   It was obvious that many men had sweated in the same jacket for many years.   The smell was powerful.   He didn't know how he was going to be able to go through with it.

At the appointed time, Santa was led to the Candyland Village on the tenth floor where his massive throne was located.   Dozens of children pulling at their parents' arms were already there, raising a cacophonous din like chickens being slaughtered.   The crowd erupted into applause and an ear splitting cheer when they spied him.   He forced a smile, waved his gloved hands and roared, "Ho ho ho".   Inwardly he was stiff.   He wore the suit but resisted it at the same time.   He sat down on the throne which proved to be not nearly as comfortable as it looked.

The routine was highly streamlined.   Workers, dressed as elves, canvassed the parents in advance to determine what they were planning on giving their children for Christmas so Santa would know what to promise them.   The parents were then handed off to the photographer's aides who in a span of a half hour wait in line, attempted to sell them as many photograph

252

packages as possible. An 8x10 package included four wallet sized pictures, one for each grandparent. The Platinum Package actually included an oil painting done from the photo, a once in a lifetime opportunity to capture the young cherub with Santa, a memory he could keep forever and show off to his own grandchildren someday for only $245 but marked down if ordered today for only $195.

The kids came in various sizes and temperaments. Some babies cried. The parents on occasion stretched their session with Santa over twenty minutes, trying to get the poor children to look excited and happy for the sake of the photograph when in fact they were terrified, forced to sit on a stranger's knee. Some kids assumed that part of the attraction was a horsey ride on Santa's lap. A few younger kids were so taken up with all the excitement that they had accidents. Robert escaped to his break times with his thighs bruised, wet, and smelly.

And Robert couldn't believe the incredible greed so early ingrained in the young children. They had long lists of very expensive items. "I want a motor powered scooter and a giant screen TV for my room and tickets to the Super Bowl, and a trip to Disney World, and uh, oh yeah, I want a brand new racing bike but not those cheap ones. I want one made out of graphite with fifteen gears like they ride in the big races."

With each child, Robert feigned happiness and excitement. "Ho ho ho, what would you like for Christmas?"

"Uh, I want, uh, I forget." Some little girl would fidget and squirm in Robert's lap as though her gyrations would somehow jog her memory. And so it went, day after day, and often Robert thought he should have opted for Albert's Alley. A couple of times fights broke out and that wasn't the kids. Parents accused others of cutting in line. One father who had grabbed the last copy of the latest video game, *Super Bloody War Games*, in a nearby toy store was being harassed by another father who was just a second shy of grabbing it for himself and carried the argument all the way to the Santa line. Some fathers watched football games on tiny portable televisions while their children pushed and shoved each other.

Somehow Robert made it through the month. This was Christmas Eve day, his last day as Santa. He watched the clock carefully. One more child to see and then he would be done. The last little girl, she looked to be about six years old, walked up to him but did not climb up on his lap.

"Don't you want to sit on Santa's lap?" he asked.

"No, Santa. You look pretty tired. Your lap must be sore from all the other kids sitting on it."

"Well, thank you. That's very considerate of you. What's your name?"

"Sandra."

"Well, Sandra, what would you like for Christmas?"

"Nothing, thank you."

"Nothing? Nothing at all?"

"I don't need any toys or anything. I have plenty of them. You can give my presents to some poor kids who can't afford them. But there is something I need."

"And what would that be?"

"I wrote you a letter about it. Didn't you get it? I want you to help my mother. She's stuck."

"She's stuck? What do you mean?"

"Well, she had an accident and she's in the hospital and she's stuck."

"I don't understand what you mean by stuck."

"She can't wake up. She's stuck. We want her to come home for Christmas but she can't wake up. I tried talking to her and telling her to wake up. Even my teddy bear, Mrs. Jones, tried."

Robert began shaking inside. Sweat was pouring down his forehead. "Wha . . .what do you want from me?"

"I want you to come to the hospital tonight and help her. I know you'll be busy and everything but you just have to come or else we won't have Christmas at all this year. I know you can help her because you're magic. If you're there I just know she'll wake up and come home to us."

Robert looked over at the elderly woman who stood patiently waiting for Sandra.

"Is that your grandmother?"

"No, that's Mrs. Jimenez, my neighbor." Robert stood up to talk to her but Mrs. Jimenez didn't speak any English.

"I have to go now," said Sandra. "I'll see you tonight at the hospital. I wrote down which one it is. See? Here's the name and a map and here's the room Mommy is in. You have to get there before seven because that's when visiting hours are over. Thank you, Santa. I knew I could count on you. I love you, Santa." She gave him a big hug and then walked slowly away toward Mrs. Jimenez.

Robert staggered to the locker room. He quickly changed clothes and left the building. He had managed to stay sober for the entire month but now he headed over to Joe's Tavern.

"Hey Bob, haven't seen you for a while. I was worried something had happened to you," said Joe the owner of the tavern.

"Set me up with a double, Joe."

"Hey, I was getting ready to close for the night. It's Christmas Eve, buddy."

"I don't care what day it is. I need a drink and I need it now."

"Okay, okay. What's going on with you? You in some kind of trouble?"

Robert related the story to Joe. When he finished, Joe rubbed his forehead. "What are you going to do about it?" he asked.

"Nothing."

"What do you mean nothing? You just gonna no show the kid?"

"Well what do you expect me to do? I can't help her. What was I thinking of taking that job in the first place? I hate Christmas and I hate hospitals, especially at Christmas. Give me another drink, damn it!"

"Hey, are you okay?" asked Joe. "You got any place to go tonight? Why don't you come home with me? We're having the family over. We can make an extra place for you."

"I want to be alone," said Robert. "I don't want to see anyone ever again. It's all a lie. It's just a big scam. As soon as Christmas is over and everyone stops pretending that everything's great they all go back to the same dark dreary world where nobody cares about anything but themselves."

"Is that what you think?" asked Joe. "Is that what you want that little girl to think?"

"I don't care what she thinks. She might as well wise up to how things are."

"You know Bobby, you've been coming in here for years now. And I've always been glad to see you but I've got to tell you something. I want you to get out of here and don't come back. Imagine breaking that little girl's heart. You're just a bitter old man. You're a worthless drunk. Go on. Get out."

Robert was shocked and hurt. He picked up his glass and threw it, shattering it against the wall. Then he turned his back and left the tavern. The alcohol helped to fight off some of the bitter cold as he made his way back toward his apartment, muttering to himself, slogging through the dirty slush. He found himself trudging past the department store. Distracted by a car going by, he slipped on the slush and fell over, sliding to a stop just under the display window. There in the window was a Santa statue with arms that moved up and down as little elves rotated around him all holding up toys. Tinkling music box music broadcasted out of tiny speakers above the window.

Robert sat himself up. People scurried around him hurrying to get home. A few stopped to help him up. One of them bent over to retrieve something. "Hey, I think you dropped this," he said. It was the amulet that was supposed to have changed his life. Robert looked at it and saw the face of the little girl smiling at him.

"I can't do it," he said. "I'm sorry. I didn't mean to let you down."

"Of course you can do it. You can do anything," she replied. "You're magic, silly."

"I can't. I . . I'm afraid. I'm afraid of hospitals."

"I'll hold your hand."

"I'm afraid of people."

"I won't hurt you."

"I'm afraid of . . . . hope."

"Hope is all we have sometimes."

"It isn't enough."

"But sometimes it's all we have."

"Hey mister, are you okay?" said the man who helped him up. Suddenly Robert was back to himself. The image of the little girl was gone and he saw only the eagle's head on the amulet.

"I'm fine. Thank you."

"Be careful now and Merry Christmas."

"You too. Mer . .Mer . . Merry Christmas." He was still in a daze. The alcohol, the fall, and the vision in the amulet all made things very fuzzy. But suddenly everything cleared. Robert looked around and found a trash can. He lifted it up and smashed it through the window. An alarm rang out. Instead of running away, Robert carefully climbed through the broken shards of glass and into the window. He trampled a few elves climbing through to the back panel and into the store. He ran as fast as he could and found the stairs to the basement employee area. Entering the locker room he quickly changed into the Santa suit. Exiting the locker room he ran down the long hallway to the back door that opened to an alley. He followed the alley to the next street over. It took him some time to orient himself but soon he did and headed toward the hospital five blocks away. He glanced at a clock and saw he had only five minutes until it was seven o'clock.

Trudging through the slush, Robert wasn't exactly an inconspicuous presence. Everyone shouted and waved to him wishing him Merry Christmas. His legs ached and his lungs burned as he ran toward the hospital. He had to stop a few times to catch his breath, wheezing and coughing and doubling over as he did so.

Finally he reached the hospital. He was greeted by the receptionist. "Well hello Santa. I'm glad to see you but I'm afraid you're too late."

"What? What do you mean? Please don't tell me I'm too late.

Please. I couldn't bear it. She's counting on me."

"But the Christmas party in pediatrics ended hours ago."

"Oh. No. I'm not here for that. I have to go to the Intensive Care Unit. There's someone I have to see there."

"Intensive Care? Is it a relative? I'm sorry I can't let you go up there. Visiting hours are over and it's only for relatives anyway."

"Yes, I'm a relative. She's my, uh, daughter. My granddaughter is up there waiting for me. Please. You have to let me up there."

"Well, seeing as how it's Christmas Eve and all I suppose I can make an exception, especially for Santa Claus."

Robert rode the elevator. His heart was still beating rapidly from running. The suit was becoming enormously heated. He got off on the fourth floor and made his way to the Intensive Care Unit, room five. Inside he saw a woman lying still in a bed barely visible under the mass of wires and tubes. An extremely exhausted looking man sat by her bed with several days' growth of beard and red eyes burning from too many tears. Sandra sat in a chair with Mrs. Jones, her teddy bear. When she saw him, her face lit up and she ran to him to give him a big hug. Her father looked up startled and then puzzled.

"Daddy, look it's Santa Claus," she said in hushed tones. "He's going to make Mommy all better."

The man stood up. "Oh Sandra, what have you done? I'm sorry to impose on you Mr. uh."

"Shh. Santa Claus is the name," he said gesturing to the little girl.

"Yeah, Santa Claus. I'm Rick. You've already met Sandra, my headstrong little menace. It was very kind of you to come. I'm sure you'd rather be with family tonight."

"That's okay. I don't really have any family anyway. What's happened to your wife?"

"She was in an accident. We don't know if she's going to pull through. Not going to be much of a Christmas this year. And uh, I don't know what we're going to do and uh. . ." And then Rick broke down weeping and fell into Robert's arms. Robert held him, not knowing what else to do.

Rick pulled away after a few moments. "I'm sorry to pull you into our family problems. I've got to say though, it felt kind of good being held by Santa Claus. I felt like I was a little boy again."

"It's time to get started," said Sandra. "You have to do magic." She told Robert to sit in the chair. "Now I sit in your lap and tell you what I want for Christmas and then we all wish real hard." Robert sat and Sandra climbed onto his lap. "Come on, Daddy. You have to come too. We all have to hold hands. Ready? Okay, I want my Mommy home for Christmas. Now everybody wish real hard for a Christmas miracle."

After several minutes with nothing happening, they slowly let go of each other's hand. Sandra had a perplexed look on her face. Then suddenly she brightened up. "Mrs. Jones! We forgot to include Mrs. Jones." Sandra scurried off Robert's lap to retrieve her teddy bear. She climbed back up on Robert's lap and held the bear tightly. "Okay, let's try it again. I wish for Mommy to wake up and come home with us. Now we all close our eyes and wish real hard."

The sound of the machines keeping Sandra's mother alive filled the room. The steady pulse of beeps and the whooshing sound of the breathing machine was all they heard. Rick opened his eyes first. Then he scooped his daughter in his arms. "I'm sorry darling. It doesn't seem to be working but it was a real good idea and I'm sure your mother would be very proud of you for thinking of it."

"But it has to be. There has to be a Christmas miracle. I wished for it and I prayed for it and I've been a good girl. Why isn't it working?"

Robert was shaking. This was all too familiar a scene.

They were interrupted by a nurse entering the room. "Oh I'm sorry Mr. Quentin. I didn't realize you were still here. I'll come back later."

Robert jerked his head up. He turned pale. "Your name's Quentin?"

"Yeah."

"You said your name is Rick. Is it, by any chance, Eric?"

"Yeah, Eric Quentin. How do you know that? Hey, who are you?"

But Robert couldn't talk. He fell back into the chair weeping.

"Don't be sad Santa. It wasn't your fault it didn't work."

"I'm not sad, darling. I'm happy. Eric, can you ever forgive me? Please don't tell me you hate me."

Eric gasped. "Is it possible? Dad? Is it you?" He ran to Robert and embraced him as tightly as he ever held anything. "I've been searching for you for years," he said. "I didn't know if you were even still alive. I don't hate you. I've never hated you. Well, it looks like we got a Christmas miracle after all."

Robert pulled the amulet out of his pocket and looked at it again with amazement. "What have you got there?" asked Eric. "Looks like an Incan stone. Where did you get it? It's supposed to have mystical powers or something."

"Daddy?"

"A friend gave it to me. He said it was supposed to help me turn my life around. I guess it worked after all."

"Daddy?"

"Yeah, I've heard about these but I've never seen one."

"**DADDY!!!**"

"What?"

"Look! Mommy's hand is moving."

It was true. Her fingers were moving ever so slightly. Eric ran out to get the nurse.

"It might not mean anything," she said. "Let's see. Helen? Can you hear me? If you can hear me, move your finger two times." The finger moved up and down twice. Helen? Move your finger three times." She did so. "I'll go call the doctor. She's coming out of it."

Helen was not ready to go home by Christmas. She was not fully alert for several more days. Eric insisted that Robert come home with them and stay as long as he wished. Eric phoned the department store and explained what had happened to their window and why. The police came by but decided not to pursue it any further, especially when Mr. Garrett refused to press charges in defiance of the advisory board.

Sandra was very excited when it turned out that she had a grandfather and that he was Santa Claus. They did some very creative explaining about Santa's helpers. Still, from that night on, Sandra always called him Grandpa Santa. Eventually Helen returned home. Sandra told her how Santa Claus had saved her life and helped her wake up. "That's very strange," she said, "because I remember having vague dreams about elves telling me to go home and trying to show me the way to the secret door where I could return to my world."

They fixed up a room in the basement for Robert and there he stayed until he died several years later. The joys of his final years more than made up for all the suffering in his early years. Robert was glad to hear that Sally was still alive too. He wrote her a letter with Sandra's help and was relieved to get a favorable reply. She was glad to hear from him. She had always worried about him and wondered what had happened to him. She was happy to relieve herself of the nagging guilt that had always hovered over her for leaving him. They slowly rebuilt a cordial friendship that they both came to treasure.

Every year at Thanksgiving, Robert cooked up the biggest roast turkey he could find and led the family in several rounds proclaiming out loud all the things they were thankful for. The day after Thanksgiving, Robert took his place on Santa's throne at Dale's Department store and loved every minute of it, often staying late into the night to make sure every child got a chance to sit on his lap and give him a hug. In his spare time, Robert volunteered at the homeless shelter preparing and serving food. And every year Miss Swanson received an anonymous Christmas card with a generous cashier's check inside as a gift.

"Hey Santa," someone asked Robert one day. "Do you really believe in Christmas miracles?"

"Not just Christmas miracles. There are miracles every day of the year. You just have to open your eyes to see them, that's all."

Acknowledgments

First I want to thank all those who have read and enjoyed my first book, "*A Drawer Full of Dreams*." It was a dream come true to write it and publish it. The feedback I have received from it helped to inspire me to try to write a second one. So thank you to all my readers and fans. Hope you enjoyed this book as much or more.

I would like to thank Gayle Harte for generously allowing me to use the image of the white chocolate moon on the cover of this book. Please visit *www.gayleschocolates.com* and see all the wonderful delicious goodies she has and order yourself your own white chocolate moon. You can find them under Special Gifts and Baskets, and then under Chocolate Boxes. And also be sure to visit the web site of the genius photographer Eric Smith, who took the photos for Gayle's web site. You can see his work at *www.ericsmith.us*.

I want to thank the wonderful contributions for ideas for the book cover that were submitted by Kelli Jansen, Melanie Daubaras, Matt Levins, and Jeanette McDonnell. You all had great ideas and you all worked very hard. It was very touching to see the dedication you put into your work.

I want to acknowledge my old friend, David Gardener. I've known you for many years through many names and incarnations. I can always see you in the background with a big smile on your face and your bright eyes that see clearly.

I also want to acknowledge Marco Alfandary, another old friend and fellow veteran of the Fresno wars, who has provided me with great wit, stimulating conversation, and loyal friendship over the years.

My friends, Jim and Cathy Beverley (and Jack and Holly too) are treasures in my life. I have appreciated and cherished your friendship and your enthusiastic feedback when a new story gets cranked out.

I have greatly appreciated the feedback on my stories from my friend Raena Balchowsky. It's been great knowing you and I appreciate your keeping Eddie alive with me as well.

Thanks again to Susan Gale Orovitz, for being my friend. I will always be grateful that you reached out to me so we could re-connect.

Thanks to Jim and Barb Ruggeri for being great friends and for introducing me to the mole people.

I want to acknowledge some new old friends, Jeffrey, Felicia, Justin, and Alyssa Pfluger. You are dear, good hearted, and talented people.

And I want to acknowledge a bright young friend, Laura Romaine who loves books so much she deserves to be mentioned in one.

I want to acknowledge a very special friend, Princess, our dog who served us faithfully for thirteen years as a friend and protector. She was one of the gentlest creatures I have ever known and she is sorely missed.

Again I want to thank my brother, Alan Levins, for always being there and always being a friend. I'm proud to be your brother.

I want to thank my parents, Milton and Mildred Levins, to whom this book is dedicated. You are both missed although you're with me every day.

I also want to thank everyone in the Krejcik family. You took me into your hearts and have held me there ever since.

Thank you to my dear son and best buddy, Matt. It's always an interesting and exciting adventure being around you. You have such a huge heart and a great demented mind. I love you dearly. Thanks for the honor of choosing me to be your father.

And finally, my utmost gratitude to my dearest friend, partner, wife, and soul mate, Sue. I am continually touched by the simplicity of your gentle nature. I am proud of and humbled by your love for me. Thank you for believing in me and allowing me the privilege of being close to you.